CONVOY HOMEWARD

CONVOY HOMEWARD

Philip McCutchan

ST. MARTIN'S PRESS
NEW YORK

CONVOY HOMEWARD. Copyright © 1992 by Philip McCutchan. All rights reserved. Printed in the United States of America. No part of this book may be used or reproduced in any manner whatsoever without written permission except in the case of brief quotations embodied in critical articles or reviews. For information, address St. Martin's Press, 175 Fifth Avenue, New York, N.Y. 10010.

Library of Congress Cataloging-in-Publication Data

McCutchan, Philip
    Convoy homeward / Philip McCutchan.
        p.   cm.
    ISBN 0-312-08168-5
    1. World War, 1939–1945—Naval operations, British—Fiction.
    2. Great Britain—History, Naval—20th century—Fiction.
    I. Title.
    PR6063.A167C644   1992   92-1584
    823'.914—dc20   CIP

First published in Great Britain by George Weidenfeld and Nicolson Limited.

First U.S. Edition: October 1992

10   9   8   7   6   5   4   3   2   1

CONVOY HOMEWARD

ONE

It was a brilliant dawn, the best time of any eastern day before the sun had had a chance to scorch away the freshness and bring lethargy in its train. From the bridge of the Commodore's ship, the former liner *Aurelian Star*, John Mason Kemp looked at the awesome colouring of the sky as the sun began to show its tip from somewhere over Burma, somewhere over the embattled troops of the Fourteenth Army, General Slim's 'forgotten army' sweltering in swamp and jungle as they fought the hordes of the Japanese emperor. Not for the first time in this seemingly endless war, Kemp gave thanks that he had made his career at sea. The sea was clean, at least until the bombs or shells turned it into a hideous hell of screaming, torn bodies and often enough – should a deep-laden tanker be hit – a murderous, burning carpet of spilled fuel oil.

But that colouring: crimson, green, orange, yellow, streaking like fingers across the lightening sky, touching the blue of the sea and turning it to gold as the convoy, behind the warship escort, moved out of Colombo for Simonstown and then the long haul up the South Atlantic and North Atlantic for the sanctuary of the Firth of Clyde.

Scottish waters, the great anchorage of the Tail o' the Bank between Greenock and the Gareloch.

Kemp turned as he heard a cough behind him. His assistant, Sub-Lieutenant Finnegan of the RCNVR – Finnegan, a citizen of the USA who had got into the war in advance of his countrymen by joining up in Canada back in 1939 and not too many questions asked.

1

'What is it, Finnegan?'

Finnegan tore off one of his curious American salutes. 'Reporting a moan from Petty Officer Ramm, sir.'

'Already?'

'Already, sir. Four of his guns'-crews, they've got the gut rot.'

Kemp grunted. Convoy Commodores had many worries, from sickness to air attack, from defaulters to bombardment by heavy ships, from bad weather to torpedoes from the ever-ready U-boat packs into which the convoy would steam once they came towards home waters. 'Hangovers from last night ashore, Finnegan?'

'Just simple Colombo tummy, I guess, sir.'

'They'll have to get on with it,' Kemp said. 'We're not going to enter the danger zone for twenty-four hours at the least. But keep me informed.'

Another salute. 'Yes, sir, Commodore.' Kemp forbore to comment; he had been totally unable to break his assistant of his habit of addressing him by, as it were, two titles at once. It was an irritation but one Kemp had learned to live with. In every other way young Finnegan was first class, and had brought an American keenness and freshness of outlook to the onerous task of shepherding the great convoys across the world's oceans, those vital convoys that had endlessly carried troops and food and the hardware of war from Canada, the USA, Australia and South Africa to the Mediterranean and the Far East, and into the Arctic Circle past the North Cape for the replenishment of the Russian armies repelling Hitler from his wintry march on Moscow.

Finnegan was lingering, staring like Kemp at the sky as the sun's rays extended to bring the first hint of the day's coming heat. He was screwing up his eyes and there seemed to be a pensive look, Kemp thought, beyond the effort to protect his eyesight.

'A penny for 'em, Finnegan.'

Finnegan nodded. 'You know something, sir?'

'Not what's in that American mind of yours, Finnegan.'

'No. Well, I guess I'll tell you, sir, Commodore. Me, I just can't wait to see the Clyde again.'

'Not the Ambrose Light . . . or Nantucket Bay . . . or the hot spots of New York?'

'Well, them too I guess. But the Clyde. It's got something, you know that?'

Kemp nodded. 'I know that, Finnegan. It's been home from so many wartime convoys. I think everyone who's ever been to sea feels something special about the Clyde. And not just the Scots.'

'I guess that's probably right, sir.' Finnegan paused. 'I've just been listening to a guy singing on the radio.'

'Ah?'

'About sailing up the Clyde.'

'I know it. Sing it, Finnegan.'

Finnegan stared. 'Me, sir?'

'Yes, you, sir.' Kemp's face was dead-pan.

'Right here on the bridge, sir?'

'Yes, right here on the bridge.'

'Well, I'll be . . . do I take that as an order, sir, Commodore?'

'Yes, Finnegan. And sing it with a Scottish accent.'

Looking as though he believed the Commodore to have gone suddenly round the bend, Finnegan obeyed orders. He obeyed them to the best of his ability.

'We're sailing up the Clyde,' he sang, 'Sailing up the Clyde . . . Sailing home tae Scotland and ma ain firrreside . . . an' a lump comes in ma throat, an' a tearrr Ah canny hide, for we're sailing hame tae Glasgie where the auld folks bide. . . .'

From the corner of his eye Kemp saw the *Aurelian Star*'s master approaching from the starboard wing of the bridge. Kemp, grinning, said, 'That was in your honour, Captain. I hope you found it nostalgic.'

Captain Maconochie, a large, jovial man whose home was in Ayr on the Firth of Clyde laughed and said, 'Music-hall Scots. Was it Will Fyffe, or Harry Lauder? Anyway – the effort was appreciated. But it's a long haul yet to the Mull of Kintyre. I hope to God we make it intact.'

Kemp said, 'Amen to that, Captain.'

A long haul by the exigencies of the wartime tracks to the Mull of Kintyre and the great seagull-whitened rock of Ailsa Craig at the entry to the Firth of Clyde it certainly was. Some fourteen thousand sea miles of hostile waters to be left behind them by the time they reached journey's end. The convoy was to proceed largely empty as far as Kilindini in East Africa; at Kilindini the

Aurelian Star would embark a battalion of the King's East African Rifles, a native regiment with British officers bound for the UK for training before being drafted for service in the Second Front against Germany, a concept not yet formalized but which by this stage of the war was on everybody's lips as an inevitable follow-up to the thrust of the Desert Rats through Italy. At Simonstown the convoy would be joined by two vessels carrying explosives, and a formation of Australians and New Zealanders would be embarked aboard the three former liners, while the fifteen cargo vessels would load mixed cargoes urgently needed in the UK. Also at Simonstown a tanker carrying sixteen thousand tons of crude oil for the refineries at Grangemouth and Milford Haven would come beneath the umbrella of the escort. From Colombo to the Cape the cover would consist of the old R-class battleship *Resolution*, the escort aircraft carrier *Rameses*, the cruisers *Lincolnshire* – wearing the flag of cs23, the Rear-Admiral Commanding, 23rd Cruiser Squadron – *Swansea, Bodmin, Marazion, Lydford* and *Okehampton*. The destroyer escort, the anti-submarine screen, would be provided by the 32nd Destroyer Flotilla. *Resolution*, on temporary detachment from the British Far Eastern Fleet and wearing the flag of the Commander-in-Chief, Admiral Sir Geoffrey Layton, would leave the convoy at Simonstown.

A large convoy; and a vital one for Britain.

This had been stressed at the sailing conference the day before departure. 'You'll not have an easy passage, gentlemen,' the Naval Control Service Officer had said. 'It's known that U-boats are operating in the southern half of the Indian Ocean, and there's this surface raider at large in the South Atlantic – the *Stuttgart*.' He addressed Kemp: 'You'll know all about surface raiders, Commodore.'

Kemp nodded. The NCS officer continued. There was going to be an unceasing need for full alertness on the part of the watch-keepers and lookouts; the destroyers of the A/S screen would need continual use of asdics to inhibit submarine attack; they would share the duties of 'eyes of the fleet' with the aircraft from the carrier. Kemp had heard it all, or something like it, countless times before since back in the autumn of 1939 he had brought the Mediterranean-Australia Lines' *Ardara* into Tilbury from Sydney via Colombo and the Suez canal, to be informed by the chairman of the Line that his peacetime days as a shipmaster were over for

4

the duration of the war. He had as an officer of the Royal Naval Reserve been called into naval service to act as commodore of convoys. Now, he found his mind going back to the convoy he had only recently brought out from the UK to Trincomalee. A difficult passage, what with air attack in the Med, the fact of having girls of the WRNS aboard, the cholera that had struck the troop convoy after leaving Port Said, and then, after passing through the Strait of Bab el Mandeb – known to seafarers as the Gates of Hell – the attack in filthy weather by the German surface raider, the *Admiral Richter*. The Commodore's ship, the liner *Orlando*, had been sunk, damaged as much by being broached-to by the sheer force of the typhoon as from the effect of the German guns. Kemp, along with many other survivors, had spent some days in an open lifeboat.

And there had been the OC Troops, Brigadier Pumphrey-Hatton, who had cracked under pressure after making life as difficult as possible for the troops under his command. Also for the Convoy Commodore.

And Pumphrey-Hatton was now bound back for the Clyde. He was to be a passenger aboard the Commodore's ship. Kemp foresaw any amount of trouble.

When on sailing day the convoy had moved out of the port, Kemp, from the bridge of the *Aurelian Star*, saw the slim figure standing in the sternsheets of a launch, touched by the early sun's rays. First Officer Jean Forrest, lately in charge of the WRNS draft . . . Kemp had not expected her to see him off, though he had half hoped she might. Now she was where she had no business to be: aboard a harbour launch belonging to the King's Harbour Master. She was following him out; but not too far. Kemp gave her a wave, resisted the temptation to blow a kiss across the water. She returned the wave and then the launch turned away, back into the port. Kemp brought up his binoculars, watched until the launch was out of sight. His hands shook a little as he lowered the binoculars to dangle at the end of their codline stay. Jean Forrest . . . they'd been through a lot together in the outward convoy and he would miss her badly on the long haul to the Firth of Clyde. He had almost made a fool of himself, not that she had been any slip of a girl infatuated by a man old enough to be her father – Jean Forrest was a little on the wrong side of forty. But it was not to be. A master mariner with a solid career behind him and a good few years to go yet, a commodore RNR in charge of a number of merchant ships in convoy, a happily married man: he had no business thinking in terms of infidelity.

He had a home in the village of Meopham in Kent, until the war so handy for the captain of an incoming liner to the London River. A happy home, and Mary now struggling with war conditions, the shortages of everything, the blackout, the air raids, the worries about a husband and two sons at sea in wartime, always half expecting the telegram from the Admiralty.

Resolutely Kemp turned his back on Colombo. There was work to be done, a war still to be fought.

Petty Officer Ramm, gunner's mate on the Commodore's staff and thereby very important in his own eyes, sucked at a hollow tooth and glared across the sea at the huge bulk of the *Resolution* as the battleship with its admiral's flag – a red St George's Cross on a white ground – took station ahead of the two columns of merchant ships, disposed abeam to starboard. Aboard the battlewagon his status as gunner's mate in charge of one of the big fifteen-inch gun-turrets would have been assured and respected. Here, he looked like being dog'sbody. The *Aurelian Star* carried DEMS ratings – standing for Defensively Equipped Merchant Ships. And there was another PO, also a gunner's mate, in charge of the DEMS party, Petty Officer Biggar. PO Biggar had refused to concede an inch to Petty Officer Ramm, who had already mentally renamed him Petty Officer Bugger.

'A matter o' seniority, chum,' Biggar had said. 'Stands to reason, don't it, eh?'

Ramm, who resented being called chum on first acquaintance, said, 'That's all very well. But me, I'm on the staff, see?'

Biggar stared rudely. 'So what? Still comes down to seniority. I got me rate in –'

'Yes, all right, all right, you've already told me that –'

'And my draft chit from Guz says I'm in charge o' the guns.'

Ramm had walked away in disgust. Guz meant that Biggar was a Devonport rating. Ramm was Pompey; and Pompey was in all things superior to Guz. And for bloody Biggar to talk about guns! Peashooters more like. Aboard the *Orlando* Ramm had had a six-inch gun. Obsolete certainly, and liable to blow up when fired, but a sight more gun-like than three-inch and two-pounders which, apart from such articles as Oerlikons, was all the *Aurelian Star* was equipped with.

The most dignified thing to do, Ramm decided, was to ignore PO Biggar as though he didn't exist. Easier said than done; and Ramm was delighted when, just after sailing, Biggar reported sick with gut rot. Immediately, Ramm had taken over. Almost as soon as he had done so, three more of the DEMS ratings turned green and were sent off to the sick bay.

All too soon, the day took on its heat. The convoy steamed over a glassy sea beneath spread awnings that would be quickly frapped if action stations were sounded. The water was of deepest blue, turquoise, cut now by the white wakes of the ships as the screws churned the water into tumbling foam and the stems cut their swathes to stream aft down either side. In his cabin, Brigadier Pumphrey-Hatton fiddled with his electric fan. There was something wrong with it; it wouldn't turn and twist as it should but remained stuck obstinately in one position, which wasn't the right position to bring comfort to Brigadier Pumphrey-Hatton, who was sweating like a pig. He had been on a search for flies, the flies that he was convinced had brought the scourge of cholera to the outward-bound convoy in the Red Sea. He could find no flies but he was convinced they lurked somewhere.

He rang for his steward. The summons was not answere ˋ Growing angrier by the minute, he rang again. Confound these seafaring people – no discipline, not like the army where everyone jumped to it instantly or else.

He went out on deck. It was almost as hot as his cabin. True, there was a little wind made by the ship's own progress through the water but it was a *hot* wind and brought out his dormant prickly heat so that he was obliged to scratch furiously.

Some things had to be brought to the attention of the ship's master. Or that of the Commodore of the convoy.

Pumphrey-Hatton made for the bridge ladder. His dark, lean face was set into angry lines. Kemp, who happened to be at the head of the starboard ladder, saw the brigadier's approach and thought: here it comes. Already.

He said, 'Good morning, Brigadier.'

'Morning. I have a complaint to make.'

7

Kemp sighed inwardly. 'Flies?' he asked.

'I've searched for flies. I've found none – so far, that is. My complaint's to do with my electric fan. It's not working as it should. I find that inexcusable – damned inefficiency if you ask me. And the blasted steward doesn't answer my bell.'

It was not Kemp's business. He glanced towards Captain Maconochie. Maconochie was checking his station, taking bearings on the flagship. Kemp wouldn't interrupt. He said shortly, 'A matter for –'

'Fiddlesticks! Kindly don't fob me off, Kemp. What do you propose to do about it, may I ask?'

Again Kemp sighed inwardly. There was no point in provoking anything. Pumphrey-Hatton was in a poor state mentally and needed kid-glove treatment. He said, 'I'll report it to Captain Maconochie. A message will be sent to the chief steward. That's all I can do, Brigadier. It's not my ship.'

Pumphrey-Hatton was trembling now. He said harshly, 'That's all you people ever say. Always passing the buck. When I commanded a brigade . . . things were very different, I assure you. It was the same with those blasted flies, even in my gin if you remember though I don't suppose for a moment you do, you were never a help, never blasted well listened.'

'I'm sorry if you felt like that, Brigadier.'

'It's a little late to be sorry now. I've no doubt you put in a word against me to that blasted medico in Trincomalee –'

'I –'

'Oh, don't bother to deny it and kindly don't argue with me. I'm not fit.'

Pumphrey-Hatton, who had remained clinging to the rails at the foot of the ladder, turned away and stalked aft, his angular body having a suddenly frail look about it. Kemp couldn't help feeling immensely sorry: it was not pleasant to be relieved of one's command in the middle of the war, to have to hand over an infantry brigade to the senior colonel until such time as another brigadier could be appointed. Kemp had been told privately (which he was aware he should not have been) of the result of the medical board: Pumphrey-Hatton had little wrong with him physically apart from the after-effects of the cholera and had in fact made a remarkable recovery considering his sojourn in the open boat in the Arabian Sea; but he was in no mental state to continue in any command capacity. The military medics in the convoy, and the *Orlando's* own doctor, had reported Pumphrey-Hatton's over-riding concern with flies, for one thing, also his lunatic behaviour in ordering the confinement below decks of the troops in the appalling heat of Port Said, the Suez canal, and the Red Sea, all in the interest of what he had believed to be secrecy. Kemp wondered now what his future would be, what the War Office would do with him after arrival and disembarkation in the Clyde. A desk job in Whitehall, probably; he couldn't do much harm pushing paper around. A sad end for an officer who had been a fighting soldier in the First World War when as a subaltern he had seen his battalion of the Duke of Cornwall's Light Infantry wiped out around him at the Marne. . . .

Kemp turned away himself and joined Captain Maconochie at the binnacle. Maconochie, his ship now in station on the flagship, handed over to his Officer of the Watch and glanced at Kemp's somewhat set face.

'Difficulties?' he asked.

'A fan that doesn't work properly. And a steward who doesn't answer bells.' Kemp hesitated. 'Look, Captain, I don't want to be a pain in the neck and I certainly don't mean to interfere, but –'

'That's all right.' Maconochie laid a hand on Kemp's shoulder. 'I've heard a lot about your late OC Troops. I dare say you and I have similar thoughts. I'll send down at once to my chief steward. We'll do what we can to make things as easy as possible for him.'

Kemp was about to express appreciation when there was a report from Yeoman of Signals Lambert taking the signal watch. 'Flag calling up, sir.'

Kemp saw the signal lamp flashing from the *Resolution's* flag deck. Yeoman Lambert's lamp clacked out the acknowledgement. Lambert took down the message on his signal pad, then reported to Kemp.

'From the Flag to Commodore, sir. Captain (D) reports single contact bearing red zero two five distant four miles. Message ends, sir.'

'Thank you, Yeoman. Repeat to all merchant ships in convoy.'

'Aye, aye, sir.'

Kemp caught Maconochie's eyes. 'The buggers are quick off the mark. This, I did not expect.'

'Nor me. Do we scatter?'

9

Kemp shook his head. 'Not at this stage, Captain. We hope the destroyers can deal with a single contact. But we'll take prudent precautions.' He turned to Sub-Lieutenant Finnegan. 'Close up guns'-crews, sub.'

'Yes, sir, Commodore.' Finnegan saluted and ran for the wheelhouse and the Tannoy. As he went, Kemp passed orders for the zig-zag to be started. The danger area had indeed come sooner than expected.

TWO

'If they're going to get us at all,' Petty Officer Ramm observed to his gunlayer, Leading Seaman Purkiss, 'they may just as bloody well get us 'ere, nice an' close to bloody Colombo. I've done my time floating around in a lifeboat.' He fished out a packet of Players cigarettes and lit up without offering the pack to Purkiss. Ramm, Purkiss thought sourly, was a man who watched his pennies: he needed them for his philanderings ashore. Purkiss, who had joined the Commodore's staff at Colombo as a casualty replacement, was a time-expired Royal Fleet Reservist like Ramm himself, and also like Ramm was of the Portsmouth Port Division. He'd come across Ramm back in the thirties, in RNB, when Ramm had been number two to the Parade Chief Gunner's Mate and a right bastard with it. Ramm had been known as Ramm by Name and Ramm by Nature and Purkiss doubted if time had dimmed his desires to any great extent.

'Zig-zagging,' Ramm said suddenly, as the *Aurelian Star*'s gun deck lurched a little to starboard. 'Increasing speed, too.' Aft, the water was churning like a mill-race, and the wake was widening as the ship turned to the zig-zag pattern. In the van the destroyers of the A/S screen were moving ahead and a little to port at their maximum speed of around 35 knots. Ramm and Purkiss watched and waited for the first of the depth charges to rip open the flat blue Indian Ocean water. Ramm began to look restive; he wasn't specially worried about a solitary U-boat, not with all the armour floating around him, but personal inaction could look bad from the bridge and he didn't want that young Yank balling him out. All subbies, in Ramm's view, were bloody

11

useless, wet behind the ears and full of bull with it, British as well as American.

He looked around for something to make his presence felt: in no time at all he found it. The panacea for all fault-finding gunners' mates: rust on the barrel of the three-inch alongside which he and Purkiss were standing. Just a pinpoint.

'Look at that,' he said in a tone of shock.

'What, PO?'

'Rust, that's what.'

'Can't see any rust.' Purkiss peered around.

'Need glasses, you do. Like a ploughed field. Get it removed pronto, all right?'

'I still can't see it, PO.'

Ramm jabbed with a finger. In so doing, he caused the rust to disappear. 'There. Blind as a bat, you are, Leading Seaman Purkiss. Should 'ave spotted it before me. Mind, it's PO Biggar's fault, that I *don't* deny, but it's your job too and if you can't do your job you're not fit to 'old your rate as a killick. Get the 'ands onto it. I'm not going into action with me guns looking like a derelict plough in a farmer's barn.'

Looking surly, Leading Seaman Purkiss detailed a hand from the gun's-crew to dig out the cleaning materials from the ready use ammunition locker. From the bridge, where he had reported back after checking that all guns'-crews had been closed up in obedience to the orders, Finnegan looked down in wonder. There were some things about the British Navy that he would never understand. It was true the limeys had a reputation for spit-and-polish, true that they were almost main deck awash with bullshit, but to see a petty officer busting his guts about cleaning a gun when within the next few minutes the ship could take a tin fish in her innards was quite something. Maybe it said a lot, but Finnegan didn't know quite what.

In addition to the zig-zag, which would now be maintained, Kemp had swung the merchant ships away from the bearing indicated by Captain (D) via the Flag and had steadied them on their original course five miles to the west of the U-boat's position. By this manoeuvre he had brought the great bulk of the *Resolution* between the convoy and the enemy while the destroyers closed in. The cruisers, under the orders of cs23, had shifted with the convoy and were guarding the flanks. From all the ships a sharp lookout was being maintained, binoculars constantly sweeping on all bearings: there might well be another U-boat, or more than one, on the starboard side, not yet picked up by the asdics.

It ended in anti-climax. Yeoman of Signals Lambert reported the next signal: 'Lost contact, sir.'

Kemp nodded. 'I fancied that might happen. She's gone deep. Stopped diesels as well. She'd probably been on the surface just before dawn, recharging batteries, and picked us up as we came out. For my money she'll let us get well ahead, then keep just out of range of the asdics.'

'Tail us, sir?' Finnegan asked.

'That's what I'm suggesting, sub. And I think the Flag has had a similar thought.' There was an exchange of light signals between the Flag and Captain (D) on the heels of which the flotilla leader began signalling himself to his destroyers. A moment later two of them began swinging heavily to port, then steadied to come up astern of the convoy to act as rearguard. Captain (D) with the remainder of the flotilla raced ahead to resume station while the cruisers remained on the flanks. Astern of the convoy, immediately ahead of the guarding destroyers, the escort carrier *Rameses* came on with her aircraft – Barracudas of the Fleet Air Arm, ranged ready for take-off on her flight deck.

Kemp left the open bridge and strode into the wheelhouse. He switched on the Tannoy. 'This is the Commodore speaking to all hands.' He paused. 'Well, it's begun. Something of a damp squib you may think. Don't be fooled. That U-boat won't go away. From now on out, we have to be ready – for her and any other U-boats that may be around. That is all.'

Kemp returned to the bridge. He swept his binoculars all around the convoy, all over the smooth, peaceful-looking Indian Ocean. The peaceful look was a mirage; it could all change within moments. A thought passed through Kemp's mind: the naval flag that was flown in peacetime when submarines were exercising in company with surface ships was a two-coloured one, blue over red. Danger under the Blue, they called it. For Danger, in wartime, read Death.

Twenty minutes later, seeing no virtue in keeping men at

action stations too long, Kemp passed the word for the guns'-crews to fall out.

The Captain's message had gone down to the chief steward, Mr Chatfield. Chatfield was an experienced chief steward; he'd seen and suffered all sorts, particularly when he'd been a dining-room steward in the liners many years before. Passengers came in all shapes and sizes, mentally as well as physically. Many of them were nice enough; many chucked their weight around and treated stewards as dirt. Haughty: they had a special inflexion in their voices when addressing stewards, like addressing shop assistants – you could hear the change, like a car changing gear, when they turned to their table companions. That had riled Chatfield, though he'd never let it show through his professional urbanity. End-of-voyage tips were important; a steward's rate of pay was poor enough. And passengers could be generous if you didn't get their backs up and did a bit of arse-crawling, much as doing that went against the grain of a self-respecting man. A few years of that before becoming head waiter (which meant even more arse-crawling) had turned Chatfield bolshie. Not exactly a communist, but certainly very red. When later, as assistant second steward, he had observed practices in the galleys that would have sent the directors of the Line into apoplectic fits, he had turned a blind eye – a red eye. Spitting in the soup destined for the first class, gobbing after a lot of hacking and hawking. The rubbing of chicken legs into hairy armpits running with galley sweat before they were delivered to the commis waiters. That and other things were passed over.

But that was in the past. As chief steward with a position to keep up after changing Lines, Chatfield had himself changed. Like many a politician, in fact. But he still didn't go much on nobs and he still didn't like that special voice. And another thing: Chatfield had had a mate aboard the ill-fated *Orlando* and this mate, who had been a survivor, had told him a lot about Brigadier Pumphrey-Hatton.

'Fans,' he said to his second steward when the message from the bridge reached his office, 'is engine-room. When will the deck department ever learn? Not answering bells – that's you. Chase up the steward on 'Is Nibs' cabin, all right? But let me know pronto if there's any trouble from Pumphrey-Hatton. I'm not having my lads turned into bloody army batmen, on duty twenty-four hours a day every day.'

The message dealt with, Chief Steward Chatfield sat back and read for the tenth time a letter from home that had come aboard with the last mail before leaving Colombo. The letter was not from his own home, oh no, it was from that scourge of husbands serving overseas, the Well-Meaning Busybody. There had been Carryings On in Southamptom, where Chatfield lived. Men had been seen coming and going; and in spite of petrol rationing there had been a Morris Eight parked outside Chatfield's house. Not once but on numerous occasions, and where was the petrol coming from was what the writer wished to know. Unpatriotic was that; the letter was about patriotism, or so it made out. But obviously what was being got at was Roxanne's virtue. Innuendoes – very nasty! Untrue, of course – Roxanne was devoted to him, he knew that because she had said so, and Chief Steward Chatfield knew he was a fine figure of a man, very little excess stomach for a man of fifty-four, a man in his sexual prime and one who brought home the bacon – like all chief stewards, Chatfield was by no means poor. In one of the liners of his former company, the chief steward, on return to their home port, used to be met by a fur-coated wife driving a car, and had once or twice given a lift to the Captain, who would otherwise have had to walk or pay for a taxi.

Roxanne wouldn't risk all that; she knew which side her bread was buttered, all right.

There was, of course, another angle: Roxanne was only twenty-six. Also, the war had meant that Chatfield was away from home for very long stretches. So in that respect, well . . . it was a worry, he had to admit that. Roxanne was very attractive, very seductive, and he'd picked her up in the first place, in the pub where she'd worked as a barmaid. People who'd been picked up once could perhaps be picked up again. Some nasty-minded, war-dodging salesman most likely, with a flattering tongue. Chief Steward Chatfield had never liked salesmen ever since his first wife, later crushed by a Southdown bus when visiting her old ma in Pompey, had been sold a very expensive lounge suite on the never-never, a suite that had collapsed under Chatfield's weight when he returned home and the firm had refused to honour the guarantee and had indeed been bloody rude about it.

If there was any truth, it had to be a salesman because salesmen had the opportunities. Chatfield ripped the letter up and dropped the pieces into his waste-paper basket. Of course it was all vicious lies, simple jealousy about the Morris Eight. But, admitting tacitly the Morris Eight, there had to be a reason for its presence. Hadn't there? Chatfield would have liked to write a stinging answer to that letter, if only to find out more, but he couldn't, because there was no address given. Nag, nag, nag – his Roxanne with a furniture salesman and a hell of a long way to the Clyde, and then the train south.

Kemp was still on the bridge when a wireless message was received in the radio room and was brought to the Commodore by the telegraphist rating on his staff.

'From NOIC Kilindini, sir.'

Kemp nodded, and read the transcript from the naval code. The message was brief, informing him that the convoy would embark two unexpected groups of people at Kilindini for transport to the UK: one, fifty-six British civilians, men, women and children, families caught in East Africa by the war and wanting to return home. This had been the first opportunity of accommodating them. Two, there would be embarked one hundred and fifty Germans, prisoners-of-war taken when an enemy cruiser had been sunk off the port some three weeks earlier. Kemp was instructed to allocate these persons among the ships of the convoy as expedient.

He passed the transcript to Captain Maconochie.

Maconochie said, 'We have spare capacity ourselves, Commodore. Some at any rate.'

'How many?'

Maconochie shrugged. 'We can take the families. Some of the Germans too. If we have to.'

'You don't sound keen, Captain.' Kemp grinned. He wasn't keen himself. Prisoners-of-war would not be popular aboard. He said, 'If you'd get precise figures from your Purser, then I'll signal the other masters and see what they can take.'

Within the next fifteen minutes Chief Steward Chatfield, on orders from the purser, had gone through his berthing lists with his second steward. He reported to the bridge that, taking into account the troops to be embarked both at Kilindini and at the

Cape, the *Aurelian Star* could take the families plus fifty of the Germans. Not a soul more. While the Commodore made signals by light around the convoy asking for berthing figures, the word spread through the ship that POWs were to be embarked for the prison camps in the UK. Petty Officer Ramm had much to say on the subject later on in the small caboosh allocated as petty officers' mess – there were just the three POS, himself and Yeoman of Signals Lambert on the Commodore's staff and PO Biggar of the DEMS contingent. Lambert, relieved from the bridge by his number two, was smoking a fag along with a cup of tea almost black in colour and syrupy with sugar.

'Huns,' Ramm said angrily. 'Buggers what 'ave bin shooting at our lads.' Too many escorts and merchant ships had been sunk by raiders in the Indian Ocean over the months of war. 'They'd best steer clear of *me*, that's for sure.' He added, 'That young Featherstonehaugh, what calls 'is bleeding self Festonhaugh. In for a commission, 'e is. WC candidate.' To the lower deck, the Commission and Warrant candidates, properly known as CWS, were known as WCS. 'On Number Two gun.'

'What about him, GI?'

' 'Is dad. Blown up aboard the old *Barham* in the Med. Blown to little pieces probably. Commander(E) 'e were, down in the engine-room when a bloody bomb went down the funnel. What's 'e going to think, eh?'

'Same as anyone with any sense,' Lambert said mildly. 'As POWs, they're out of it, facing God knows how many years of being shut away somewhere where it's not nice. No use blaming 'em for what bloody Adolf made 'em do.' He drank tea noisily. 'Me, I won't let it worry me.'

'Your dad didn't get killed by the sods, Yeo. Anyway,' Ramm added with a smirk, 'you still got other worries, I s'pose. Get any mail in Colombo, did you?'

'No, I didn't. Would you believe it, eh? Not a thing all the way from the Clyde.'

'Maybe she's still chocker,' Ramm said, smirking again. 'Teach you not to be bloody careless another time.'

Lambert made no reponse; it was a very personal matter and no business of Ramm's to go on and on about it and never mind that he, Lambert, had sought consolation in sharing his worries with Ramm in the first place. That had been a mistake: Ramm, a salacious man, had merely thought it funny. To Lambert it was very far from funny. During his leave immediately prior to rejoining Commodore Kemp for the long eastbound convoy, a french letter had popped out of his top pocket when he'd brought out his pen. Explanations had been useless. Lambert had bought the object years ago, before the war, when as a young signalman in a cruiser on the China station he had been advised by an older shipmate that matelots should always take precautions. Just In Case, Like. You Never Knew, his mentor had said, poking him in the ribs with a heavy hand. Situations could arise, and then what? Nasty diseases was what. Or even, if the woman concerned was not a Chinese prozzie but a respectable young girl who'd let a matelot go too far, children. Bastards, like. Lambert had taken this good advice but had never used the french letter, which had in fact perished. It had remained a virgin packet, if you could use the word virgin, to the day his wife had found it. By the time he had been given the advice, Lambert had already been a married man, the wedding having taken place just a week before his draft to China. He had never had any intention of being unfaithful, certainly not with a Hong Kong or Wei-hai-Wei prostitute. When he had explained this, fervently, to his wife, she had not unreasonably asked him why, if such was the case, he had equipped himself with the offending object?

There had been no really convincing answer to this. Lambert had mumbled the words of his shipmate: Just In Case. You Never Knew. This had made things worse. By the time he had left Pompey by train for Greenock and the Tail o' the Bank Doris was still nagging. Currently, Lambert had no idea how the land lay. But there was one thing he did know, at any rate about Ramm, because Ramm had come out with an anxiety of his own. Ramm's worry centred around a barmaid in the Golden Fleece in Pompey who had discovered not only that Ramm was married but Ramm's address as well. Ramm's anxiety could be summarized in the words of the traditional wardroom toast always drunk after dinner on Saturday nights at sea: 'Our wives and sweethearts – may they never meet.'

Ramm, Lambert thought, was a bloody hypocrite, his pot being slightly blacker than Lambert's kettle.

Others aboard the *Aurelian Star* were concerned about the

Germans. Several of the crew had lost fathers, sons or brothers in this war, not all at sea – there was the army and the RAF, and there had been the ferocity of the air raids at home in which in many cases wives or mothers or sisters had also died or been horribly wounded.

The ship's Chief Officer, Andrew Dartnell, spoke of this to Maconochie. 'Bad blood, sir,' he said. 'There could be trouble.' At sea, you didn't come into much physical, personal contact with Germans. They just attacked from a distance. 'When they're here in the flesh –'

'I don't think you need worry, Mr Dartnell. There'll be a perfectly adequate military escort.'

'They'll have to be allowed on deck for exercise, sir. The Geneva Convention –'

'Yes, that must be observed, of course. There'll be a conference with NOIC and the army people on arrival in Kilindini. Just start planning for it, and any difficulties'll be sorted out then.'

Dartnell had to be content with that. He had his own conference with the junior deck officers and with the bosun, the ship's master-at-arms, the chief steward and the carpenter, the latter likely to be required to carry out structural alterations on deck or below. Meanwhile Kemp had his own reservations about the Germans and to a large extent agreed with Dartnell's ideas. Also, he'd already been informed about Featherstonehaugh and his loss – throughout his seafaring life Kemp had made a particular point of knowing the details so far as he could – the worries, the hopes and ambitions – of all the men under his command. Featherstonehaugh had been very deeply upset about his father's death in action and when Kemp had spoken to him in private, man to man, he had sounded bitter. Kemp hadn't been surprised; but he hoped the bitterness would pass. Now, the advent of Germans aboard would be exacerbating. Kemp considered young Featherstonehaugh – he was little more than nineteen years of age – promising material and in due course hoped to forward his recommendation for a commission as sub-lieutenant RNVR to the Admiralty. Featherstonehaugh was in the position of not being able to put a foot wrong if he wished, as of course he did, for that recommendation to go through. He would need to watch himself when it came to the German POW presence. If Featherstonehaugh had a fault it was a tendency to

19

impetuousness and an over-eagerness. If he became over-eager on his dead father's behalf, as it were, there would be trouble. Kemp decided to have a word with Petty Officer Ramm.

In the meantime he had reports to write up: reports on the departure of the convoy from Colombo, on the contact with the U-boat, and on the preparations for the reception of civilians and POWs at Kilindini.

'I'll be in my cabin,' he said to the Officer of the Watch, 'chasing bumph. I'll be up inside thirty seconds when I'm needed.' He went below, clattering down the starboard ladder to the Captain's spare cabin beneath the wheelhouse, which had been placed at his disposal. Kemp detested paper-work, tended to put off the task whenever possible. Today he sighed and temporized: first, he would start a letter to Mary his wife, for landing with the mail at Kilindini. At Colombo, just before leaving with the convoy, Kemp had had depressing news in a cable sent by Mary via the good offices of the chairman of Mediterranean-Australia Lines and addressed to him c/o the naval base. The cable had brought the news that his grandmother, who lived with them in Meopham, had died. She had gone peacefully whilst asleep. Kemp, who had so often reflected that he must be the only Master Mariner in his fifties to have a grandmother still alive, would miss her. On the early death of his mother, Granny Marsden had brought him up as her own son, and later when she had become unable to cope on her own, the Kemps had given her a home. At ninety-two she'd had a good innings and was probably better off where she had now gone. On getting the news John Kemp had gone down on his knees in the privacy of his room and had offered a prayer for her to the God in whom he very strongly believed. He had always thought Granny was wonderful. But it had been, of course, Mary who had borne the brunt of a very old lady's whims and fancies, a very old lady's constant demands on her time amidst the wartime worries and privations, Mary who had mostly answered the call of the walking-stick constantly banged on the floor of Granny's bedroom after she had become bedbound, Mary who had patiently listened time and again to often-repeated, rambling stories from the long gone past, stories about how little Johnny had been a naughty boy and so on.

Sighing again, Kemp unscrewed his fountain pen and began the letter by thanking Mary for all she had done for so long. He made a guess that she might even miss that walking-stick; at least Granny had been company in a house otherwise empty except when either he or one or other of the boys had been home on leave. Now Mary would listen alone to the bombings as Goering's *Luftwaffe* loosed off its remaining bomb-loads before streaking home across the Channel for the airfields in Occupied France.

THREE

Ashore in a hotel in Mombasa, not far from the port area of Kilindini, the families for UK had assembled to await the arrival of the convoy and the long, dangerous voyage home. They were a fairly typical representation of British Colonials, Britons who had come out over the years before the outbreak of war, in a number of cases shortly after the end of the First World War, to make their fortunes in the ownership of coffee or tea plantations or merely to enjoy a better way of life than had become possible in England where servants were often unreliable or less hard-working than once they had been or were simply less and less easy to find. Income Tax, too, had a lot to do with their seeking a new life. Now they were going back, for a whole variety of reasons. The younger menfolk to join up and fight for the country their parents had left, the older ones either because the war had put an end to profit or because they, like the sons and daughters, felt they should rally round in Britain's hour of need.

Old Colonel Holmes and his wife were going because they were old enough to know that death was not far away and they preferred to die in their native land. Colonel Holmes, formerly of the Royal Berkshire Regiment, had had himself seconded years before the war to the King's East African Rifles where the chances of promotion were better; in the British regiments of the line, it was a case of waiting for dead men's shoes and if men didn't die you could remain a captain until into your forties.

Colonel Holmes reached out a hand as thin as paper and rested it on his wife's knee. He said gruffly, 'It's a wrench, of course, Mildred. I realize that. So many years.'

'Yes.'

'Still, the regiment's being embarked with us. There'll be things to talk about.'

'There's nobody left, Stephen.'

'Nobody that we served with, my dear. But there have been friends.'

'Yes, Stephen.'

'So we shall be in good company.'

Mildred Holmes nodded but didn't comment further. It would never come from her lips that the present officers of the regiment looked upon her husband as a fuddy-duddy, a relic of the past, a dug-out who appeared at guest nights in the mess, was politely talked to for as short a time as possible and then disregarded. Stephen had never seen that for himself; he had continued to believe as the years went by that his stories of garrison life before 1914, of the Flanders trenches, and of gay days in the twenties were well received and of interest to a totally different generation. Year after year after their retirement she had tried to dissuade him from accepting the polite invitations but his reply had always been the same: 'Oh, nonsense, my dear. They'd be disappointed.' This had invariably been followed by a gentle laugh. 'I'm a tradition, don't you know.'

A traditional bore: even as the thought came to her Mildred was distressed at her own disloyalty. Now there would be no more guest nights, no more dinner-jackets and evening gowns. In England they would be nobodies at last: an ancient colonel and his wife in a private hotel in Cheltenham, which was to be their destination. Destination, she thought, and final resting place. That was, if the Germans didn't get them first. Mildred half wished they would. They had little money beyond her husband's minuscule army pension, and the five guineas a week for the two of them in the Cheltenham hotel would absorb virtually all of that. But Stephen was determined to go home so that was that. He had been born in the North Riding of Yorkshire and had gone to public school at Sedbergh. Until Sandhurst, he had never been out of Yorkshire and now he wanted to see it again. They would have found a hotel up there if Mildred hadn't for once been adamant and made it plain that after Kenya she would be unable to stand the northern climate, the long winters, the snow that regularly blocked the roads for weeks on end.

Colonel Holmes gave a wheezy cough and fingered his close-clipped white moustache. 'I had words with Oliphant just after breakfast.' Captain Oliphant was the Naval Officer in Charge of the port. 'Very helpful. Told me we'll be going aboard the Commodore's ship. I regard that as an honour, don't you know. Told me the name of the Commodore, too.'

'Really?' Mildred wasn't particularly interested.

'Kemp,' Holmes said, as though she was expected to know the name. There was no response. 'Don't you remember?'

She shook her head. 'Kemp,' he said again. 'The time we went home via Colombo. British India to Colombo. Then the *Ardara*, Mediterranean-Australia Lines. Surely you remember, Mildred?'

'Well, of course I —'

Holmes shifted irritably in his basket-work lounge chair. 'We were at his table in the saloon. *Kemp*. Staff Captain, he was then. You *must* remember, my dear.'

Mildred's face seemed to vanish in fresh wrinkles. 'Yes, I think

'Very good chap – Kemp. Took to him immensely. First-class feller and a fine seaman. RNR, don't you know – that accounts for him having a naval appointment.'

'Yes, I see. Do you think he'll remember us, Stephen?'

'Oh, I should think so. Even —'

'Liner captains must meet a very large number of people,' she said warningly. Stephen could be in for a snub and she wouldn't care to see that; besides, the Commodore of a convoy would presumably be a very busy man.

'I had many yarns with him, my dear. Many. He was in the last war. I remember we talked about that.'

Mildred reached into a motheaten bag beside her chair and brought out some knitting. Something for a baby. The Holmeses had no children of their own, thus no grandchildren, but there was a great-niece of whom Mildred was fond and this great-niece had a baby of six weeks. Mildred was very anxious to see her; the little scrap, a boy, would make a long sea voyage worthwhile.

Kemp said, 'I wonder who they've got for us, Finnegan.' He lowered his glasses. The *Aurelian Star* was making her approach to Kilindini now. She and two more former passenger liners would enter the port to embark the native troops, the POWs and

24

the families, while the remainder of the convoy stood off with the naval escort. Kemp added, 'The civilians, I'm referring to.'

'A bunch of expatriates, sir. Empire builders, I guess.'

'You sound disparaging, Finnegan.'

'Maybe I do, sir, Commodore. The British Empire, it's kind of a sore point, back in the USA.'

Kemp grunted. 'Don't let it show, then. They may be touchy, and they're packing up a whole segment of their lives.' He paused. 'Not that I don't know what you mean, or what I think you mean, sub. They can be a difficult bunch, used to chivvying natives around, plenty of servants, that sort of thing. Stiff-necked very largely.' Kemp's liner experience had all been on the Australia run, and passengers going to Australia had on the whole been of a different sort from those going to, say, India. They had mostly been going out on business trips, or conversely returning from visits to families who had emigrated and had become absorbed into the Australian way of life and outlook. As for the Australians themselves, they were a very free-and-easy bunch and had no time for the snobbery that they associated with the English. Most voyages had been good fun, with a good social life for the ships' officers when off duty. The India-bound ships were very different. Kemp had had a number of friends in the P & O and B. I. Lines, and he'd heard enough about the sahibs and mem'-sahibs, the colonels and their ladies, the gentlemen of the India Office and the civil servants going to and from Bombay to make him glad he'd chosen the Australia run on which to build his career. The British Colonial families he was about to embark could have at least a touch of India about them. Also, he was apprehensive about carrying children to sea in wartime. The German U-boat captains, even supposing they knew, would not hold back on account of children. Kemp reflected that on the heels of the outbreak of war back in 1939, the *Athenia*, carrying predominantly women and children seeking safety in the USA, had been attacked and sunk.

Captain Maconochie conned his ship in, his engines reducing to slow as the liner neared the berth, where numbers of native dockers stood ready to act as berthing parties and take the ropes and wires from for'ard and aft. Below, Chief Steward Chatfield was engaged with the Purser, John Scott. The full details of the families, the breakdown of sexes and the number of children, had not reached the ship until, half an hour earlier, the nominal lists had been put aboard from the pilot boat. The lists showed a predominance of women: eighteen men, twenty-five women, thirteen children, six male, seven female, ages ranging from four to eleven.

Chatfield said, 'The women without husbands, sir, they'll have to share.'

'Yes. How many without husbands, Mr Chatfield?'

'Nine I make it, sir. The younger gentlemen appear to be mostly single.' Chatfield tapped a pencil against his teeth. 'All those excess women travelling single, sir. A bit of a problem. If you see what I mean.'

Scott looked up, grinning. 'We've all travelled with excess women, Mr Chatfield.'

'Yes, we have. But in peace. Not war. There's a difference.'

'What difference? Oh, all right, don't bother to explain. War loosens morals, though there's never been any noticeable tightness even in peacetime. I imagine it's not the troops you're worried about?'

'Not the Kilindini lot, sir, no, being as they're black.' Chief Steward Chatfield, bolshie as he might have been where self-important passengers were concerned, knew the status of persons with black faces. 'The ladies is white, sir. There won't be any hanky-panky there, stands to reason. After the Cape, it might be different, of course. All them Australians and New Zealanders.'

'Well, we'll cross that bridge when we come to it, Mr Chatfield. For now, the women without husbands go into two four-berth cabins.'

'Which leaves one, sir.'

'Damn, so it does. Put the lady in a double berth for now, and we'll take another look after Simonstown.'

Chief Steward Chatfield went down to his own office. His second steward was there, going through his overtime lists. Chatfield passed him the berthing plan for the Kilindini embarkation. 'I see trouble,' he said.

'Women?'

'What else, eh?'

The second steward gave his own version of what Purser Scott had said: 'Perennial problem, Chief. No good looking for trouble till it strikes.'

'Well, maybe not, but I dunno . . . a lot depends on who gets the berth in the double cabin. There's going to be nine men on their tod, missing it.' Chatfield went across to his desk and sat down heavily, wiping sweat from his face. 'I heard a good one from the chef this morning. Want to hear it?'

'Go on?'

'When royalty has a baby, they fire a twenty-one gun salute. When a nun has a baby, only a dirty old canon gets fired.'

The second steward's face was deadpan. 'One of the single women a nun, then, is she?'

Chatfield made a swiping motion towards his assistant. 'Trouble with you, Charlie, is you've no bloody sense of humour.'

Brigadier Pumphrey-Hatton was on deck a little later as the troop embarkation began. He looked down critically as the native soldiers of the King's East African Rifles were marched by companies onto the jetty. They were smart enough, he thought, marching as he had marched with the DCLI to the light infantry and riflemen's step of 130 to the minute. As ever, the tall ones looked stiffly uncomfortable – it was hard on a tall man, and some of the natives were very tall. The companies were halted and turned into line and reported by the sergeants, who were black, to the Regimental Sergeant-Major, who was white. The RSM reported to the Colonel, who was also white of course. Pumphrey-Hatton feared that one day after the war was over and everything had gone to pot – just look at some of the appallingly common temporary officers that had been foisted onto good regiments already – at some future date officers might be black. Pumphrey-Hatton shuddered at the very thought. Black men in the mess when His Majesty's health was drunk, black lips around glasses that might next be used by white ones. It would be the end of the world for such as he.

Pumphrey-Hatton lifted a hand to his uniform cap, a hand that shook badly, and eased the leather band on his head: it was giving him a headache and he didn't feel at all well after a sleepless night during which he had got up to pursue what he had believed to be a fly, one bearing disease. He had not found it, and had rung for his steward. A nightwatchman had answered and had clattered in heavy boots about the cabin, without

27

success. The man had been polite enough but had seemed to treat Pumphrey-Hatton as though he were not a brigadier who had been oc Troops aboard a transport but as a child who had had a bad dream. Pumphrey-Hatton was still thinking angrily about this when he spotted something. A movement in the ranks of riflemen, a black man picking his nose. Pumphrey-Hatton saw red, a sudden blinding light of fury at everything in sight.

'That man,' he roared out in his parade-ground voice. 'Number Four, front rank, B Company. Hand to his blasted nose. Stop it instantly!' As he finished shouting there was a dead silence all around. The RSM looked startled but quickly recovered his composure. The Colonel looked up at the liner's deck, opened his mouth, shut it again when he saw the red tabs. But he looked extremely angry. Into the silence Pumphrey-Hatton was heard to say something about blasted black beetles then, as though suddenly becoming aware of an unforgiveable *faux pas*, he put his hands over his face for a moment, recovered himself, and marched stiffly below and out of sight.

'Not my affair or yours,' Kemp said to Maconochie. 'We leave this to the military. It was damned embarrassing,' he added. 'He'd never have done it if he'd been in his right mind. It's all very unfortunate and it could lead to a lot of friction if he ever gives a repeat performance. But I say again – it's not our affair. We can't interfere.'

'You could, if necessary. As Commodore –'

'I have a responsibility to maintain the peace – if necessary, as you said. But only if it's represented to me by the Colonel of the rifles, who'll be oc Troops as far as the Cape.'

'The brigadier permitting,' Maconochie said with a grin. Kemp nodded; the remark had been tongue-in-cheek but there was a serious side to it. Pumphrey-Hatton was just the sort to pull rank and make things awkward, notwithstanding the fact that he was on the sick list for home. As to the Colonel, now seeing his troops aboard, all Kemp knew about him was that his name was Carter and that, from Kemp's brief sight of him from the bridge, he looked a reasonable sort, young for his rank and thus – or so Kemp hoped – not verging on blimpishness like Pumphrey-Hatton. With luck, Colonel Carter would have come up against senior officers like Pumphrey-Hatton before now, and would know how to deal with them. Tactfully.

28

For a while longer Kemp and Maconochie watched the native troops streaming up the embarkation gangway to the gunport door, then went below to meet the various port officials and deal with yet more bumph, the inevitable accompaniment to any ship's arrival in any of the world's ports.

One of the visitors from the shore was the Naval Officer in Charge, Captain Oliphant, wearing on the shoulder-straps of his white uniform the four straight gold stripes and curl of a captain RN. After a formal conversation with the ship's Master and the Convoy Commodore he offered a silver cigarette-case to Kemp and Maconochie and accepted a light from Kemp. Blowing smoke he asked, 'How is your memory for things past, Commodore? Or should I say, persons from the past?'

'Fair,' Kemp said. 'Who have you in mind?'

'The name's Holmes. Colonel Holmes.'

Kemp shook his head slowly. 'Can't say I recall anyone of that name.'

'Another clue, then: *Ardara*, Colombo home . . . several years ago.'

Again Kemp shook his head. 'I'm sorry, Captain. The penny fails to drop.'

'Well, do have a good think – and don't let on you don't remember him. He's embarking here with his wife, for UK. He's a decent old stick. They both are. Pretty far gone in years, and the old lady's apprehensive about the voyage. I told them I'd put in a word.'

Kemp said, 'I'll look out for them. But they'll have to accept that this is no peacetime liner. No question of being necessarily allocated the Captain's table in the saloon, that sort of thing.'

'Oh, I'm sure they'll realize that.' Oliphant added, 'It was at your table – Staff Captain's table – in the saloon that they met you. See if that aids the remembering process, Commodore.'

Kemp would do his best. But there had been so many Staff Captain's and Captain's tables over so many years, outward and homeward bound, so many dozens of faces of which only a very few were really memorable. What was much more on Kemp's mind was the content of a w/t signal from the Admiralty passed to him by Oliphant when he had come down from the bridge. This signal was addressed to Commander-in-Chief, Far Eastern Fleet, repeated NOIC Kilindini and Commodore Convoy sw03. It indicated that survivors from a merchant vessel sunk by gunfire confirmed the presence of the German raider *Stuttgart* two hundred miles east of the port of Durban in Natal.

Not so far off the track of the south-bound convoy.

Petty Officer Ramm's face was sour as the decks of the *Aurelian Star* filled with the native troops, now being chivvied by their corporals and sergeants, none of whom seemed able to find their way below. There was a lot of eyeball rolling and a lot of unintelligible chatter.

'Don't know if they're on their arse or their elbow,' Ramm said to no one in particular. He was responded to by the ship's bosun, a grizzled seaman who had done time in sail, in the old windjammers that had battled their way through the everlasting storms off Cape Horn, from Liverpool to Australia the long way, the hard way.

'Not surprising, is it? Never been aboard a ship before, and they don't know what to expect, none of 'em.'

Ramm sniffed. 'Puke their guts up, soon as we put our nose into the 'oggin outside, that's what I reckon. *And* run amok if we meet a Jerry.'

Bosun Barnes disagreed. 'They're soldiers, never mind if they've got black skins, mate. Me, I've known blacks before. We had 'em from time to time in the windjammers –'

'Well, bully for you,' Ramm said sarcastically. 'Any use, were they?'

'When they'd learned their trade, mate, they made bloody good seamen, and strong with it. Talk about muscle. A lot of 'em came from Sierra Leone – Kroos. Fishermen, used to boats from the start, they were.' Barnes paused and rolled a cigarette with a flick of his fingers. 'Mind, there was always the odd black sheep that got shanghai-ed aboard in places like Iquique or Valparaiso, you can't –'

'Black sheep, eh? That a joke, bose?'

Barnes gave him a hard look. 'Not meant to be, no. I reckon you got black on the brain, Mister Ramm. Prejudice, that is. Know that bloke Kipling, what wrote poems? "For all 'is dirty 'ide, 'e was white, clear white inside, when 'e went to tend the wounded under fire." Gunga Din, that was. North-West Frontier of India.'

'My, my,' Ramm said, eyebrows lifted. 'Walking bloody encyclopaedia, you are, mate.' He stepped backwards suddenly as some of the natives came past and he almost got a kitbag in his gut. 'Watch it, you lot,' he said in a harsh voice, and gave the offending kitbag a shove. The native stumbled and fell heavily against the guardrail of a hatch down which a steel ladder led into the bowels of the ship. He let go of the kitbag in trying to right himself, and the bag went down the hatch, making a lot of noise in its descent. The soldier seemed distraught; there was fear in the rolling eyeballs. Ramm laughed coarsely.

'Be on a charge, you will,' he said. 'Up before the Colonel an' all, just you see.'

The transports, the embarkation completed, moved off the pierhead and re-joined the rest of the convoy and the warship escort. The ships formed up again in their allotted stations and when Kemp had reported by flag to the *Resolution* there was immediate activity on the flagship's signal bridge, her chief yeoman of signals personally using the all-round masthead lamp to send the general message to all ships from the Commander-in-Chief informing them of the Admiralty's wireless signal. On the admiral's bridge of the flagship, Sir Geoffrey Layton, a short, very thick-set officer, had conferred with his Flag Captain, the Fleet Gunnery Officer, the Fleet Signal Officer and the Master of the Fleet, a specialist navigating officer.

'Not much change,' he'd said. 'We knew the raider was out, though we didn't expect him here. I'm not unduly worried. But I shall bear in mind that we may have to alter nearer to the coast and farther from the bugger's track.' He moved up and down on the balls of his feet, like a policeman in a shop doorway, resting from his beat. 'I'm not running from a fight, gentlemen. I trust you know me better than that. But my first responsibility is the safety of the troops and the convoy as a whole. In the meantime, we're ready for anything that may happen, and if we fall in with the *Stuttgart* my fifteen-inch batteries will blow the bugger out of the water. Understood, Fleet Gunnery Officer?'

'Understood, sir.'

'Good!' The Admiral rubbed his hands together and grinned, a somewhat impish grin. 'It's getting dark, Flag Captain. I suggest a further signal to all ships: *good night, sleep tight, mind the bedbugs don't bite.* I'll be in my sea cabin if I'm wanted.' He turned away and was saluted down the ladder.

When Kemp was informed of the last signal from the Flag, he said, 'For bedbugs read U-boats.'

The convoy steamed on into the gathering night, all ports and deadlights clamped down hard, no lights showing anywhere except right aft where the shaded blue stern-lights enabled the convoy to maintain station. But there was plenty of light all around, too much light for the safety and the peace of mind of any convoy commodore or any shipmaster in time of war: as the night wore on the stars shone out like beacons, glittering with an intensity that made them look so close that a hand could reach them. Thousand upon thousand of them covering the arch of heaven, and with them the moon, hanging low and large, a lantern to silhouette the ships and bring them to the immediate attention of any U-boat's captain, watching through his periscope beneath the flat calm of the Indian Ocean's surface.

Half asleep in the stifling heat of the seamen's messdeck deep down in the ship, Ordinary Seaman Featherstonehaugh sweated like a pig into his pyjamas and listened to the irregular snore coming from the wide open mouth of Able Seaman Sissons who, like himself, had been drafted to the Commodore's staff back in Colombo to replace casualties caused to the guns'-crews aboard the ill-fated *Orlando* when under attack in the Arabian Sea. Able Seaman Sissons was a three-badgeman – three good conduct chevrons on the left sleeve, gained, as it was popularly said, for thirteen years' undetected crime – and was thus by tradition known as Stripey. Stripey, an RFR man recalled for service in 1939, was well on the wrong side of forty and, like virtually all lower deck men, was accustomed to sleep either in the bare buff or in his vest and pants. Featherstonehaugh's pyjamas had been the cause of a good deal of mirth on the part of Stripey Sissons, who thought them pansy and had said so. Real men, he said, wouldn't be found dead in such. Only officers wore them, and officers were pigs. Saying this, Stripey had addressed Featherstonehaugh by his name, as spelled.

Featherstonehaugh had at once put both feet in it. 'Festonhaugh, actually. That's how it's pronounced. And my father's – my father was an officer.'

'Was 'e – actually? Was. Got disrated, did 'e?'

The young OD had flushed at that. 'He was Commander(E) in the *Barham*.'

32

'Oh. Lorst, was 'e?' Sissons changed his tone.

'Yes.'

'Sorry, lad.' Stripey put a hand on his shoulder. 'Didn't mean no offence. But do I take it you're one of them WCs?'

'If you like to put it that way, yes.'

'I do like. So don't get uppity with me, lad o' your age. And if I want to call you – whatever your bleedin' name is, in full, well, that's what I shall do. An' for Gawd's sake chuck them bleedin' pyjamas in the 'oggin.'

Featherstonehaugh had not done so. Back in his training establishment and in RNB Portsmouth most of the others in the new entries' mess had also worn pyjamas, having only recently left their civilian status behind them. Now, in the Indian Ocean night punctuated by Stripey Sissons' snores, he came fully awake. He listened to the steady beat of the engines, the slight swish of the sea against the ship's plates, and he thought of the Mediterranean and of the horrific end of the old battleship *Barham*. The *Barham* had gone up, like the battle-cruiser *Hood*, in a split second, there one minute, gone the next, in a shattering explosion, a sheet of flame and clouds of thick, heavy smoke, the guts blown out of her. He thought of what the end must have been like for his father, caught on the starting-platform below in the engine-room, caught in the fires, the escaping steam under immense pressure that could strip the flesh from a human body in seconds, the total dark as the ring main went, the tangle of steel ladders that would have been twisted into unrecognizable shapes, the inrush of water from gaping plates that would douse the fires but drown anyone still left alive.

To think of his father in that context was shattering; but the image kept recurring, and with it the memories of past days in their home in Southsea, memories of his father coming back from foreign commissions – two years with the Mediterranean Fleet, three years China-side in the light cruiser squadron – opening up wooden chests to bring out presents for the family, exotic things to Paul Featherstonehaugh as a child, things of jade and pressed Chinese silk, ornate daggers from North Africa, opium pipes . . . and over-ridingly of his father himself, smiling, happy to be home again, making them once more into a complete family unit until, inevitably, his leave was over and another ship was waiting to snatch him away. Paul had determined to follow his father into the Navy, either as an engineer or executive officer; but his maths had not been up to the standard required and he had failed to get a naval cadetship. But by this time the war had started and on his eighteenth birthday he had volunteered for the Navy as a hostilities-only ordinary seaman. Shortly after joining HMS *Royal Arthur*, the 'stone frigate' that had in pre-war days been Butlin's holiday camp, Skegness, he had been recommended by his Divisional Officer as suitable for training for a commission. His father had known that before his appointment to the *Barham*.

Paul Featherstonehaugh knew by now that the path of the CW rating was not an easy one. To attain a commission you had to stand out, to know your job better than your contemporaries, and to keep your nose clean. The fact that your father was an officer and you spoke the King's English and had been to a certain kind of school was a help in getting the first recommendation, but after that it was up to you.

Stripey Sissons' snores continued but despite them sleep came as the past images faded. He was woken again by the torch beams of the ship's master-at-arms making night rounds, then again drifted off to sleep. His next awakening came when the urgent sound of the action alarm broke the peace.

FOUR

The first alarm had come from the *Aurelian Star* herself, a report to the bridge by telephone from the masthead lookout. The senior second officer, Officer of the Watch, immediately called the Captain.

'Masthead lookout, sir, reports a feather of spray two points on the port bow. I've not picked it up myself yet.'

'I'll be right up,' Maconochie said. 'Call the Commodore at once.'

Maconochie was on the bridge inside thirty seconds, his uniform jacket over his pyjamas. Bringing up his binoculars he scanned the area around the given bearing. He found nothing. As Kemp joined him he called the masthead lookout.

'Captain here. And you sure of your report, Jones?'

'Dead sure, sir, but I've lost it again.'

'Right.' Maconochie swung round on the Commodore. 'Evidently no contact by the asdic screen. Could be imagination.'

'Or could be that she'd been lying low and had only just come to periscope depth. We'll go to action stations just in case, Captain.' Kemp added, 'We'd better report by lamp to the Flag – shaded lamp. If there's a U-boat there, we'll obviously have been seen already so nothing's lost.' The signalman of the watch was already at his side with his signal pad; Kemp passed the message for the Flag; even as the signalman was passing it, a blue lamp was seen flashing from Captain(D) in the flotilla leader. This was read off by Yeoman of Signals Lambert as he reached the bridge.

'Contact bearing red four five, sir, distant ten cables. Am attacking.'

'Thank you, Yeoman. Finnegan?'

'Sir?'

'Inform the guns'-crews. Use the Tannoy.'

Finnegan went into the wheelhouse at the double. Kemp, watching through his binoculars, saw the destroyers altering course to port and increasing speed. They were clearly visible in the moonlight; and the kerfuffle of their streaming wakes stood out in bright green phosphorescence as they hurtled towards the given bearing. As the reports came in from Petty Officer Ramm that the guns'-crews were closed up at action stations and had swung onto the bearing, the series of splashes on the convoy's port flank indicated that already the destroyer screen was attacking with depth charges from the chutes and throwers; and shortly after that the ocean seemed to rip apart as the charges exploded, great spouts of water flinging up astern of the racing destroyers. The hull of the *Aurelian Star* shuddered to the shock waves; and below decks cork insulation showered down from the deckhead of Brigadier Pumphrey-Hatton's cabin. Having slept through the stridency of the alarm rattlers, he had been woken by the racket from the depth charges and had sat up in his bunk with a jerk.

He fumbled around for the bunk-side light, cursing as at first he couldn't find it, then seized the cork life-jacket from the hook on the cabin door. The ship vibrated to more underwater explosions; and a moment later both the three-inch guns went into action overhead. Pumphrey-Hatton pulled on his khaki drill, felt around for his shoes, struggled into the life-jacket and left his cabin. In the alleyway outside, the recently embarked families, men, women and children, seemed largely to be in a state of panic. Boat drill had been held as required by Ministry of War Transport regulations as soon as the *Aurelian Star* had cleared away from Kilindini and all passengers, the military contingent included, had been fully instructed by the ship's officers. But now there was a strong degree of uncertainty in the air. Pumphrey-Hatton compressed his lips, showing anger and frustration. He pushed at an elderly man who was shepherding an old woman, presumably his wife, towards the companion-way at the end of the alley.

'Kindly get out of my way,' he snapped.

Colonel Holmes looked round. 'Really, I – '

'Kindly don't argue with me. I happen to be Brigadier Pumphrey-Hatton.' He pushed again and Holmes stumbled aside, protesting at a lack of manners. Pumphrey-Hatton continued to thrust his way through, calling out loudly that he was trying to reach the bridge. When he reached the companion-way and climbed it to the deck above he was virtually submerged by the press of native troops. He began shouting for a sergeant, but there was no NCO to be seen. There were more sharp cracks as the three-inch guns continued firing; and as Pumphrey-Hatton struggled in a sea of black men sweating with terror of the unknown, there was a whistling sound followed by a rush of air close overhead as a shell from a U-boat scored a near miss on the *Aurelian Star.*

'Commodore, sir – Flag reports more contacts on the starboard beam.'

Kemp nodded and ran across to the starboard wing of the bridge. To port, the original contact had come to the surface, forced up by the depth charges. One up to the convoy; but the German was not quite finished yet. Her fo'c'sle-mounted gun was in action, as was the machine-gun mounted on her conning-tower, and her fire seemed to be directed towards the Commodore's ship. Kemp was relieved when Maconochie, from the port wing, called out that two of the destroyers were closing the U-boat and, a moment later, reported that a direct hit had been scored on her conning-tower, and she was already beginning to settle low in the water.

As more depth charges exploded to starboard Brigadier Pumphrey-Hatton, his uniform awry, was seen coming up the starboard ladder to the bridge. Eyes blazing, he approached the Commodore.

'Now look here, Kemp –'

'Not now, Brigadier. Please leave the bridge. Unless,' Kemp added, just in case, 'you have something relevant to report?'

'You're damn right I have! Those native troops, blasted well indisciplined, never seen such a shower. I was almost trampled under foot. And there's another thing. My bedside light. Very badly positioned. You have to *grope* for it. In an emergency –'

'The point is noted, Brigadier. Now leave the bridge, if you please –'

'I *don't* please,' Pumphrey-Hatton interrupted in a shrill tone. 'I have come to state a complaint and I shall not leave until –'

'The ship, the convoy, is in action, Brigadier Pumphrey-Hatton. I am ordering you to leave the bridge. If you don't do so immediately I shall have you placed in arrest and then confined to your cabin once the attack's over. I trust you understand.'

Pumphrey-Hatton gaped. Kemp's face was set, icy. He would carry out his threat. Pumphrey-Hatton waved a fist in his face. He said hoarsely, 'I intend to break you for this, Kemp. Be very sure of that. My God, you'll be sorry for what you've just said.' He turned away and went down the ladder, every inch of him bristling.

Kemp was joined by Maconochie. 'I heard that, Commodore. Does he carry any weight?'

'If he does,' Kemp answered evenly, 'I can take the strain.' A moment later there was a loud explosion on the starboard bow, followed by a brilliant sheet of flame from one of the cruisers of the escort. The first explosion was followed by others, smaller ones, and the cruiser's quarterdeck was seen to be on fire. Her after turrets stood out in the flames, one of them wrenched from its position, the guns twisted and broken.

'*Bodmin*, sir,' Lambert reported.

Kemp lifted his binoculars. He could see bodies draped across mushroom ventilators and lying below the turrets as the flames spread. There was a signal being flashed to the Flag from the cruiser's bridge. Lambert was able to read it off. He reported to Kemp. 'Am able to steer and maintain way.'

'Maybe he is,' Kemp said grimly. 'But if that fire reaches the magazines . . .' He had no need to say more; imagination completed the thought. The shell-handling rooms, deep down in the ship, were approached by way of steel-lined shafts topped by heavy hatches which, when the clamps were put on, were fully watertight. In action, the shell-handling parties were sent down these shafts and the hatches were clamped down after them, leaving no escape. There might come a moment when the cruiser's captain would see the urgent need, if the fires encroached, to flood the magazines and shell-handling rooms. When such an emergency struck there was seldom time to open up the hatches and bring out the seamen of the shell-handling parties. The valves would be opened by remote control and the men would drown, forced up on the deepening water until they met the unyielding steel of the clamped-down hatches, openable only from above. As Kemp faced these thoughts, there were more explosions and the cruiser seemed to glow throughout her length as her plates grew red-hot from the fires that had now made their way below. Then the inevitable final explosion came, a great blast of noise and flame, and the ship disintegrated, became nothing more than flying chunks of metal outlined in the blaze, metal and bodies together, raining down on the Indian Ocean. As the *Bodmin* died, the destroyers continued their attack. Two more U-boats were forced by the depth charges to the surface and were then despatched by gunfire. An eerie peace, a calm, descended. Fifteen minutes later a laconic report came from the *Resolution*: lost contact. The convoy, minus the *Bodmin*, steamed on for the Cape. Fifteen more minutes and the order came from the Flag to secure from action stations. At the after three-inch Petty Officer Ramm removed his steel helmet and wiped at his forehead. The hard rubber band of the tin hat always gave him a nasty headache when worn for what he considered too long.

He spoke to Featherstonehaugh. 'First taste of action, lad? Didn't do so badly, I'll say that. Bet you was shit scared, though, eh?'

'No, PO, I –'

'Don't tell bloody lies! *I* was. Reckon you never get really used to it, wondering if your name's going to be on the next projy. Though sometimes you think to yourself, maybe that'd be the best bloody way out of it.' He gave a guffaw.

Featherstonehaugh asked, 'Out of what, PO?'

'Never mind that, you're too young and bloody innocent to appreciate it.' The barmaid at the Golden Fleece was still much on Ramm's mind. If she made an approach to Ramm's old woman, well, the old woman in action was a sight worse than anything Adolf Hitler could chuck at a matelot. He'd sooner face the enemy any day of the week.

As ever when a ship went down in wartime, there was, afterwards, a man's conscience to plague him. It was in fact very unlikely that many of the *Bodmin*'s company would have survived that final explosion that had ripped the cruiser apart. But there might have been a handful. This was the Indian Ocean, not – for instance – the Denmark Strait where the mighty *Hood* had gone down, leaving only three survivors out of a ship's company of some sixteen hundred men. There had in fact been some who had been thrown clear but all except for those three had perished quickly in the icy waters. The three had been picked up by the destroyer escort in the nick of time before death came. Here, south of Kilindini, that would not have happened. On the other hand, there would be the sharks, scenting blood. But in any case you didn't hazard a vital convoy by stopping to pick up possible survivors – not in a situation where other U-boats could be closing in, as yet beyond the range of the asdics, or a surface raider might be lurking. You didn't turn a convoy into a sitting duck, a perfect target for attack. This was true; but it was a facet of the war that all hands detested, however inevitable it might be. This was far from the first time Kemp had been faced with such a situation; but he had never grown inured to it. He suffered each time. With two sons at sea, there was a personal angle to it in addition to his own sense of inadequacy to help: would another ship one day steam away from a sinking and leave one or other of the boys to drown?

He became aware of Finnegan at his side as he stood there on the bridge, not going below again to resume his sleep. Already dawn was not far off; soon the brilliance of the stars would start to fade as the eastern sky lightened, and the guns' crews would be at routine dawn Action Stations. He said, 'It's a rotten business, sub.'

'Yes, sir, Commodore. Nothing you can do about it, though. What it comes to is . . . it's up to the Flag.'

Kemp sighed. 'Admirals have a hell of a lot of gold braid. They also have a hell of a responsibility. They earn their privileges.'

'Yes, sir, I guess they do.' Finnegan had, very briefly, met the Commander-in-Chief at a reception held in Colombo before the convoy had left. Kemp and his assistant had been invited along with Captain Maconochie whose ship would wear the Commodore's broad pennant, and the commanding officers of the escort. Admiral Layton had taken pains to talk to Finnegan, to congratulate him on being almost the first citizen of the USA to join the war. The Admiral had seemed immensely human, with a kindly twinkle in his eye, although he had a reputation for being a strict disciplinarian. Sir Geoffrey Layton had altered Finnegan's view of British admirals, whom he'd imagined would be a remarkably stuffy bunch of self-important shellbacks who wouldn't dream of speaking on friendly terms with a mere sub-lieutenant of the RCNVR. There was nothing stuffy about Admiral Layton. He had asked a lot about America; he had great admiration for President Roosevelt, and was appreciative of the immensity of America's war effort which was largely due to Roosevelt himself. And he had seen to it that Finnegan's glass was topped up with gin while they had been talking.

Finnegan knew that the Admiral would be feeling as bad as Kemp about steaming away from the *Bodmin*.

The Commodore did not attend meals in the saloon: the Captain's table remained the Captain's table. Kemp had had enough of that during his years as Master with the Mediterranean-Australia Lines, where he had had to suffer many bores along with more congenial voyagers. But he did not forget the recommendation of NOIC Kilindini that he should spare some of his time for old Colonel Holmes and his lady wife. During the forenoon of the day after the U-boat attack he sent Finnegan down with an invitation to the Holmeses. He would be delighted if they would come to his cabin for a pre-luncheon drink.

They would indeed be delighted; but only the Colonel would come. He asked for his wife to be excused; she was feeling a little off-colour.

At eight bells in the forenoon watch Kemp left the bridge and waited in his cabin for Colonel Holmes. He arrived very formally dressed in a white sharkskin suit with a stiff white collar and his regimental tie, the Berkshires, to which parent regiment he had mentally reverted on retirement. To Kemp, who quite failed to recognize him, he looked thin and papery. He apologized again for his wife's absence. 'The racket, you know, Captain. The gunfire and all that. Not used to it. We've lived a pretty quiet life since I retired.' He gave a somewhat croaky laugh. 'Quiet! Certainly no heavy gunfire. Or depth charges.'

Kemp smiled. 'I imagine not, Colonel. It would have been upsetting, naturally.'

'Yes.' Holmes, who had not yet made any reference to their

41

previous, peacetime meeting, took a glass of gin-and-bitters from a salver held out by Kemp's steward. 'Thank you, steward,' he said.

'It's a pleasure, sir.' The steward handed his salver to Kemp: Kemp's glass contained only orange squash, something he more or less detested but he seldom drank alcohol at sea in wartime and never in company with passengers. When the steward had returned to his pantry Holmes said, 'As a matter of fact . . . there was something else that upset my wife. Not that I'm making any formal complaint, nothing of that sort. It's not really important. But it was upsetting.' Holmes took a sip of his gin and swallowed. A large adam's-apple rippled in a scrawny throat. Then he asked, 'Who is this Brigadier Pumphrey something?'

'Pumphrey-Hatton. He –'

'Ah, yes, that sounds like what the feller said. I remembered the Pumphrey part. By association, really. When we were serving with the Berkshires in Colchester . . . my wife had a cat named Pumphrey. Tabby.'

'Really?' Kemp sat forward in what he hoped was an attitude of interest.

'Yes. Now, who is this officer? Do I take it he's OC Troops?'

Kemp felt he had to go carefully, act with due caution when speaking of Pumphrey-Hatton. He said, 'Not OC Troops, Colonel. He's a passenger, the same as you.'

'That's odd. He appeared to be wearing a uniform. And he doesn't strike one as retired. What's up with him, Commodore?'

'In what respect do you mean?'

'Feller's a boor,' Holmes said briefly. 'Damned rude to me and my wife.' He explained about the shove in the back from Pumphrey-Hatton and the way in which the brigadier had spoken and had forced his way through the passengers. 'Quite unnecessary,' he said. 'Is he going to the Cape?'

'No,' Kemp said. 'All the way to the Clyde.'

'Home? Do you know why?'

Kemp shook his head: it was not his business to reveal anything about Pumphrey-Hatton's recent past. 'I really can't say, Colonel –'

'Or won't? As the Commodore of the convoy, you're surely . . . well, I won't press. It's not my pigeon, of course. But the feller didn't strike me as normal somehow.'

Kemp thought it time to alter the course of the conversation. He said, 'I understand we've sailed together before, Colonel. I have to confess I didn't remember you at first.'

'Yes, I was coming to that – our previous voyage together.' Holmes waved a thin hand. 'It's natural enough not to recall . . . so many faces, don't you know, in between. And I dare say I've grown older.'

Kemp murmured some polite disclaimer of age. After that the old man did most of the talking. Did Kemp remember . . . various names from that long forgotten Staff Captain's table were trotted out and remarked upon. When that was exhausted Holmes turned to other aspects of his life, mainly military. Many names were mentioned, people whom Kemp was not remotely likely to have met. Good old Bill Palmer of the gunners: when stationed in Victoria Barracks in Southsea, good old Bill, who was a real character apparently, had by some subterfuge managed to switch off all the lights at a Kimbell's dinner dance and had then hurled rolls of toilet paper across the dark dance floor, with hilarious results when he switched the lights on again. Did Kemp know Kimbell's? No. It was the fashionable place to go to, in Osborne Road. Good old Bill was followed by Arse-end Portlock of the KOSB, so called because he was always late on parade and had to be covered for by his company sergeant-major. General Montgomery, whom Holmes remembered as a subaltern in the Warwicks, right back in the First World War . . . Holmes couldn't recall just where he'd met Monty, and he cudgelled his brains for a while before deciding that it didn't really matter. He mentioned a few other names and then went back to good old Bill and Arse-end Portlock, both of whom had retired some years before the war and had been recalled to the colours to act as Railway Transport Officers, good old Bill at Crewe and Arse-end Portlock at Paddington, where he had been killed by a bomb in an air raid. Late again: Holmes said he'd been slow to reach the air-raid shelter. He'd been, after all, pretty elderly, though younger than Holmes himself.

Somehow, Kemp was unable to tie up the old man with people such as good old Bill with his toilet-paper japes, and Arse-end Portlock. But he reflected that everyone had been different in their salad days, himself included.

Colonel Holmes' visit was terminated by the luncheon bugle:

43

war or no war, the *Aurelian Star* maintained at least some of the niceties of a first-class peacetime liner.

In the saloon, Holmes was joined by his wife. 'Charming feller, Kemp,' he said as he sat down in the chair withdrawn for him by the saloon waiter. 'Just as I remember him. Sad to say, he didn't remember me, but that's understandable, as I told him. Pity you couldn't have come along, my dear. Anyway – it's nice to see you better.'

'I'm afraid I shan't eat anything, Stephen.'

'Oh, dear.' He looked at her with concern. 'Think you ought to see the ship's doctor? Or perhaps Kennedy would stretch a point.' Major Kennedy was the MO of the native battalion. 'I can have a word, Mildred, if –'

'No, no.' She shook her head vigorously. 'I really don't want to bother anyone, Stephen.' She changed the tack of the conversation somewhat quickly. 'What did you and Commodore Kemp talk about?'

'Oh, this and that.' Holmes waved a hand. 'Reminiscences, don't you know.'

'Yours?' There was an affectionate amusement in her eyes.

'Well – yes. Largely. Kemp was never a particularly talkative man as I remember. Not a man for small talk.'

'You told him about Captain Portlock I dare say.'

'Oh, yes. He was very amused. Or was it the story about good old Bill . . .'

There were no further attacks; a sense of peacetime began to descend on the liner as with the accompanying ships she continued on her way south for the Cape. The zig-zag was being maintained despite the absence of any submarine contact: no chances were being taken. Kemp kept his personal staff and his guns'-crews at a high pitch of efficiency. Ramm was constantly, as it seemed to the gunnery ratings, exercising the three-inch crews, largely under the surveillance of Sub-Lieutenant Finnegan which Ramm didn't go much on and said so to Leading Seaman Purkiss.

'Gets on me wick,' he said. 'What's 'e know about gunnery, compared to a Whale Island gunner's mate. Eh?'

'He's an officer,' Purkiss said, tongue-in-check. 'Got to know best, hasn't he?'

Ramm's breath hissed between his teeth. 'You,' he said. 'Featherstonehaugh.'

'Yes, PO?'

' 'Ow long before you aspire to the bleedin' wardroom, lad?' Featherstonehaugh shrugged. 'I don't know, PO. It depends on more recommendations, and on –'

'All right, lad. Reckon you know more about gunnery than I do, do you?'

'No, PO –'

'Dead right you bloody don't,' Ramm said grimly. 'So just learn while you can, eh? Before bloody 'Itler says it's too late, like. Shift round, take Leading Seaman Purkiss' place on the gun. We'll see how you make out.'

As gun-drill recommenced, Finnegan was seen once again making his way aft. As Ramm began shouting orders to bring the three-inch to bear on imaginary targets, Finnegan kept a special eye on Ordinary Seaman Featherstonehaugh as per orders from the Commodore. Watching, Finnegan reflected that the limeys made heavy weather for themselves even over their own names. Not only their own names but trade names too. Even Dooars whisky: the limes called it Dyouars . . .

That afternoon the wireless office received a WT signal from the Admiralty, a Top Secret classification addressed to the Flag repeated Commodore. The signal being in cypher and not plain naval code, it was decyphered by Sub-Lieutenant Finnegan. He handed the plain language version to Kemp in the latter's cabin.

Kemp read: the surface raider *Stuttgart* was no longer in the Indian Ocean. Intelligence reports indicated that she had rounded the Cape of Good Hope, having kept well to the south, and was now believed to be back in the South Atlantic.

Kemp tapped the message form. 'This could mean she's waiting until we've embarked the main troop draft at Simonstown. A more worthwhile kill, sub.'

'Yes, sir. And I reckon there could be another angle to it.'

Kemp looked up. 'Well?'

'*Resolution*, sir. She's due to leave us at Simonstown. With her escort. It's likely the Heinies know that, wouldn't you say?'

Kemp nodded. 'It's possible. Damn spies everywhere, and big mouths not taking in the message of the posters. You know – Be

Like Dad, Keep Mum.' Kemp got to his feet. 'I'm showing this to Captain Maconochie. I'll be with him on the bridge. My compliments to OC Troops . . . I'd be grateful if he'd join us right away.'

When the three senior officers conferred within the next few minutes, Kemp put forward his assistant's guess. Colonel Carter, OC Troops as far as Simonstown, concurred but made the point that the reduced convoy escort was bound to be reinforced with another battleship.

Kemp was not so sure. The briefing at Colombo had made no mention of a replacement for the *Resolution*. There was in any case a shortage of heavy-gun ships and many of those that might be available – might being the operative word – were old and slow like the *Resolution* herself and their presence would slow the convoy when eventually it moved into the principal operating area of the U-boat packs – the North Atlantic. He added, 'It was known from the start that *Resolution* would be leaving us –'

'But surely this makes a difference, Commodore? The fact of the *Stuttgart* going back around – ?'

Kemp gave a hard laugh. 'It ought to. Perhaps it will. It'll be on the minds of the staff in the Operations Room at the Admiralty. But staff minds are unpredictable, and a lot depends on what other uses they have for the heavy ships. Don't forget, there's been a lot of talk about a second front in Europe. I have it in mind, and so will the staff, that the battlewagons are going to be needed to bombard the coasts, soften up for the landing craft to disembark the troops.'

'So what you're saying is this: the convoy could be left without proper protection, set at risk in the interest of something bigger?'

Kemp said, 'I'm not saying that, Colonel. All the same . . . it's happened before. All we can do is – wait and see. You can be dead sure Admiral Layton will make urgent representations to the Admiralty just as soon as we reach Simonstown. Until then, he can't break wireless silence.'

Three days later the convoy and escort reduced speed for entry to the base at Simonstown. Shortly after the ships had secured at the berths, Brigadier Pumphrey-Hatton, who had lain low ever since the contretemps with Kemp on the bridge, was observed making his way ashore.

FIVE

'Gibraltar,' Pumphrey-Hatton said reminiscently. 'Eight years ago. Or was it nine – one's lost count of peacetime years, I find. It all coalesces. I see you have flies here too,' he added, sweeping a hand across his face. 'Damn brutes! It was they that brought the cholera, back there in the Red Sea.'

Pumphrey-Hatton was seated in the office of a rear-admiral, who held the appointment of Senior British Naval Officer, Simonstown. Pumphrey-Hatton, then a major, and Rear-Admiral Thomas, then a commander, had met in Gibraltar when Pumphrey-Hatton had been stationed in Buena Vista barracks with the foreign service battalion of the DCLI; Thomas had been Executive Officer of the battleship *Queen Elizabeth*, flagship of the Mediterranean Fleet. They were both men of a largely similar outlook and they had got along together when they had met at the various social occasions that had been part and parcel of naval and military life in peacetime. There had been drinks at the NOP, the Naval Officers' Pavilion, swimming at Rosia, parties at Government House, functions at the Royal Gibraltar Yacht Club and so on. There had been expeditions across the guarded frontier into Spain. Now, Pumphrey-Hatton spoke of some of this.

'Lamorna,' he said. 'No blasted flies. You'll remember, of course.'

'I do indeed.' Lamorna was the name of a guest house where many service families had stayed when out from home on a visit to their husbands – mainly naval wives since the army families mostly had quarters in the garrison. Commander Thomas' wife and children had stayed there on two or three occasions when the flagship had been in the port; and Pumphrey-Hatton and his wife had dined with the Thomases. Pumphrey-Hatton remembered what he had privately called 'the Thomas woman' as a somewhat faded beauty who spent much of her time talking about horses and had a voice and a laugh to match.

Now, he enquired after her.

'Oh, she's very well . . . when I last heard, that is. Sent her off to a sister in the country when the war came. Plenty of riding, that sort of thing.'

'Yes, quite. There's another fly.' Pumphrey-Hatton swatted again.

The rear-admiral raised an eyebrow. 'Flies really bother you?'

'Yes, they damn well do.' Pumphrey-Hatton spoke viciously.

'Don't let them, then. They don't bother me, so long as they keep out of the gin.' The rear-admiral gave a hearty laugh.

'That's just it – they damn well don't! I had them in my gin in the Red Sea, you know. Really damnable – I've had the devil of a time I don't mind telling you. What with the cholera and the sinking. Of course, you'll have heard I'm being invalided home.'

'Yes. I'm very sorry – rotten luck, that.'

'And all because of flies. Largely, anyway. And other things that are just as bad. Confounded inefficiency. And *damned impudence!*'

'I'm sorry, my dear chap. I agree things aren't what they were in peacetime, but . . .' He glanced at a clock on the wall to his right: he was verging on an appointment with a member of the South African government. He continued with what he had been about to say. 'We have to make the best of things as they are. It's been good to meet you again, old boy. We had some wonderful times in Gib. If there's anything –'

'I've not finished yet,' Pumphrey-Hatton said. He brought out an envelope and handed it across to Rear-Admiral Thomas. 'In there is a report, compiled by myself, on the conduct of the Convoy Commodore. Kemp's his name as I dare say you're aware. Confounded inefficiency is rampant, *absolutely rampant*, in that man's ship. Not just the flies. Other things. Electric fans that don't work, stewards who fail to answer bells. And personal rudery to boot. The man had the blasted cheek to order me off his bridge – and then threatened me with arrest! It's all in

48

there. I'm asking you to read it and then forward it to the Admiralty.'

At Simonstown, the mail came aboard. Kemp read five letters from his wife. The death and funeral of his aged grandmother was gone into; the Chairman of the Mediterranean-Australia Lines had attended the funeral out of respect for Kemp who had been one of his senior captains. There were also letters, one each, from his sons at sea on naval service and unable to write much about their lives on account of the censorship; but both were in good spirits and, so far anyway, safe and well.

Yeoman of Signals Lambert also had a letter from his wife. Just the one, and a little restrained in tone: reading between the lines Lambert believed the episode of the french letter had not been entirely set aside. The letter seemed to contain a rueful sniff, a sort of self-pity that didn't exactly help a man thousands of miles away across the sea.

For Chief Steward Chatfield there was a long letter, heavily scented, from Roxanne in Southampton. It was very loving and there was no mention of a salesman but she did say she was having as good a time as was possible in wartime and without him by her side. A friend (what sort of friend?) had managed to get her a bottle of gin, rare as nectar these days, and each supper time she gave herself a teensy-weensy one and drank to hubby's safety at sea. She hoped – and he could almost hear the coy giggle – that he wasn't going after all those uninhibited popsies out east, the word 'east' being heavily scratched out and 'where you are' substituted.

There were other letters for Chatfield: a reminder that the rates hadn't been paid; a bill for a wireless repair; an invitation from Dr Barnardo's to make a donation. These had all been forwarded by Roxanne. There was one that had not been: one from the anonymous busybody. The Morris Eight had been seen again, many times. Its driver had been seen: a man of around thirty, maybe a little less, who should have been in uniform but wasn't. He was handsome if you liked that sort – rather slick with Brylcremed dark hair and padded shoulders – and he hadn't looked short of a bob or two, or of petrol either come to that.

As before, Chatfield ripped the letter up angrily. He turned his attention to his stores list. There was quite a bit to come aboard in

Simonstown, including booze for the passengers and ship's officers. Chatfield also had his own personal stock to consider: he was very partial to van der Humm, the very excellent brandy that they produced at the Cape.

Petty Officer Ramm's wife had also written. So had the blonde bombshell from the Golden Fleece. Ramm opened each letter to the rapid thump of his heart, but all was well so far. And never the twain must meet . . .

During the afternoon Kemp made his formal call on SBNO – Rear-Admiral Thomas. After his morning appointment, Thomas had read Pumphrey-Hatton's lengthy report. It was a diatribe of complaint, an extension of what the brigadier had already reported verbally: flies, fans, stewards and rudery, right back beyond Colombo where the current convoy had originated, back to the Red Sea, the Suez Canal, and the Mediterranean. It seemed to substantiate what Thomas had gleaned about Pumphrey-Hatton's mental state. Nevertheless, it was a report officially delivered from a senior military officer who until disaster had struck had been OC Troops aboard the Commodore's ship.

After Kemp had made his formal report, also for transmission to the Admiralty, of the conduct of the convoy from Colombo to the Cape, the rear-admiral mentioned Pumphrey-Hatton.

'How,' he asked abruptly, 'do you get on with Brigadier Pumphrey-Hatton?'

'In what respect do you mean, sir? Socially – or in the course of duty?'

'Let's say both, Kemp.'

'I'd say he's fairly typical of a certain sort of army officer.'

Thomas gave a short laugh. 'And what's that supposed to mean?'

Kemp said, 'I rather think you get the meaning – don't you?'

'Perhaps. Not all beer and skittles. Of course, there's no question of duty for Pumphrey-Hatton now. I find it all rather sad. He's a prickly character.' Thomas got to his feet and took a few turns up and down the room. He seemed about to say something further but thought better of it. He returned to his desk and sat down. 'Question of your escort,' he said. 'There'll be the usual sailing conference with NCSO but I thought a word first . . . you'll know you're losing *Resolution* and her destroyers, of course.'

50

Kemp nodded.

'Admiral Layton will leave Simonstown after refuelling. And I dare say you've noticed there's no other battleship in the port.'

Kemp said, 'Yes, I had noticed that.'

'With some misgivings, I suspect?'

'Yes, sir, you could say that.'

'Well, we can't produce battlewagons out of thin air. Layton's destroyers will be replaced and there'll be one additional cruiser, a heavy one – *Vindictive*. Ten thousand tons. She's been down here boiler-cleaning. *And*,' Thomas added with a grin, 'replenishing her wardroom wine stocks. She's normally based at Freetown in Sierra Leone and that's where she's bound. She'll detach at the latitude of the Rokel River.'

'And be replaced?'

'No, I'm afraid not, Kemp –'

'But that German raider, the *Stuttgart* –'

'Yes, we know all about the *Stuttgart*. Except, that is, her current exact position and course. But you've not been forgotten. The Admiralty's well enough aware of the risks. C-in-C Home Fleet has been ordered to detach a battleship from Scapa and steam her south to rendezvous with the convoy. We don't yet know where the rendezvous will be nor which ship C-in-C will detach, but it seems likely it'll be the *Duke of York*. And that's all I can tell you for now, Kemp.' He paused. 'By the way, your report didn't have much to say about those POWs. I take it you've had no trouble?'

'None at all, sir.' Kemp hesitated. 'Nothing beyond a few long faces amongst the merchant crew. And my own staff . . . nothing that can't be contained, of course.'

The rear-admiral nodded thoughtfully and after a pause said, 'You have a CW rating aboard. Featherstonehaugh.'

'Yes, I have –'

'How's he making out?'

'I've only had him since Colombo, sir. But I've no complaint to make. He does his job, according to my assistant and the gunner's mate.'

'Keep an eye on him, Kemp. I knew his father – commander(E) in the *Barham*. Lost, of course. I met the boy on a couple of occasions before the war. Seemed the right type. No favouritism, of course – but keep an eye open whenever you can, Kemp.'

Kemp promised to do so. But if that eye detected any shortcomings, it would not be the Nelsonic blind eye. Too many men's lives depended in war and peace at sea on the efficiency and personal qualities of those set in authority over them for high-ranking connections to over-ride any defects.

After Kemp had left his office, Rear-Admiral Thomas read again through the report prepared by Brigadier Pumphrey-Hatton. It was, in his own unuttered phraseology, a load of bullshit. Flies and faulty fans might be irritants but personal comfort had no place in a formal report from a brigadier. Thomas had more than a suspicion that Pumphrey-Hatton wouldn't bat an eyelid at flies and airless heat along the troop-decks. And any commander at sea had the unassailable right to chuck anyone off his bridge if he felt so inclined. The threat of arrest was perhaps, but only perhaps, going a little far. But from what he had just seen of Kemp, Thomas was inclined to believe that his judgement was unlikely to have been at fault. In other words, Pumphrey-Hatton had asked for it. Thomas had played with the idea of telling Kemp about that list of complaints but, since it had been delivered in confidence, he had felt his hands, or his tongue, to be tied. Which he very much regretted. Pumphrey-Hatton and he had got along together in those pre-war days. Pumphrey-Hatton had been a keen soldier and dedicated to his regiment. A harsh disciplinarian, or so it had been said, but there was nothing wrong in that. Something of a nit-picker, but then so were many regimental officers with little to occupy their time on foreign service. Thomas recalled that his wife hadn't really liked him. Too starchy, she'd said, and no interest in horses. Now, sitting brooding in his Simonstown office, Thomas believed that that ill-natured report, when received eventually at the War Office via the Admiralty, might prove to be the final nail in Pumphrey-Hatton's military coffin.

Leading Seaman Purkiss, right-hand man of Petty Officer Ramm, had gone ashore just as soon as libertymen had been piped. He had gone ashore with two objectives: to get drunk, and to find a popsie, black, coloured or white didn't matter all that much. By the time Commodore Kemp was on his way back, in a taxi, to the *Aurelian Star*, Purkiss was well on his way to achieving his first objective, having consumed several pints of beer, six gins, and a couple of large Van der Humms. There was, however, still some spare capacity, and it was while that capacity was waiting to be filled that Leading Seaman Purkiss left the bar where he had been seated on a high stool and made his way to the gents to empty tanks, a precautionary move on his part.

On emerging he bumped into a uniformed figure. Swaying, he blocked the way, uttering a belch of fumes.

'Get out of my way,' Brigadier Pumphrey-Hatton said.

Purkiss lurched and almost fell against the brigadier. 'An' 'oo says so?'

'I'm Brigadier Pumphrey-Hatton.'

'I don't give a fish's tit if you're Pontius bloody Pilate, mate –'

'You're stinking drunk, man, and a disgusting sight. If you don't get out of my way immediately, I shall call the Military Police and have you arrested. *Move!*'

Purkiss remained where he was. He was seeing two if not three Pumphrey-Hattons now. 'Look, mate –'

'Don't call me mate!' Pumphrey-Hatton said in a voice that was becoming frenzied. 'I shall charge you with lack of respect in addressing an officer and I warn you –'

'Bollocks,' Leading Seaman Purkiss said loudly, and as another person loomed up behind the brigadier he shoved a fist forward into Pumphrey-Hatton's face. Pumphrey-Hatton stepped sharply back, at the same time flinging out an arm. Losing his balance, he not only cannoned into the person behind but managed to strike this person a blow in the face with his outflung hand. The newcomer happened to be Petty Officer Biggar of the *Aurelian Star*'s DEMS contingent. Biggar lost his footing and fell flat, with Pumphrey-Hatton coming down on top of him. As the two struggled to their feet, Biggar became aware of the identity of the rating who had caused the fracas.

'You, eh. Just bloody look at what you done now, you bleedin' object. Striking an officer. Thus causing the officer to strike a rating. Me. Court Martial charges both. What a fuckin' awful potmess, begging your pardon, sir.'

He saluted. Pumphrey-Hatton stared, his face working with a number of emotions. Then tears began streaming down his face and suddenly he pushed past Biggar and vanished along the passage. Petty Officer Biggar pulled out a handkerchief and wiped at his face. 'What I'd call embarrassing,' he said. 'Poor sod's likely had a hard war. You didn't ought to 'ave done what you did, Leading Seaman Purkiss, putting me in a bloody pickle an' all. I reckon we keep mum, hope 'e don't recognize either of us. An' don't you do any more drinking, Leading Seaman Purkiss, an' that's an order, right?'

'Right,' Purkiss said in a slurred voice. 'Got other things to do now anyway.'

'Oh, yes? Such as?'

Purkiss gave a leering laugh. 'One guess, PO.'

'Bollocks. In your state? You'll never make it, boyo.'

Early the following morning, the Commodore of the convoy along with the masters and chief officers of the merchant ships and the Commanding Officers and navigators of the escorts attended the briefing by the Naval Control Service Officer. There was no fresh information so far as Kemp was concerned: what the rear-admiral had already told him was still virtually the extent of current intelligence. The whereabouts, in any precise sense, of the *Stuttgart* was still not known. The raider apart, there would be the usual hazards of any ocean convoy: the hunting packs of U-boats as the ships came towards the latitude of Freetown, where the *Vindictive* would detach into the Rokel River. The one fresh piece of information available was that the Home Fleet battleship would make a rendezvous three hundred miles to the north of where the *Vindictive* would detach. Also it was confirmed that the battleship would be HMS *Duke of York*, wearing the flag of the Vice-Admiral Commanding, 1st Battle Squadron, together with her own destroyer screen and two light cruisers, *Caradoc* and *Cardiff*. As Kemp returned from the conference with Sub-Lieutenant Finnegan and Captain Maconochie, there was movement in the port: HMS *Resolution* was moving out with her escort, the Admiral's flag fluttering from the masthead in a strong southerly breeze. With her went her escort: as Maconochie remarked, it left them fairly naked.

'Like the mistress of the Alsatian,' Finnegan said with a straight face.

'I beg your pardon, Finnegan?'

'A filthy story, sir. Told me by a guy in a bar –'

'I don't think we want to hear it, Finnegan.'

Finnegan waved a hand. 'Just as you like, sir.'

The taxi deposited them at the gangway of the *Aurelian Star*; as they climbed Kemp saw the *Vindictive* moving across the harbour towards the fuelling berth. Her boiler-cleaning completed, the cruiser was entering the final stages of her preparation for sea. Big and well-armoured, one of the last of the heavy cruisers, she was a reassuring sight. But she was no battleship.

The returning officers were saluted aboard by the Chief Officer and the quartermaster at the upper platform of the accommodation ladder. Captain Maconochie took his Chief Officer aside.

'Prepare for sea, Mr Dartnell. We leave at 2200 tonight.'

'Aye, aye, sir.'

'And a message to the Chief Engineer. My compliments – and I'd like him to come to my day cabin.' With the Commodore, he climbed the ladders to his accommodation below the bridge. In the space allocated as seamen's messdeck for the RN ratings, Leading Seaman Purkiss was nursing a head that still clanged like a bell at the slightest sound. He had little recollection of what he'd done in the later stages of the day before, no recollection at all of having been brought back aboard by the naval patrol and more or less poured into his bunk. He had been apprised of this by Petty Officer Biggar early in the 'morning after'; charges, PO Biggar said, pended. Purkiss knew that he stood to lose his rate as leading seaman but Kemp might be lenient and merely put him under stoppage of leave for a while, which wouldn't be any hardship once they'd gone to sea. His worry was Brigadier Pumphrey-Hatton. If *he* pressed charges, then this current voyage would end for Purkiss in the Naval Detention Quarters in RNB Pompey. Ninety days was the least you could expect for striking an officer. Another thing that bothered him was a very personal matter: he had not the remotest idea as to what kind of woman if any he had eventually landed up with. He might have got himself a dose, and what would his wife say to that? Edith was the jealous sort and weepy with it. Also, her old man, an ex-chief gunner's mate, was still alive and active and had once been the heavyweight champion of the Navy.

Purkiss had consulted PO Biggar, whose advice was to see the quack and set his mind at rest. Or not, as the case might be. But Biggar had also offered consolation. 'Like I said back in that bar. A pound to a penny you 'ad the droops. Not that I know where you went after, but I reckon you're safe enough. Anyway, you were so bleedin' pissed not even a prozzie would have taken you on. Not beyond taking your cash off you.'

At 2130 special sea dutymen were piped throughout the warship escorts, the cable and side parties were closed up, and the ships that had been at anchor shortened-in and prepared to weigh, while those at the berths alongside cast off wires and ropes fore and aft, retaining the springs until the word came from the various navigating bridges to let go all.

Kemp was at Maconochie's side as the final order was passed. Below on the starting platform, Chief Engineer French stood by as on the bridge the handles of the telegraphs were pulled over, the repeaters below calling for slow ahead both engines. As the order came the great shafts began turning to bring the former liner off the wall for the long haul to the Firth of Clyde, the really dangerous part of the voyage beginning. On the troop-decks above the engine-room the Australians and New Zealanders, who had been embarked late that afternoon, were still settling in and sorting themselves out for the last long leg before they joined in whatever awaited them thousands of miles from home.

In his cabin Chief Steward Chatfield grew maudlin on Van der Humm and thought about Roxanne and the hypothetical bloody salesman. At this stage there was really no point at all in writing, since he would be in touch by telephone from Greenock long before any letter could arrive. He began to rehearse that telephone call: he would be all nonchalance, simply asking in an innocent voice if Roxanne had gone and spent all the money that went by monthy allotment from his pay to her bank account in Southampton.

'Whatever makes you think,' she would reply, 'that I gone and done that?'

'Oh, nothing really,' he would go on to say. 'But I s'pose you'll be meeting me at the Central station . . . with that Morris Eight you just got with my spondulicks?'

That would put the fox among the chickens, all right; especially if the bloody salesman happened to be there when he rang.

Chatfield felt the sea movement as the *Aurelian Star* came out from the lee of the breakwater, felt the lurch as she met the ocean swell and more than a little of a seaway. Roll on the Clyde, he thought, the Tail o' the Bank and a touch of vengeance. He drank more Van der Humm. Spanking, that was what was called for. Women liked the firm approach. Put her across his knee, and wham. After that, well, she'd come to heel, and the salesman, who was likely enough married and wouldn't want his old woman to get to hear, would scarper into his bloody Morris Eight and vanish . . .

There was quite a weight of wind outside the port as the merchantmen and warships turned to starboard to come past the Cape, the actual Cape of Good Hope itself.

'The Cape of Storms,' Kemp said.

'What was that, sir?'

'History, Finnegan. Vasco da Gama called it the Cape of Storms when he discovered it. It's pretty appropriate tonight – or it will be in an hour or so. The wind's freshening fast from southerly.'

'You can say that again, sir, Commodore.'

Kemp sighed. 'Two Americanisms in one sentence, Finnegan, is a bit much. I've no desire to say it again. However, I gather it's registered, right?'

'Right, sir –'

'So gather your wits, young man, and check that Petty Officer Ramm has taken due precautions with the ship's armament.'

'Or Petty Officer Biggar, sir?'

'I said Ramm, and I meant Ramm. He can sort out the niceties with Biggar.' Kemp lifted his binoculars around the assembly of ships, no more than blacker bulks in the night's darkness, showing only the usual shaded blue stern-lights. Dimly he could see the bow-waves of the vessels on either beam, could see the bones in the teeth – as the saying went – of the destroyers as they raced ahead to take up their stations to act as anti-submarine screen. Already the water was heaving over the bows of the *Aurelian Star*, and spray was flying over the fore cargo hatches to reach the bridge, where canvas dodgers had been rigged. It was going to be a dirty night, with the wind slap on the port beam, making the ship roll badly. Kemp spared a thought for the troops crammed in along the troop-decks: never mind that they'd already made the voyage from their Australian port of embarkation, they still wouldn't really have their sea-legs, not in many cases.

Below, Finnegan made contact with Petty Officer Ramm.

Ramm, surly at being chased, went in search of PO Biggar. Well away to the north, and standing handily to the west of the northbound shipping lanes, the *Stuttgart* received word by wireless that Convoy sw03 had left the Simonstown base and was steaming for the Firth of Clyde with no escorting battleship.

SIX

The German prisoners-of-war, under guard of sentries found by
the King's East African Rifles, were mainly a surly bunch, not
liking their lot and not liking the fact of being under native
control, an unseemly thing for pure-bred Aryans, members of the
master race, sailors of their Führer. But, up to the present
anyway, they were behaving themselves. Sergeant Jeremiah
Muhoho of the Rifles, who with Sergeants Mgala and Tapapa
took his watch as NCO of the guard, was a diligent man who took
his duties very seriously and would stand no nonsense. None of
the Germans would risk a tongue-lashing from a native. But
beneath the surface there was a stir of hatred for the British, for
the newly embarked Australians and New Zealanders, and for
the natives themselves who had taken King George's shilling
against the might of Adolf Hitler and the German Empire that the
Führer had stated would last a thousand years.

OC Troops – Colonel Harrison of the Australian Army who had
now replaced Colonel Carter – was aware of the feeling as he
made rounds of the troop-decks and POW accommodation on the
first day after leaving Simonstown. He remarked on it to his
adjutant: Captain Mulvaney agreed, pushing his bush hat to the
back of his ginger hair and wiping sweat from his face.

'Right you are, Colonel. They want to hit back at the poms.
Can't say I blame 'em and that's fair dinkum. You met that
pommie brigadier?'

'I have. Point taken, Mulvaney. But don't forget this: pommie
brigadiers are going to be a fact of life once we hit the Clyde –'

'Take me back to bloody Wagga Wagga.' Captain Mulvaney

blew out a long-suffering breath. 'Why did I ever join up?'

'Because you had to,' Harrison said with a grin. 'Why did I, come to that? Anyway – those Krauts, they aren't allowed to have hate feelings, not to let it show anyway. Same applies to you.'

Mulvaney said, 'And that's an order. Right, Colonel?'

'Dead right, Captain. So watch it. Meantime, I'm going to have a word with the Commodore.' Harrison paused. 'For a pom, he's a good bloke.' Leading the way out from the POW accommodation, low down in the ship, Colonel Harrison returned a smart salute from the native NCO. 'What's your name, son?'

Standing rigid at attention, Sergeant Muhoho answered. 'Muhoho, sah! Jeremiah Muhoho, sergeant, sah, the King's East African Rifles.'

'Uh-huh. At ease, Sergeant. Well now, son, I'm relying on you and your mates to keep that bloody bunch under full control. I note you speak English. Some English anyway. How much?'

'Plenty good English, sah! Very good speaker, learning from British officers, sah, all white.'

'Well, good on yer, bloke.' Colonel Harrison fished in a capacious pocket of his khaki-drill tunic and produced a packet of cigarettes. 'Take a fag, bloke. Go on, they won't bloody bite.'

'Sah! I do not smoke, sah.'

'Oh, well, that's your loss. Not that some people don't call 'em coffin nails.' Colonel Harrison laid a hand on Sergeant Muhoho's shoulder and grinned in his shining face. 'Don't look so bloody shit scared, bloke. Like the fags – I don't bite.'

'Sah!' To Sergeant Muhoho's immense relief, the Colonel moved away, undoing the buttons of his tunic and giving a loud belch before sticking a cigarette in his mouth. The Australians were a very curious species, Sergeant Muhoho thought in perplexity, very different from the officers of the King's East African Rifles and as if from a different form of life from the very old officer, Colonel Holmes. Never in all his life had an officer addressed Sergeant Muhoho as 'bloke'. He wasn't sure that he liked it, in front of the rank-and-file, the riflemen. He was, after all, entitled by long and faithful service to be addressed as Sergeant.

Colonel Harrison climbed to the bridge. As OC Troops, he was permitted so to do. He was greeted by both Maconochie and

Kemp. Waving his right arm in a kind of salute to the Convoy Commodore he started right in, no small talk about Colonel Harrison when he was being official.

'Those Germans, Commodore. Pretty rat-faced bunch if you ask me. And a shade too bloody quiet. If you get me.'

'Still waters?' Kemp suggested.

'Eh?'

'Still waters that run deep.'

'Oh, right, I get you. Sums it up. They're fermenting. Or that's what I think. Waiting their chance. Thought I'd mention it.'

Kemp said, 'They're well guarded, Colonel, and all the regulations regarding the conveyance of prisoners-of-war have been complied with and their officer – a *kapitan-leutnant* named Stoph – has been informed of them.' Kemp, who had been given the bumph at Kilindini, ran through it even though Harrison probably knew it all. 'No cutlery such as could be used as weapons allowed, no pepper that could be thrown into the eyes –'

'Sure thing. Done me homework too.'

'Good. Well, whatever chance they're waiting for, they'll not get it. I repeat, that guard's strong.'

'So let's hope you're right, Commodore. They're a tough bunch . . . and what worries me is this bloody raider that's loose around here. If the shooting starts, they c'd be well placed to make any God's amount of trouble. With the ship's crew at action stations. If you get me.'

'Yes, I do. But the native battalion won't be part of action stations –'

'You mean they stay guarding the POW contingent?'

Kemp nodded. 'That's the idea, yes. They'll guard the Germans with their lives. The native troops . . . they're among the loyalest of all the regiments. But don't let me teach my grandmother,' Kemp added with a smile. 'You know the army. I don't.'

'Just a simple sailorman?' Harrison returned the grin.

Kemp laughed. 'You could say that, Colonel. But don't you worry about the Germans. I don't.'

Colonel Harrison reached forward and dug Kemp in the chest with a thick, nicotine-stained forefinger. 'Maybe you should.' Kemp, who disliked being dug in the chest, moved back a

61

fraction. Harrison went on, 'On a point of protocol, Commodore. One thing wasn't made too bloody clear back in Sydney. To be fair, they may not have known about the POW element, not then. But whose are they? Yours or mine? Eh?'

Kemp said, 'In the first instance, they're Captain Maconochie's as Master of the ship. In a sense they're his passengers. I'm merely the Convoy Commodore. In no sense do I command the ship. But to the extent that I have a responsibility for the convoy as a whole, the POWs are mine.'

'Because they're seamen, not pongoes?'

'Not exactly that. Because they're part of the convoy.'

'But in a sense, they're part of the troop draft. Even if they're seamen. Now, that'd make them mine. Eh?'

'There's another angle,' Kemp said, and said it firmly. 'In any passenger ship – currently, any troopship, the responsibility is the Master's. That includes the troops, I have to say – except in regard to internal matters of military organization and discipline, of course.' He was unable to resist adding, 'If you get me.'

There was a glint of something like anger in Harrison's eye. He said, 'Get you, eh? Does anyone outside Britain ever get a pommie? Answer: no, they bloody don't. What you said . . . it sounds like a load of gobbledegook if you don't mind my saying so.'

Kemp's response was a laugh; he intended to keep the peace, not wishing for any repeats of the Pumphrey-Hatton situation. He said, 'I know all about the shortcomings of pommies, Colonel. I spent the peace on the Australian run – Mediterranean-Australia Line. I've spent more time down under than I have at home.'

'Well, I'm blowed! Know Sydney well, do you?'

'Like the back of my hand. And Melbourne and Fremantle. And the outback to a lesser extent.'

'My oath! Well, Commodore, reckon that makes us mates. Why let a bunch of lousy Germans come between us, eh?'

'Why indeed?'

A possible disagreement had been neatly averted. But Kemp was well aware that there could be some truth in what the Australian had said about the Germans taking advantage of any attack. A word with Colonel Carter might not come amiss. And frankly Kemp was not entirely sure of whose initial responsibility the POWs might be. He had not been given a clear answer in Kilindini, nor when he had raised it at the Cape. If all poms used gobbledegook, then officialdom and the top brass used it three times over. Not that it was worth losing any sleep over; when the chips were really down, they were all literally in the same boat. And enemy seamen though they were, the Germans would be accorded the lifeboats or rafts, if it ever came to abandoning, as surely as anyone else aboard after the women and children of the returning British families.

Brigadier Pumphrey-Hatton, the red tabs of the staff adorning the open collar of his khaki-drill tunic, walked the promenade deck as the sun went down, keeping to leeward to avoid the wind and spray and muttering to himself as he paced back and forth. He was still seething about the fracas that had taken place back at the Cape. He had no idea who the drunken man was; nor had he recognized Petty Officer Biggar. The men could have come from any one of the many warships in the port of Simonstown. After the occurrence he had made no report ashore; neither had he done so on his return aboard the *Aurelian Star*. He was aware that he had not come very well out of the encounter; a weeping brigadier was something to be concealed. But he brooded: the whole world as he'd known it was going downhill, heading straight for hell and the devil. There was no respect any more, no discipline in a pre-war sense. Of course, Pumphrey-Hatton knew quite well why that was: the influx of civilians, persons with no concept of service life. Counter-jumpers, clerks, artisans, labourers . . . bolshies all of them very likely. It took years to make a soldier from scratch, and the younger they joined the better. Drummer boys and so on, brought up from a tender age to obey their officers and NCOs instantly and without question. And some of the people with temporary commissions were of course utterly impossible, not fit to enter any officers' mess. It had become a disgraceful state of affairs when men virtually straight from civil life, with no public school and Sandhurst behind them, were put in charge of troops. That alone had led to the decline in discipline: it was a fact that the men had no respect for them and the rest followed from that.

It was cold on deck now. Pumphrey-Hatton entered the shelter of the B deck lounge. As he did so, he saw that the old man,

Colonel Holmes, was getting to his feet and trying to catch his eye. Holmes called out, 'A nightcap, Brigadier. If you'd care to join us my wife and I would be delighted.'

Pumphrey-Hatton gave a nod. He'd spoken on a few occasions to the Holmeses, who had decided to forget the incident of the shove in the back. He'd found the old man a bore but at least he was a gentleman and had been a soldier, so they spoke the same language. He thanked the old man and sat down beside the wife, who smiled at him. 'We always indulge ourselves in a nightcap,' she said.

'Very civilized, Mrs Holmes.'

'A long-standing custom,' Holmes said. 'In East Africa, don't you know –'

'Yes, yes.' Pumphrey-Hatton's tone was brisk: he wanted no more monologues. He said, when asked, that he would like brandy. Not Van der Humm: a genuine brandy, from France. The lounge steward was already waiting with a tray. The order was given: both the Holmeses asked for whisky. Whilst awaiting the drinks, they chatted desultorily. Mrs Holmes was worried about the sea passage. There had been rumours about a German surface raider being at large.

'Do you know if that is correct, Brigadier?'

'Can't discuss that,' Pumphrey-Hatton said briskly.

The old lady seemed disconcerted at the abruptness, but she said, 'No, of course not, I'm so sorry. Careless talk – I really shouldn't have.'

'Better not,' Pumphrey-Hatton said. 'Get in the habit – when you reach UK you'll find you need to be very careful. England isn't East Africa, you know.'

'Yes. Such a pity. We shall miss the life. We had some very good days, such very *happy* days.' Mrs Holmes was growing a shade maudlin; she brought a wispy handkerchief from her handbag and wiped at her eyes. The old colonel became gruff.

'Yes, yes indeed, my dear.' He raised the glass that had just been brought by the lounge steward and looked across at Pumphrey-Hatton. 'Your good health, Brigadier.'

'Good health,' Pumphrey-Hatton said automatically, reflecting that a temporary officer would almost certainly have said 'cheers'. As he drank, a gust of wind came into the lounge. A door had opened to admit a man in naval uniform, a rating, who

64

after a look around headed for the ship's Chief Officer who was sitting with Colonel Carter of the rifle regiment. Some sort of report was obviously being made; the Chief Officer excused himself and made his way towards the door to the open deck, followed by Petty Officer Biggar.

Pumphrey-Hatton stared at the PO. Biggar stared back briefly, seemed to blink a little, looked away, then recovered his poise and moved on. Blood coursed through Pumphrey-Hatton's head and his face became flushed. At his side Colonel Holmes was going on talking. 'I said, Brigadier, that the Germans –'

'Never mind the Germans, man, or what you were saying about them.' Pumphrey-Hatton jerked to his feet, leaving his brandy mostly untouched. 'I wish you goodnight.' He went at a jerky walk across the lounge, leaving by the door opposite that taken by Biggar.

'Well, I'm damned,' Holmes said in some agitation. 'What on earth did I do to bring that on?'

'I don't believe it was anything you said, Stephen. It was when he saw that naval man.'

'But surely –'

'Who was the man, do you know, Stephen?'

'Oh . . . the PO in charge of the DEMS people, I believe. Don't know his name.'

'I think,' Mildred Holmes said in a quiet voice, 'that Brigadier Pumphrey-Hatton knows him. I wonder . . .'

'What do you wonder?'

'Nothing, really. Nothing that I can lay a finger on. But it was really rather curious.'

'Nothing to do with us, Mildred.'

'No, of course not. But I do dislike bad manners, Stephen.'

'Well, yes, so do I. The staff always did think a lot of themselves though, and tended to be brusque – even rude.' Holmes sighed. 'They're all so damned *young* these days compared with what they were before the war. Insolent puppy was what we'd have called the feller once.'

Later that night, when the guns'-crews were relieved by the oncoming watch at eight bells, Petty Officer Biggar approached Petty Officer Ramm, oozing unctuous intent not to prod his nose into a fellow PO's territory. 'Mind if I 'ave a word with one o' your party, eh?'

'Fill your boots,' Ramm said off-handedly, then added on a note of suspicion, 'What about, then?'

'Not official, this isn't. We 'appened to meet ashore, an' I got a message for him after he'd gone on his way like. Your leading 'and it was, Purkiss.'

Ramm wasn't particularly interested in anything but getting turned into his bunk. Petty Officer Biggar drew Purkiss aside and muttered into his ear, 'Best watch it, Purkiss.'

'Watch what?' Leading Seaman Purkiss was sorting out his anti-flash gear, the gloves and face protection that were required when the guns opened fire.

'Pumphrey-Hatton. He recognized me, that's what. No doubt about it at all.' Biggar elaborated on the exchange of looks. 'He may make something of it now he knows, or again he may not. Both ways there's reasons, see. An' just you remember, you 'it him. Struck an officer.'

'He hasn't recognized me yet, PO.'

'Maybe not. But now 'e'll be poking his nose around the ship, won't 'e?'

'What am I supposed to do about it, then, eh?'

'The obvious: keep your 'ead down, all the bloody way to the Clyde. Request permission to grow a beard p'raps – something like that. Basically, you just keep out of 'is way.'

'What about you, PO?'

Biggar shrugged. 'I'm not worried. I didn't strike him, did I? 'E struck me . . . in a manner o' speaking. Sort of lashed out blind. So 'e won't want that to come out, not if 'e's got any sense 'e won't. But I don't want it to come out neither, and for why you might ask? Reason's obvious. As a PO I should 'ave shoved you in the rattle, 'ad you up before the Commodore one-one-two. Which I didn't. Which makes me an accessory after the bleedin' fact or whatever it is them legal johnnies call it. See?'

Leading Seaman Purkiss gave a long sniff and then, blocking one nostril, expelled air through the other one, leaning over the ship's side as he did so. He said, 'I don't reckon you can keep out of the way of anybody, not aboard a ship you can't.'

Petty Officer Biggar made his way for'ard, checking right round the guns, surface and ack-ack. He had come to an accommodation with Ramm: they shared the duties of gunner's mate and that satisfied both of them. More or less; PO Biggar still thought of himself as being in overall charge.

SEVEN

When the noon sight was taken next day, the second officer fixed the ship's position in longitude 33°40' south, latitude 10° east. They had made good some 540 sea miles from the Simonstown departure and were steaming on a north-westerly course that would take them clear of the coast of South West Africa towards, eventually, the Cape Verde Islands off French West Africa, a long way ahead yet. Many miles of ocean, and many hours of tension for the civilian passengers, the homeward-bound families. Tension and in many cases boredom: there was little to do but worry about the surface raider and later the U-boat packs. There was plenty of drinking time for those who were most at home propped on a bar stool.

One of these was Gregory Hench. Hench had owned a coffee plantation back in Kenya, not a very successful one, the lack of success having been mostly due to a lazy disposition and a liking for whisky. At thirty-nine he was returning home a failure: the plantation had gone bankrupt and he had just about raked up the fare for UK plus enough to keep his thirst at bay. In point of fact he had no need to pay over the bar: he signed chits. He would probably not have enough to cover them at the end of the voyage, but saw no need to cross that bridge for some while yet. In any case, you couldn't get blood out of a stone. He'd made that point to the bankruptcy court. He'd had few assets beyond the run-down plantation and he'd had a number of debts. It had not been until after the proceedings that he'd cabled his old mother for the fare home plus expenses. Longing, as she'd said, to see him again, the cash had been instantly forthcoming. The fact that she couldn't afford to part with it without sacrifices was just too bad. What were parents for?

Hench pushed his empty glass across the bar. 'Same,' he said.

'A large one, sir?'

'That's what I said. Same.'

'Coming up, sir.' The bar steward, a cheerful-looking Scot who had been with the Line since the middle thirties, studied Hench in the mirror behind his optics. He saw a man with a florid face, a disagreeable expression, a man as thin as a rake whose fingers shook as he fumbled with a propelling pencil and a book of wine chits. Steward MacInnes was pretty adept at summing up his customers. He foresaw trouble with Mr Hench, who would be truculent when drunk, really drunk – he'd not been exactly drunk since embarking at Kilindini, just very well oiled, but give him a few more days and he might go over what appeared to be his set limit. Four large whiskies at the lunchtime session, six large whiskies at the evening session, two large brandies after dinner. MacInnes had already made a mental note to have a word with Chief Steward Chatfield about the future: MacInnes reckoned Mr Hench might well default on his booze chits. He didn't give the impression of being well lined; his khaki shirt and shorts had seen better days and his shoes were scuffed and his hair too long and ragged, as though he economized on the barber.

'There we are, sir.' The glass was pushed across. The response was a grunt; never a thank-you from Mr Hench.

Hench took a gulp from the glass and set it down again. His fingers seemed a shade less shaky: MacInnes had noted that the shake tended to subside after the second large whisky. As the steward polished glasses with the cloth that he always carried over his arm he saw another passenger joining Mr Hench at the bar. Miss Gloria Northway, aged at a guess thirty-five. She too had a good intake – gin in her case. She also had a predatory look, one well known to Steward MacInnes. Women at sea – single women or women travelling without their husbands, it came mostly to the same thing – were different from women ashore. Different in that they really let their hair down as though it didn't matter a tinker's cuss. Aboard a ship they were divorced from shoreside life, no one ashore need ever know what they'd been up to at sea, and they lived in a sort of safe cocoon within which they could behave as maybe they'd always wanted to behave but hadn't dared to. Grinning to himself as Mr Hench looked around at the newcomer and made welcoming noises, a grunt of a different sort from that used to stewards, MacInnes wished Miss Northway luck with Mr Hench but didn't reckon she would achieve much. A pound to a penny Mr Hench suffered from distiller's droop.

'Morning, Gloria.'

'Is it?' Her voice was hoarse.

'Hangover?'

'Bloody awful. As per usual. Steward?'

'Yes, madam?'

'Hair of the dog. Fast before I die. And have one yourself.'

'Thank you, madam. I'll take a pale ale.' MacInnes, knowing the particular dog, mixed gin and grapefruit in a long glass with a straw. Gloria Northway sucked avidly and said something about the bottom of a parrot's cage.

'I've a good mind to go on the wagon,' she said, still hoarse, 'but I don't suppose I will. Too painful. Got a cigarette, have you, Gregory?'

Hench produced his cigarette-case. Silver, salvaged from the wreck. He flicked a lighter and Miss Northway blew smoke towards MacInnes. Stale breath accompanied it. With a long finger-nail she removed a fragment of breakfast from a tooth and deposited it in an ashtray. She said suddenly, 'Sod the war.'

Hench looked surprised. 'Why, in particular? I mean – just like that, out of nowhere so to speak?'

'Oh, I don't know.' She shifted about on her stool; her breasts wobbled, more or less tantalizingly. 'Just sod it, that's all. All the shortages, and the dangers, and everyone here today and gone tomorrow, you know what I mean.'

Hench nodded but didn't comment.

'Take you and me. Waifs of the war.'

'Yes.'

'Funny we never met in Kenya.'

'You said you'd been in –'

'Nyasaland, right, so I did. And was. Anyway, we've met now and that's something good come out of the war. Coffee, didn't you say?'

'Yes,' Hench said.

'Coffee's good and safe. I just drifted and I don't mind

admitting it, Gregory, I don't mind at all. I suppose you could say I was a bit of a bum, actually.'

Kept woman was more like it, Hench thought, but he said, 'Oh, no, surely . . . you shouldn't say that –'

'I do say it.' She reached out a little unsteadily and laid a hand on his arm. 'Someone like you is good for little me,' she said.

'Think so?'

'Damn right I do.' She belched, put a hand to her mouth and said, 'Pardon me, so sorry. Where was I?'

'I'm good for you. May one ask why?'

She waved her cigarette in the air. 'Morale. I'm not proud, I've had a few rejections. Could be I drink too much, but so what?'

Hench grinned. 'Have another,' he said, noting that her glass was already nearly empty.

'Don't mind if I do.' Miss Northway drained the glass and pushed it across towards MacInnes. 'That's what I meant,' she said to Hench. 'You don't criticize.'

He shrugged. 'Live and let live.'

'And so say I . . . dear Gregory. Oh God – my head.'

She would very probably be willing. Hench was willing, at any rate in spirit; any port in a storm and Gloria Northway wouldn't expect to be – what was the word – wooed. No need for extended preliminaries. But there was a snag, an overwhelming one. Hench, who had never married, had had sundry brief affairs over the years, mostly with the wives of fellow planters until they found out he was no use in bed, however strong and urgent the desire. With deadly accuracy, Steward MacInnes had put his finger on it. Desire, heightened by the treacherous effects of whisky, was always frustrated by its own bolsterer and Gregory Hench had come to dread the moment when a woman showed signs of being ready.

Once again he pushed his glass across and recommended Miss Northway to take a couple of aspirins.

Below in his cabin, Bridadier Pumphrey-Hatton found that once again his electric fan was not turning properly. He muttered furiously to himself, then, with hands that shook badly, he took hold of the fan, jerked it hard so that the flex parted, and cast it down on the deck by his bunk. The moment he had done so, he regretted it. There would now have to be explanations to his steward and he was damned if he was going to explain himself to

71

anyone of that sort. He slumped into the hard, upright chair that was all he had to sit on, and put his head in his hands. The business at the Cape was much on his mind, having seen that petty officer. He should be taking action over that, should be making a formal report to the Commodore, or Captain Maconochie if the man turned out to be one of the DEMS party. Ratings should never be allowed to get away with crimes . . . but if he made a report far too much would come out. In the meantime the man was no doubt sniggering away behind his back, knowing that he had him by the short hairs.

'Cypher, sir.'

Kemp turned, lowering his binoculars. The report came from the leading telegraphist on his staff. The leading telegraphist said, 'From Flag Officer West Africa, sir. Freetown, sir.'

'Thank you, Phillips.' Kemp took the cypher, passed it to Finnegan who had come across from the starboard wing of the bridge. 'Over to you, Finnegan. Break it down straight away – the prefix is urgent.'

'Okay, sir –'

'Not okay, Finnegan. Dammit, you've been long enough with the British Navy!'

'Sorry, sir.' Finnegan grinned. 'For okay, substitute aye, aye, sir –'

'Oh, just get on with it,' Kemp said irritably. Americans were irrepressible, though God alone knew how Britain would have survived without them. Kemp, pacing the bridge in deep thought, pondered on the likely purport of the signal, which was in fact addressed to the senior officer of the escort, cs23, the prefix indicating that it was repeated to the Convoy Commodore. In naval signalling procedure, this meant that any action required would be taken by the naval escort commander; the Commodore was merely being informed. But to Kemp, the urgent prefix meant that it was a report of enemy activity somewhere in the vicinity of the convoy's north-westerly course.

He had a word with Maconochie. 'There may be an alteration signalled from the escort. He may move us farther west.'

Maconochie nodded. 'That's about the only option. Are you expecting word of the raider?'

'It could be, yes. Or submarine packs farther south than was thought likely back at the Cape. Let's take a preliminary look at the chart, Captain.'

They went into the chart room just abaft the bridge. The chart of the area was laid out on the polished mahogany table, a pair of dividers and parallel rulers laid upon it, and the ship's position at the last fix noted by a small pencilled cross inside a circle. Kemp scanned the area; the South Atlantic was vast, but both Kemp and Maconochie knew from long experience that in war there was little enough of the needles-in-haystacks element. A determined enemy had ways of making contact however immense the area of operations. Long-distance radar, intelligence passed from the German Admiralty in Berlin, intelligence passed by a great network of operators – spies was the better word – throughout the world; and intelligent guesswork and anticipation by the enemy captains to fill any gaps. Kemp, as he waited for Finnegan to report back to the bridge with the broken-down, plain language version of the signal, found his mind going back to the days of peace when the great liners kept to their regular schedules without any need to deviate, any need to cover their tracks, any need to wonder what intelligence agents were reporting behind their backs. All the way – in his case – from the locks at Tilbury, all the way to Sydney via the ports of call – Gibraltar, Port Said, the Suez Canal, Aden, Colombo, the long stretch across the Indian Ocean to Gage Roads at Fremantle, round stormy Cape Leeuwin and across the Great Australian Bight and the Southern Ocean to Adelaide and Melbourne, through the Bass Strait and round Cape Howe for Sydney Heads and the berth at Woolloomooloo or Circular Quay or under the harbour bridge to Pyrmont. All that way like clockwork, the whole voyage worked out minutely months before so that the Line could publish its passenger schedules well in advance. Long before you dropped the mud-pilot at the Downs, you knew the precise moment you would, four weeks ahead, pass into Sydney's Port Jackson harbour.

They had been fabulous days in many ways, and Kemp doubted if after the war was over they would ever be quite the same again even if there were any liners left. For years now, the pilots and crews of, for instance, Imperial Airways had been predicting the end of the ocean liner. Speed was to be the watchword of the future, the great god of speed and never mind the comfort and atmosphere of a liner. Attentive stewards, excellent and varied meals in the saloons – mess dress at night for the ship's officers, dinner jackets and evening dresses obligatory for first-class passengers, a bugle blown warningly for dinner and all that went with all of that. So many ports with excursions laid on for those that wanted them . . . and the glamour of the sea itself, the low-slung stars in the night skies of the Mediterranean, myriads of them like glowing lanterns, a sight never seen beneath British skies; the moon sending its beams over the violet waters of the Indian Ocean, and then the contrast, after Cape Leeuwin, of the grey, heaving seas – often majestically spectacular – of the Bight.

Kemp had never grown tired of the sea's variety, of the satisfaction of bringing his command into each port with miles of safe steaming behind him. He thought now, in the *Aurelian Star's* chart room, of many years ago and his very first sight of the great Rock of Gibraltar, the bastion that now guarded the Mediterranean from entry by Adolf Hitler's warships. Turning between Algeciras on the Spanish coast and Europa Point at the southern extremity of Gibraltar he had seen with awe the immensity of the Rock, green and brown looming into the sky above the white buildings of the town behind the breakwater guarding the naval port, looming huge and impressive as though to block out the very sky. The winking lights of the port and town as the scented dusk descended, the sound of bugles and Royal Marine bands as the battleships and cruisers of the Mediterranean Fleet struck their colours for Sunset. Or in the daytime the evocative sounds of the fifes and drums, or when a Scots regiment was in garrison the pipes and drums, from the parade grounds of South Barracks, or Buena Vista Barracks, or Red Sands fringed with palms, pepper trees and eucalyptus. They were the sounds to stir the heart, the sounds of Empire and a long history of valour and sacrifice.

But such thoughts were best put behind him for the duration of the war. Kemp straightened and returned to the bridge, leaving Maconochie to confer with his second officer, one of whose responsibilities was the navigation of the ship.

There was a blustery wind coming up from southerly, taking the ship on her port quarter and causing her to roll somewhat heavily as her course took her across the wind and a rising sea.

The men on the troop-decks would be having an uncomfortable time. Kemp hunched himself into a corner of the starboard bridge-wing and used his binoculars to scan the horizons all around. Still peaceful, and the convoy was maintaining its formation well, no need for chasing by signal from the Commodore or from the escort, which was often the case when unwieldy cargo vessels fell behind their station or surged ahead of it to lie dangerously close astern of their next ahead. Convoys could become a nightmare: each ship was an individual with her own characteristics of handling, very different from, say, a cruiser squadron each member of which had similar power and helm-answering habits, even though it was true enough that no two ships of the same class handled precisely the same. Merchant ships came in all shapes and sizes, the average convoy containing some deep-laden, some in ballast, some big, some smaller – tankers, dry-cargo ships, transports, some liable, simply because of the unending sea-time that the merchantmen were putting in now, to sudden and unpredictable engine-room breakdowns, usually at impossibly awkward moments.

No picnic; and it looked as if it would go on for ever, world without end.

'Mind if I join you, eh?'

Pumphrey-Hatton looked up from some notes he was making. He was sitting in the B deck lounge with a gin-and-bitters, and jotting down items for the rough draft of a list of complaints that he proposed submitting to the War Office when he reached London. Unless you made notes, you forgot. You forgot even important things, oddly enough, though certainly you couldn't forget the damn flies. Fortunately the flies had by now been left behind, but there was still the electric fan and the attitudes of various people, and various lapses in efficiency . . .

Looking up, he saw the Australian colonel. Harrison, now OC Troops.

'I'm rather busy. Surely you can see.'

Harrison wasn't in the least disconcerted. Australians, Pumphrey-Hatton thought, probably never were; they were much too brash. Harrison grinned and said, 'Sorry about that. Just wanted to ask your advice, that's all. But if you're writing your bloody memoirs, or your love letters, why, I reckon –'

'You are damned impertinent, Colonel Harrison.' Pumphrey-Hatton half rose from his chair. 'I would expect –'

'Sorry again, mate. Just take it easy, eh? Reckon I didn't intend any disrespect, nothing like that. Only you're experienced in things I'm still green at and I don't mind admitting it.'

Pumphrey-Hatton made a sound like, 'Hah.'

'Me first go at OC Troops. I need to get the oil.'

'Oil?'

'The dinkum oil. You know? The . . . gen. The bloody know-how. Don't want to go and make a duck's arse of it.' Colonel Harrison turned to a hovering lounge steward. 'A refill for the brig,' he said, 'and then there's me, eh? Got a Foster's, have you? Swan beer, eh?'

'I think we can manage, sir.'

'Good on you, bloke. Let's have 'em.' Harrison sat down, pulling up a chair close to Pumphrey-Hatton, who looked furiously angry and was in fact quite speechless at the fellow's effrontery. And the appalling modes of expression, of terminology – duck's arse, bloody love letters, dinkum oil, the brig, mate, and take it easy! It was utterly grotesque that such a person should be found wearing the crown and two stars of a full colonel even in a colonial army. Trembling as if with a high fever, Brigadier Pumphrey-Hatton hoisted himself to his feet, spilling his gin-and-bitters as he did so. He stuttered incoherently with sheer fury, unable at that moment to express himself. Muttering, he moved away, out of the lounge, while Harrison mopped the spilled gin off his uniform trousers. Pumphrey-Hatton heard the shout just as he reached the door.

'Clumsy bloody bastard! Bloody pommie snob.'

That, too, would go in the report for the War Office. The man was obviously totally unfit for the position of OC Troops. A moment later, Pumphrey-Hatton faced another upset. Moving with his jerky walk aft along B deck, he came face to face with Petty Officer Biggar, proceeding for'ard from aft. Stiff-faced, Biggar saluted and moved past.

'You, there. That petty officer.'

Biggar turned. 'Yes, sir?'

'Name.'

Biggar licked at his lips. 'Biggar, sir. PO, Royal Fleet Reserve.'

'That will be noted. You may carry on.'

Biggar remained where he was. 'Sir, I –'

'That will do. You may carry on. Is it necessary for me to repeat my orders?'

'No, sir. I'm sorry, sir, but I –'

Pumphrey-Hatton lifted a foot and stamped it on the deck. 'Hold your tongue and do as you're told!'

Petty Officer Biggar's face flushed. As a petty officer, the equivalent of a sergeant, he was not accustomed to be bawled out publicly – bawled *at* publicly – nor to be told to hold his tongue. He had a bloody good mind, he told himself, to make an issue of it and report to that Mr Finnegan for transmission to the Commodore. As Pumphrey-Hatton marched away aft, Petty Officer Biggar continued angrily but thoughtfully for'ard. It needed reflection – that it did. There were many angles to it, and he had to consider Leading Seaman Purkiss.

Sub-Lieutenant Finnegan reported back to the bridge with the plain language version of the Admiralty signal.

Kemp and Maconochie read it together. The estimated position of the *Stuttgart* was indicated: Kemp and Captain Maconochie, with Finnegan, went back into the chart room and laid off this position on the chart.

Maconochie said, 'Her superior speed's taken her a long way nor'-nor'-west.'

'But she's on a closing course. More or less. A little north in fact.'

'So as to cross our track?' Finnegan suggested.

Kemp nodded. 'Looks like it, sub.' He glanced again at the signal. 'No information as to whether or not it's suspected that the *Stuttgart* knows our position currently. But we can certainly assume she knows we've left the Cape – and what our present course will be.'

'So what do we do?' Maconochie asked.

'Mastery inactivity for the moment, Captain,' Kemp said with a grin. 'We wait for orders from cs23. If his signal officer's as quick off the mark as young Finnegan, we'll know any moment now.' He added, 'And to forestall what I think you're going to ask, Captain, we announce nothing to the troops and other passengers about the raider. Not yet, that is.'

EIGHT

The reaction came quickly from the senior officer of the escort, in a signal made by lamp addressed to the Convoy Commodore and repeated to all ships. *Convoy will alter ten degrees to port on the executive and will steer 320 degrees until further orders. Ships to maintain second degree of readiness continuously from now.*

Kemp nodded at Yeoman Lambert. 'Thank you, Yeoman. Acknowledge.'

'Aye, aye, sir.' As Lambert went back to his signalling projector, the alter-course signal was hoisted from cs23's flag deck to her fore upper yard, being held at the dip. When all ships had made their acknowledgements, the signal was hoisted close-up to indicate the executive order for the turn to port. Kemp nodded at Maconochie, who passed the orders to his Officer of the Watch. The ships came round, and for a while the convoy was in some disarray as each vessel altered its speed either up or down to resume the original formation. Across the bows of the Commodore's ship came a big freighter – dangerously close in Kemp's view. Maconochie reacted fast.

Moving at the double to the wheelhouse he shouted the orders. *'Emergency full astern, wheel hard-a-starboard!'*

Kemp held his breath, hands gripping the bridge guardrail until the knuckles showed white. If two big ships should hit . . . but Maconochie's instant reaction had saved them from that, if only just. As the stern pull of the engines took effect and the *Aurelian Star*'s head began to pay off, the freighter slid past to safety with what looked like only inches to spare.

When the next order reached the engine-room by the

78

telegraphs, the order to resume normal speed, the Chief Engineer let out a long breath and wiped a fistful of cotton-waste across his forehead. A moment later the Captain came on the sound-powered telephone from the bridge. 'A near miss, Chief. All's well now, thanks to your engines.'

Chief Engineer French grinned into the mouthpiece. 'We try to give satisfaction, sir.'

'I know you do, Chief. What's more – you succeed.'

French clipped the telephone back on its holder. He was lucky in the Old Man. With some masters, it was a case of running warfare. Many deck officers regarded what they called the black gang as beneath their notice, nasty foulers of God's good fresh air with the smoke that they sometimes made, especially when more oil fuel was fed to the furnaces when the call came for extra speed. Not Maconochie: he recognized that in the last resort it was the engines that got the ship home. As from the starting platform John French surveyed his noisy, pulsating kingdom, watched his engine-room ratings moving about the great spinning shafts with their long-necked oil-cans, he thought of home and of homecomings. Thirty-three years at sea, Chief of the *Aurelian Star* since the outbreak of war, he'd had more homecomings than he could remember. As many departures too, leaving home life and his family behind while he set out on the world's oceans, living a bachelor existence for months on end until his next leave, seldom more than a fortnight before the next departure.

A hell of a life for a married man.

Daft, really.

Absolutely potty. That was his wife's term for it. Monica hated those departures that came like the clockwork that regulated the Line's sailings. But John French had seen no alternative. When he'd married he'd been senior third engineer, which meant many years in the Line's service, too many years to throw away in an attempt to find a job ashore where he'd have had to start all over again, at the bottom. He'd left the bottom behind a long while ago, signing as a junior engineer, little more in truth than an oiler or greaser, with a tramp shipping company running out of Cardiff. There was a world of difference between a junior engineer in a tramp line, and senior third in a liner. So he'd stayed at sea, because of that and because, despite the absences, he liked the sea and its variety, its challenges when something went wrong and he was able to put it right.

But Monica, now. When the war had come she had been devastated. She lived a nightmare all the time he was away, always fearing the worst, always dreading the telegram that would come without warning from the Line or maybe from the Admiralty. She'd had a cousin who'd been an engine-room artificer in the RN. He'd been aboard an aircraft-carrier that had been hit by a torpedo and had then taken an eight-inch projy from a German cruiser, slap in her starboard engine-room. The cousin had in fact survived, but only by a miracle, and survival hadn't been worth while. He was now confined to one of those contraptions made of basket-work, bed-length, on four wheels, paralysed from the neck down, couldn't do anything for himself and a pittance of a pension from the Admiralty. John French had been at sea when the cousin had been brought to the Royal Naval Hospital, Haslar; and he hadn't been there to stop Monica hearing all about it when she visited her cousin.

She knew the horrors now. The scalding, escaping steam, the raging fires as the oil fuel spilled, the oil fuel that covered men's bodies, spewed into their mouths and nostrils, the twisting of the network of steel ladders that led from the deck of the engine-room to the air-lock at the top, the only way out from hell. She heard about the burns suffered by the cousin before he had managed to reach the air-lock, only to lose his grip and fall from the upper platform, back down into hell, to break his back on one of the shafts before being hauled to safety by a heroic stoker petty officer.

Since then, she'd been a bag of nerves. Not surprising, of course; but that had reacted badly on their two children. They had become tearaways as a result of too much protective mothering that had never let them out on their own. Taken and fetched to and from school, inquisitions every time they were asked home by a school friend, every movement to be accounted for in detail, that sort of thing. They'd rebelled and that wasn't surprising either. With dad away at sea, there was no one to appeal to. The family home was in Southampton, and both sets of grandparents were in Sunderland, right up north and too far to visit in wartime, travel being not all that easy.

And now they'd both fallen foul of the police. A long and rather hysterical letter had reached John French in Simonstown: Alan and Billy had been caught shoplifting in Woolworth's. The case was pending.

A worry he could do without as the troop convoy steamed for home.

Sighing, John French wiped his hands on a fresh bunch of cotton-waste and told his senior second engineer that he would be in his cabin if wanted. He had, he said, reports to write. What he really wanted to do was to read Monica's letter again.

'We seem to have altered course,' Colonel Holmes remarked to his wife. He had noted that the sun was in a slightly different position relative to the ship.

'It's probably after that scare,' Mildred said. 'When that ship –'

'No, no, it's not that. The whole convoy's altered.'

She looked up at him. 'Why's that?'

'I don't know, my dear.'

'There's obviously a reason.'

'Yes. But I don't know what it is.'

'You could always ask the Captain, couldn't you?'

'I suppose I –' Holmes broke off, feeling irritated by his wife's non-perception of their status as passengers, nosey ones they would be considered. 'One can't bother busy people with questions they probably don't want asked. We'll be told in due course.'

'Yes, but when?'

'When the Captain considers it necessary. Not before.' The old soldier believed the convoy's alteration to have more than a little to do with the lurking enemy, but he wasn't going to say so to Mildred, there being no point in worrying her too soon. Hearing footsteps on the deck behind him, he turned his head then turned it back again. In a low voice he said, 'There's that damn cad Hench. And that appalling woman.'

'Which –'

'Don't look now,' Holmes hissed urgently, but there was no avoiding an encounter when Hench stopped by the rail and leaned over alongside Mrs Holmes.

'Something going on, Colonel,' he said, speaking across Holmes's wife. She moved back a little; the smell of stale whisky was strong.

'Yes,' Holmes said briefly. 'We seem to have altered course, but not by very much.'

'I didn't mean that, though I expect it's connected. I meant all the signalling. Flags, and flashing lights. See it, did you?'

'Yes, I did –'

'Something's up,' Hench said. He sounded nervous. 'As I was saying to Gloria –'

'Gloria?'

'Miss Northway. You've not met?'

'Not formally,' Holmes said.

'I'll rectify that.' Gregory Hench made the introductions. 'Gloria Northway . . . Colonel and Mrs Holmes.'

'How d'you do?' Holmes said perfunctorily.

'Fine, thanks, and you?'

There was really no answer to that, and neither of the old couple gave one. Miss Northway went on to say, anyway, she was pleased to meet them. She hoped to God they would all reach the UK safely but now she was worried because Gregory had said the flags and lamps and so on meant that the escorting warships had had word about an enemy attack. Everybody knew there were hundreds and hundreds of U-boats at sea and what did Colonel Holmes think?

'For a start, Miss Northway, I doubt the hundreds and hundreds. In the South Atlantic, anyway. Hitler has other fish to fry. Not just our convoy.'

'Well, maybe, but it's terribly scary. I'll bet your wife's having kittens right now.'

Holmes glared. 'I beg your pardon?'

Hench said, 'She meant Mrs Holmes must be worried, Colonel –'

'I gathered that, thank you, Hench. Naturally my wife is anxious. But we are a military family, which perhaps Miss Northway doesn't understand. Doesn't understand the significance of the fact of coming from a military family.' He looked Gloria Northway directly in the eye. 'Stiff upper lip, you know. All that sort of thing. Face up to the enemy. It's a British characteristic. I have every confidence that we shall reach the Clyde in safety.' He turned away and stared out to sea.

'Weird old couple,' Miss Northway murmured as Hench, taking her arm, drew her away from the Holmeses. 'Stiff upper lip, my *God*! What next?'

'Colonial forces,' Hench said. 'Bred in the bone. Used to kicking the natives around. They're sort of . . . cocooned from reality. Flies in amber.'

'Stiff upper lips don't stop torpedoes,' Miss Northway said. 'Or do they, in the minds of ossified old fuddy-duddies like those two?' She added, 'The old girl never opened her mouth. I reckon she has to wait for orders . . .'

The word had gone from the Chief Officer via the bosun to all hands of the troopship's deck department that extra vigilance would be required from all watchkeepers, the lookouts especially; Chief Engineer French was warned that within the next few hours there might be a need for sudden alterations of speed and that extra revolutions might be wanted at short notice. He in turn passed orders for the remaining boiler to be flashed up in readiness. Finnegan spoke to the two petty officers: the guns'-crews would now be working in two watches, which meant that extra guns would be manned at all times.

'Meaning the Nazis are around, sir?'

Finnegan nodded. 'We've had a report that the *Stuttgart* is not all that far off. That's for the information of the guns'-crews only. The Commodore doesn't want the civilian passengers alarmed, get it?'

Ramm said, 'Got it, sir. We keep mum. What about them other Jerries? The POWs?'

'That's another reason the Commodore doesn't want any loose talk.' Finnegan added, 'If it seems inevitable that we're going to fall in with the raider, an announcement will be broadcast from the bridge, okay?'

Finnegan moved away, making back for the bridge. He found the Commodore deep in conference with OC Troops and Colonel Carter of the rifles. The subject under discussion was the one that had been raised by Petty Officer Ramm: the POW contingent, under guard below the troop decks. Kemp was concerned as to the possibilities of a breakout if and when the German raider was encountered. Harrison didn't believe there would be any trouble. The Germans were, he said – and Carter agreed – under strong enough guard to ensure that they would remain firmly below in action.

'Unless they have to be brought up,' Kemp pointed out.

'You mean if we have to abandon?'

'Yes. In fact I'd prefer not to leave them below once action starts. There's always a chance it'll be too late as things develop. I don't like to take that chance. So what I'm suggesting is this: the Germans should be brought up under escort and held in, let's say, the в deck lounge, which of course will have been cleared of all passengers, the civilians. They'll be in the firing line as it were, but so will we all be, and it's better than being confined below if anything happens suddenly. Which is a fair enough prognosis, I think.'

'Reckon you c'd be right at that, Commodore,' Harrison said. 'But I'd call it not all that *likely*. Because I don't reckon that Nazi raider's going to attack a convoy with a strong cruiser escort. Isn't it a fact that the surface raiders concentrate on the less well-escorted convoys?'

'Yes and no,' Kemp said. 'Don't forget, we're a prize target. Troop convoys always are. There would be a lot of prestige and a lot of celebration in Berlin after a successful attack on a troop convoy.' He paused. 'Normally, I agree, I'd not expect an attack by a single surface raider even on a troop convoy.'

'So what's different this time?' the Australian colonel asked.

Kemp spoke quietly. 'The Admiralty signal indicated something extra. There's known to be two U-boat packs operating off Freetown – off the Rokel River. They don't know the strength of these packs, but going on general intelligence knowledge of the German submarine command, they could be of six boats each. Now, if those packs are operating – and this isn't known for sure either – if they're operating with the *Stuttgart*, that puts a very different complexion on what might be going to happen.'

Harrison nodded thoughtfully. 'Reckon you'll get any further intelligence, do you, Commodore?'

Kemp shrugged. 'That's in the lap of the gods. If I do, you can be sure I'll pass it on, Colonel. In the meantime – and I'm confident I don't really need to say this – not a word to anyone outside your own trooping staff. I don't want to cause any worry to the civilians over something that may never happen.'

Again Harrison nodded. 'What do you reckon yourself?' he asked.

Kemp said, 'I think we're going to have a fight on our hands. And just as soon as I'm able to make a positive appreciation, everyone will be fully informed.'

*

'Off your arse, *Featherstone*haugh.'

Featherstonehaugh jumped to his feet as though stung by a wasp; he had been sitting on a fairlead alongside his gun, day-dreaming. 'Sorry, PO.'

'You'll be sorrier,' Petty Officer Ramm said, and went on to diagnose what the OD had been doing. 'Dreaming oh my darling love of thee. Dreaming of thee. Right?'

'Just thinking, PO.'

'Oh, yes! You're not supposed to bloody think. Got it? Here to do a job, you are. In case you don't know, there's a war on.'

'I know that, PO.'

'Eh? Now and again I doubts it.' Ramm ticked over. 'Sorry, lad. Your dad. Don't take all I say too much to 'eart. That said, remember the ship needs all the eyes it's got. To spot bloody Adolf that is. Got a fag, have you?'

Featherstonehaugh produced a packet of Players. Ramm took one and flicked a lighter for himself and Featherstonehaugh. He blew a cloud of smoke and wondered how the armed services would ever manage if the brass hadn't insisted on a constant supply of cigarettes being made available to the troops and seamen. Life itself depended on a quick draw, it took the tension out of things and all sensible officers turned a blind eye to smoking on watch other than at night when the flick of a lighter or even the glow of a cigarette-end could be seen through a periscope. The fag in his mouth, Ramm went on with his job, which currently was to inspect the guns, make sure that all was shipshape and that all moving parts were greased and ready. Not that the *Aurelian Star*'s armament would be any use against the *Stuttgart*: the Nazi cruiser was a big job, around 11,000 tons with a main armament to match – eight 8-inch guns in twin turrets, a secondary armament of six 5.9s plus ack-ack and six torpedo-tubes, all of which she could carry around the oceans at some 27 knots.

But of course they had the escort.

With any luck, the Nazi wouldn't risk it.

The POW contingent had in fact been brought on deck daily for the exercise period laid down by the Geneva Convention for the treatment of their ilk. They were herded from their accommoda-tion by a company of the African riflemen, and another company stood by on the boat deck as extra security, all the natives carrying rifles with bayonets fixed.

On the day of the early-morning receipt of the Admiralty's signal the regimental sergeant-major of the Australian trooping staff watched as the German naval ratings emerged on deck. RSM Treddle was a formidable-looking man, tall, hefty and imposing in his bush hat and khaki-drill shirt and shorts, bunches of hair visible at the open neck of the shirt and the Royal Arms that denoted his rank as a Warrant Officer 1 prominent and shiny on the leather strap that secured it to a thick, hairy wrist.

'Look almost human, eh?' he remarked to Harrison's adjutant.

Captain Mulvaney nodded. 'Some do. Some don't. Scraggy, some of the bastards.'

RSM Treddle went on watching. He observed that the native troops were treating the Germans with caution, very trigger-happy he reckoned, but at the same time seeming almost apologetic in their roles as guards on white men, as though they sensed the anger of the prisoners at being herded by men with black skins. RSM Treddle remarked on this to Captain Mulvaney.

'Reckon they know about Hitler's ideas, do you?'

'What particular ideas?'

'Race. The pure-bred Aryan idea. All others being inferior.'

Mulvaney gave a coarse laugh. 'I doubt it. Reckon they don't have enough bloody English for that, Sar'nt-Major. But I reckon I get what you're driving at: the blacks expect trouble. But I doubt that too. The Jerries won't start anything aboard a ship crammed with troops.'

'Tempers,' RSM Treddle said, 'can erupt, Captain Mulvaney. Sudden incidents deliberately inspired, eh? Look at that bloke over there – see him? The tall bloke at the back end of the deck. By the rail.'

Mulvaney looked. The tall German, by his dress a petty officer, was getting up on the rail and looking forward towards the bridge. As the two Australians watched the German gave a Nazi salute, arm extended, hand palm down. They heard his shout: 'Heil, Hitler!' A number of other Germans followed suit, and there was a general stir from the prisoners.

Mulvaney met the RSM's eye. 'Not really our patch,' Mulvaney said. 'Not really. But let's get in there just the same, eh?'

'Right with you, Captain,' Treddle said.

They moved aft, RSM Treddle in the lead. As they reached the native escort, the riflemen parted to let them through. They pressed on through the bunched prisoners. The man who had given the Nazi salute watched their approach, smiling, still in his position on the rail.

RSM Treddle halted in front of him. 'You,' he said.

'Yes, Sergeant-Major?'

'So you speak English, eh?'

'Yes.'

'Well, good on yer, then. Pull your ears back and we'll see if you understand Australian too.' RSM Treddle took a deep breath that visibly increased his chest measurement. Staring the German in the eye he said, 'You're aboard a pommie ship and you bloody respect the fact, right? For a start, you'll not mention the name of fucking Hitler, never again. We don't want to bloody hear about that little bastard. And if you give the Nazi salute in my presence again, I'll wrench your fucking arm from its fucking socket with my own fucking hands. Got that, have you?'

As he finished, he moved closer, flexing his muscles. The German flinched away, lost his balance on the guardrail, and fell straight down to the after well deck, a long drop. Breathing hard RSM Treddle said, 'I hope he's bust his fucking neck.'

'For your sake, Sar'nt-Major,' Mulvaney said, 'let's hope he bloody hasn't.'

They each drew their revolvers and began the move back through the prisoners. They made it in safety; but the mood of the Germans was obvious enough.

Major Kennedy, the medical officer of the native regiment, was quickly at the scene. A moment later he was joined by the ship's surgeon, Dr Grant. An examination was made: it didn't take long. Their eyes met over the broken body: there was no need for speech. Death from a broken neck was all too obvious.

It was now a matter for higher authority: in the first instance Colonel Carter commanding the riflemen, the official guard on the POWs. And then OC Troops. And an unwelcome worry for the Commodore. Whoever was ultimately responsible for the safe conduct of the prisoners to the UK, the authorities in London were not going to be happy with any breach of the Geneva rules.

*

87

There would be an enquiry. In the meantime RSM Treddle went about his duties, supervising others doing theirs. Each day, after the POWs had been taken back to their quarters below, there were parades of the Australian and New Zealand contingent. Parades for the inspection of arms and equipment, parades for physical training, parades for this, that and the other, anything to keep the troops on their toes and as fighting fit as possible. When inactive for too long, men grew soft. It was RSM Treddle's mission in army life to stop them getting soft and he was pretty good at it, inventing all manner of things to keep them on the hop. Also being there in person to make sure the sergeants and corporals kept them at it. It was no use giving orders and then not see them carried out.

This morning Treddle was pre-occupied following upon a preliminary interview with OC Troops. Colonel Harrison had turned the air blue in the privacy of his stateroom and Treddle was still smarting. He'd held nothing back; and he knew he hadn't laid a finger on the man. If the Nazi wanted to move away from him, that was his own choice and his own bloody fault, Treddle had said. Harrison had more or less agreed but had said the matter could obviously not end there. There would be shoals of reports to be written to all sorts of authorities, Harrison said, and RSM Treddle had been a bloody nuisance, while Captain Mulvaney was initially at fault in suggesting a move into the ranks of the prisoners. It was, Harrison said, a bloody fuck-up he could well do without. Treddle would hear more about it shortly.

It was in the middle of one of his parades and around half an hour before Captain's Rounds of the troop decks that RSM Treddle was bidden to the bridge. This order was almost immediately negatived. In the short interval that had elapsed between the two messages, the Commodore had had a report from the senior officer of the escort, made by light and repeated from the leader of the anti-submarine screen: the Asdics had picked up two echoes. U-boats were in the vicinity.

NINE

'Action stations, if you please, Captain.' Kemp found this one of the unwelcome irritations of being the Convoy Commodore; he was not in command of his own ship and it was the Captain's responsibility to handle her and pass the orders. A moment later the action alarm sounded throughout the ship. By Kemp's order passed earlier, the B deck lounge was cleared for the reception of the German prisoners. Gregory Hench was sitting on a bar stool when Steward MacInnes began lowering the metal cage over the bar in protection of his stocks and to indicate that no more drinks would be served until orders came from the Purser.

'Just one more,' Hench said, holding the descending cage up by thrusting his hand through, the hand holding a glass.

'Sorry, sir.'

'Come on, man. Be a sport.'

'Sorry, sir,' MacInnes said again. 'Orders, sir.'

'Whose orders?'

MacInnes stared him in the eye. Hench was already a little tiddly. 'Captain's. You heard the alarm, sir. Ship's at action stations. You'd best get –'

'Bugger that,' Hench said in a harsh tone. He made as if to force the cage up, turned with a start as he felt a hand on his shoulder. He faced Purser Scott, three gold rings on his shoulder-straps. white cloth between. 'Leave the bar, Mr Hench.'

MacInnes completed the lowering of the cage. Hench said in a hectoring voice, 'So they don't teach you manners, Purser, in this Line. I happen to be a fare-paying passenger, not some uni-formed bod in a military draft.'

'Everyone aboard is under orders, Mr Hench, you included. Leave the bar immediately or I shall send for the master-at-arms to escort you out.'

Slowly, Hench slid off the stool. His voice slurring a little now, he said, 'Don't think I won't be reporting this to the Line in London. Because I shall.'

He moved away towards the open deck. MacInnes said, 'We get all sorts, sir.'

Scott nodded. Any complaint to the Line's head office would get the reception it deserved. A few minutes later the German prisoners began streaming in under guard of the rifles and bayonets. Going below, Purser Scott saw Gregory Hench going along an alleyway, his own cabin alleyway. With him was Miss Northway. What a time to choose, John Scott thought, if that was what was intended. On the other hand, it could be a pleasant way to die.

Finnegan had asked if the Commodore intended to scatter the convoy. Kemp's answer was no. The ships were better off keeping within the guns and depth charges of the warship escort. If they should encounter the surface raider, then would come the time to scatter.

The reports were coming in now: all watertight compartments sealed, fire mains ready, fire hoses run out. All the military draft and civilian passengers mustered at their boat stations, Hench and Miss Northway included. Their station happened to be under the orders of one of Scott's assistant pursers and when Scott checked round he saw Hench and Gloria Northway struggling with their cork lifejackets. He grinned to himself: he'd obviously been wrong, maybe they'd just been going below for the lifejackets.

At the guns, the crews were ready for action. Petty Officer Ramm spat on his hands and observed that he hoped they'd spot a Jerry, forced to the surface by the depth charges.

'Sink the bugger by gunfire,' he said with advance satisfaction.

'Probably a false alarm,' Leading Seaman Purkiss said.

'Trust you to spoil the fun, Purkiss. Not that I'd mind all that much, not being keen to get bloody sunk if they get us first like.'

'Which they probably will. If they're there.'

'Defeatist talk, Leading Seaman Purkiss, so can it.'

'Whatever you say, PO.'

Ramm moved to the ship's side and stared out over the water. By this time there had been a good deal of signalling between the destroyers of the A/S screen and the senior officer, and between the senior officer and the Commodore. Already the destroyers had moved ahead at full speed, creating big bow waves and wakes that streamed astern to mingle with the kerfuffle kicked up by the churning screws. The cruisers of the escort were maintaining a close screen on the merchantmen, steaming at convoy speed on the port and starboard beams. As Ramm watched, the great humps of water began spouting into the air as the depth charges from the racks and throwers began exploding at their set depths beneath the sea.

'Contact's real enough,' Ramm said, and moved back to his gun. 'Stand by, you lot, you never know. I reckon –'

He was interrupted by Featherstonehaugh. 'Something moving, PO!'

'Where, lad?'

Featherstonehaugh pointed away on the starboard bow. 'Just astern of the *Vindictive* –'

'God almighty, lad, that's not a something, it's a bloody tin fish!' Before he had finished speaking Petty Officer Ramm had grabbed the sound-powered telephone to the bridge. 'Torpedo bearing green one five,' he reported. He had just replaced the hand-set on its hook when there was a heavy explosion from the starboard beam, a merchant vessel that had strayed outwards from her station and was, or had been, moving on steadily astern of the *Vindictive*.

Now she was virtually gone.

'It's the ammo ship,' Ramm said in a shaking voice. 'Poor sods. There won't be any survivors from that lot.' A moment later the debris from the massive explosion began dropping in the water all around, some of it landing on the decks of the *Aurelian Star*. Blazing pieces of woodwork, white-hot metal fragments, parts of dismembered bodies blown through the air with tremendous force. Ramm ordered the gun's-crew to get below the shelter deck. Leading Seaman Purkiss, Ramm noted, was there already.

On the bridge, Captain Maconochie had lost no time when the report had come in from Petty Officer Ramm. He had ordered thirty degrees of starboard wheel, following the proper procedure so as to present as small a target for the oncoming torpedo as was possible: bows-on. Steadying his course when the torpedo's track was still a little on the starboard bow, he waited, watching narrowly as the menace sped towards his ship. Kemp stood by the rail in the starboard wing, found himself clutching the rail like a vice. Then came the shattering explosion as the big ammunition ship blew sky-high and the debris began to fall. Kemp's and Maconochie's whole attention remained on the approaching torpedo, evidently one of two – maybe more – that had been fired. Kemp blew out a long breath of relief when the tin fish passed down the troopship's starboard side. He found his whole body soaked with sweat.

'Well done, Captain,' he called. 'Very nicely timed.'

Maconochie was also wiping away sweat from face and neck. 'We had better luck than those poor beggars,' he said, waving an arm to starboard. There was drifting debris, and flames shooting up from what was left of the ammunition ship. Some ten thousand tons of munitions had gone up, lost to the Allied war effort, but it was the fate of the men, the human factor, that was on all minds. Husbands, sons, fathers. So many families ashore whose lives would be in ruins.

'Bugger this war,' Kemp said. His voice was filled with anger. Then he stiffened. Incredulously he said, 'Did you hear that, Maconochie? *Cheering!* From the B deck lounge.' His face was unbelieving. 'Finnegan, restrain me from going below with a revolver!'

Finnegan said, 'I feel the same way as you do, sir. So I guess we restrain each other, okay?'

There was another thought in both their minds: at any moment they might go the same way as the ammunition carrier. If that happened, there wouldn't be much help given to the Germans.

The Commodore's ship under port wheel moved back to her course and carried on. The detonations of the depth charges continued, one after the other. Kemp remarked that it seemed likely there was a whole pack of U-boats attacking.

'Jumping the gun, sir?'

'What gun, Finnegan?'

'Not waiting for the *Stuttgart*. One of the theories was that the *Stuttgart* would attack together with the U-boats.'

'Correct, Finnegan. But they're always full of theories, shore-side.'

'Guess that's right, sir, Commodore. But this one was yours. The conference with oc Troops –'

'All right, Finnegan, I've never pretended to be an oracle. But just bear in mind that there may be, probably will be, other packs around.' Kemp swung his binoculars, scanning the assembly of ships ploughing doggedly along beneath a clear blue sky with enough breeze to ruffle the sea's surface and make the spotting of periscopes difficult. He said, 'Whoever picked up that first torpedo was a live wire. We failed to spot it from the bridge.'

'Guess we did, sir.'

'When this is over, find out who it was.'

'I'll sure do that thing, sir.'

'Just aye, aye, sir is quite enough, Finnegan. Three words instead of . . . how many was it?'

Finnegan counted on his fingers. 'Six, sir.'

Kemp grunted. 'Verbal diarrhoea, Finnegan.'

'Why, I guess you could be right at that, sir, Commodore –'

'Shut up, Finnegan.'

The convoy steamed on. Inside the next two minutes there was the whine of the sound-powered telephone from the lookout at the foremasthead. Finnegan answered and reported to the Commodore. 'U-boat surfacing, red four five, sir!'

Kemp swung round. A long black bow was starting to emerge, to be followed by the conning tower breaking through the water. 'Damaged by the depth charges,' Kemp said. 'But she can still be dangerous. Warn the guns'-crews, Finnegan.'

Finnegan ran to pass the word fore and aft. The U-boat was on a clear bearing from the *Aurelian Star*'s decks and was within gun range of both the three-inch. Two destroyers were moving towards her but were still some way off. As Finnegan reported the Commodore's message passed, a stream of machine-gun fire arced towards the *Aurelian Star*, and there was a puff of smoke from a gun mounted just for'ard of the conning tower.

Kemp said, 'Open fire, Finnegan.'

'Open fire!' Ramm roared out. The gun went into immediate action, as did the for'ard gun under Petty Officer Biggar. There were sharp cracks and a shudder ran through the ship; down below cork insulation was brought down in showers from the deck-heads immediately beneath the gun-mountings. A rapid fire was kept up. The first shots from both guns went over the target. The next shells fell short.

'Straddled,' Ramm shouted in high excitement. 'We'll get the bastard with the next.'

They didn't; there was another shortfall. But after that they had the range more closely and a shell took the upward-canted bow of the U-boat. There was an explosion, and the bow slewed to port. Two more that were near misses; and then there was a further explosion, this time slap on the conning tower. There was a burst of smoke and flame. Ramm had the impression that the conning tower and its adjacent gun had ceased to exist. On the heels of the strike another shell took the base of what had been the conning tower, ripping away the plating of the pressure hull.

The order came from the bridge to cease firing. As the guns fell silent there was a further tongue of flame from the gap left by the shattered conning tower and this was followed by a burst of pressurized steam just before the U-boat settled in the water and then, her broken bow lifting to point upwards like a finger, slid back beneath the sea.

'Let the bloody Nazis cheer that one,' Ramm said with a great deal of satisfaction. 'One up to us, eh? Well done, lads.'

Purkiss said sourly, 'Bet you a day's pay PO Biggar'll claim it as his.'

'Put a sock in it, Leading Seaman Purkiss. Biggar can claim what he bloody likes. I see *our* shell 'it.'

'Ha, ha,' Purkiss said, but he said it *sotto voce*, very much so.

The guns'-crews were kept closed up; the action was not over yet. Ahead of the convoy another U-boat was brought to the surface and despatched by gunfire from the *Vindictive*. One of the cruiser escorts, HMS *Okehampton*, was taken by a torpedo on her starboard bow. Her Captain reported damage and casualties but indicated that he could proceed at slow speed while makeshift repairs were carried out. The cruiser was given orders from the senior officer to detach from the convoy once the U-boat attack was over and to enter Freetown. In the meantime a destroyer would be detached from the A/S screen to stand by her to the Rokel River. On urgent representations being made by the Commodore, the senior officer indicated that he would break wireless silence, the position of the convoy being already known to the Germans now, and request back-up from Rear-Admiral West Africa in Freetown.

When the asdics of the escort reported lost contact Kemp said, 'Either there were just the two, or the rest took fright. We'll keep the ship at first degree of readiness for a while longer, if you please, Captain. The Germans don't usually get cold feet. There could be a boat lying deep with engines stopped.'

Kemp went round the upper decks, having a word here and there with the troops and the civilian passengers, doing his best to allay fears. The blowing up of the ammunition ship had had its effect on morale in a number of cases. Old Mrs Holmes was shaking and pale, and her husband was doing his best with her. There was a good deal of stiff-upper-lip about Colonel Holmes. War was war and had to be faced up to. And he was certain they were all in good hands. The Navy would never let them down.

Kemp agreed heartily with this, though he doubted if the crew of the ammunition carrier would take quite the same view.

Moving aft, Kemp spoke to Ramm and his gun's-crew.

'Very well done, all of you,' he said. 'We don't know if it was this gun or Petty Officer Biggar's that got the U-boat, but –'

'This one, sir, for certain sure. I see the projy 'it like, sir.'

Kemp concealed a grin. 'I've no doubt Petty Officer Biggar saw his do the same thing. Let's say it's honours even. The result's the same and you all contributed. Which of you was it who saw the torpedo track?'

Ramm said, 'It were Ordinary Seaman Featherstonehaugh, sir.'

Kemp reached out and shook the OD's hand. 'Splendid,' he said. 'I'm proud of you. It's not too much to say you may have saved the ship.' He would have liked to add that he would be putting in a word to the right quarter, but he refrained. The young man was in for a commission and there must be no suggestion of anything that might be construed by his messmates as favouritism, or any apparent leaning over backwards to commend an ordinary seaman destined for the wardroom. Kemp was well enough aware of jealousies along the lower deck and indeed he could understand them. Often he had reflected that it must be galling for, say, any PO such as Ramm or Biggar, men of long sea experience in the fleet, fine seamen all of them, to see a youngster virtually only just out of school vault over their heads to the wavy gold stripe of a sub-lieutenant RNVR. He had occasionally overheard the comments: 'Bin in the Andrew 'alf a dog-watch and just look at 'im.' That he, Kemp, could understand the feelings was not to disparage the RNVR – far from it. The green sub-lieutenants learned from experience and became as reliable as anyone else, and quickly too. Moving on again, Kemp grinned inwardly at another thought: the green sub-lieutenants not infrequently equipped themselves with two officers' cap badges and kept them alternately in glasses of salt water to make them look as though they had faced years of bad weather . . . and reflected also that he had done the same thing himself years before when he had first joined the Mediterranean-Australia Lines as a junior fourth officer.

Going back for'ard Kemp met Brigadier Pumphrey-Hatton at the foot of the starboard bridge ladder. Pumphrey-Hatton said, 'A word in your ear, Kemp.'

Kemp waited. The brigadier went on, 'That RSM. You'll know what I'm getting at. Of course, the feller's the responsibility of his own OC Troops, I know that. But as Commodore you may come into the picture. Or Maconochie might, as Master. I just wanted to have my say. I'm not inexperienced when it comes to men, you know.'

'Of course not, I appreciate that. I'll be glad to have your views, Brigadier.'

Pumphrey-Hatton looked at him sharply. 'Do you mean that, Kemp?'

'I do.'

'Very well then, here they are. Try to get that Australian colonel to play it down. Regimental Sergeant-Majors are the back-bone of any army. Damn fine fellows, with a damn hard job to do. Follow?'

Kemp nodded. 'Yes, I do. The Navy's never had quite the equivalent. We have warrant officers, but they don't entirely equate. Nevertheless –'

'Nevertheless, what the fellow did was wrong. Dead wrong – I know that. If you look at it that way – as death caused to a prisoner-of-war. Personally, I do not. The RSM never laid a hand on the man. And the RSM's reaction was perfectly understand-

96

able, don't you see, a natural response to the giving of the Nazi salute. Don't tell me you'd not have done the same.'

Kemp said, 'That's possible.' He laughed. 'Oh, I'd have had the initial urge, I expect, but I'd like to think I'd have exercised more self-control.'

'Ah, but you're not an Australian. I've fought with the Australians – the Australian Division at Tobruk, under Morshead. Their discipline wasn't that of the British infantry-men, but, by God, they achieved results.' Pumphrey-Hatton paused. 'I'm just asking you to put in a word if you get the chance. Not that it's any business of mine. Except that I'm a soldier too.'

He turned and walked stiffly away. Kemp remained for a moment at the foot of the ladder, staring after him. Pumphrey-Hatton hadn't seemed the sort to intercede on behalf of anyone not of commissioned rank . . . or had he? Kemp recalled the events of his previous convoy, the outward convoy from the Clyde to Trincomalee when Pumphrey-Hatton had been oc Troops. The Regimental Sergeant-Major of the trooping staff, Mr Pollock late of the Border Regiment, had fallen victim to the cholera that had raged throughout the Commodore's ship and other vessels of the convoy and escort. Kemp had heard via the galley wireless that Pumphrey-Hatton, visiting his RSM's sickbed, had found two of the ship's crew, one a man who had been a sailmaker in the days of the old square-riggers, already measuring the dying man for the canvas shroud in which he would shortly be slid overboard. Pumphrey-Hatton had been outraged and had booted the pair of them out of the cabin in no uncertain fashion. And when Mr Pollock had died, it had been Pumphrey-Hatton who had insisted that the regimental depot at Carlisle Castle be informed and urged to do all they could for Pollock's family.

Pumphrey-Hatton was a long-serving officer. He'd soldiered through the peace between the wars. He had, no doubt, a fierce pride in the British Army and in its regimental system where all the members of the regiment formed a family, very much along feudal lines – the squire, the parson, and, below the salt as it were, the villagers. But a source of great strength and pride and, by and large, fairly benevolently conducted. Kemp guessed that what got under Pumphrey-Hatton's skin were the civilians turned soldiers, men who hadn't at all the same outlook, and in many cases were villagers transported to the Hall.

Kemp climbed the ladder to the bridge. There were other matters that he had learned about, sketchily, from the galley wireless: trouble ashore at the Cape, involving Pumphrey-Hatton and two of the *Aurelian Star*'s naval party. Pumphrey-Hatton had never said anything about that and although Kemp was very curious to know he didn't intend to get involved with any galley wireless or tales told out of school.

Reaching the bridge, he saw signalling from the senior officer's flag deck, an Aldis lamp trained on the *Aurelian Star*'s bridge.

Yeoman Lambert reported, 'Commodore from cs23, sir. Enemy drawn off, am resuming cruising stations.'

'Thank you, Yeoman. Captain, I suggest we follow suit.'

Captain Maconochie passed the word by Tannoy throughout the ship. On the starting platform below in the engine-room, Chief Engineer French eased his cap on his head, wiped his forehead with the inevitable ball of cotton-waste, and gave silent thanks to God that he'd survived another U-boat attack and would live to face the next, and the next, and the next . . . there was never any enduring let-up in this war, only when you were on leave at home in UK and even then the buggers got at you with their perishing *Luftwaffe*, night after night of air raids that got a weary man and his wife out of conjugal bliss and sent them down into the shelters to listen to the crump of bombs, the ringing of bells from the fire appliances as the incendiaries rained down along with the high explosive, police whistles, the crying of young children, and then, when you emerged, the terrible sights of the smashed and gutted buildings, all the rubble and the bodies, and more cries, this time the pathetic cries of people buried beneath the fallen masonry, the results of Adolf Hitler's night's work.

In the B deck lounge, Steward MacInnes re-opened his bar.

'So what about it, Greg?' Gloria Northway asked.

'Yes . . .'

'What d'you mean, yes?'

'I mean yes.' Hench shifted uncomfortably.

'But.'

'But?' Hench stared, rather glassy-eyed.

'Yes, but. There's always a "but" in your voice. You don't really want to, do you?' She looked at him accusingly. 'Well, go on, do you?'

'Of course I want to, Gloria. Only . . . well, the way I see it . . . to take advantage of – of the sea surroundings and all that, if you follow, the build-up of tropical seas, and the moon . . .' He waved a hand around, vaguely. 'Phoney romance,' he said. 'You'd come to regret it. When we reach UK, you see.'

'Bollocks.'

Hench was a little startled. 'What?'

'You heard. You're just being stupid, Greg, really stupid. Taking advantage my bottom, I've been taken advantage of too many times to bother and I don't mind admitting it. I *like* being taken advantage of. I thrive on it, as a matter of fact. So don't worry about me, I'll not follow you crying my eyes out all the way from the Clyde to wherever it is you're going. Worthing, isn't it, your dear old mum?'

'Yes.'

'Well, then.' She sighed impatiently. 'Look, Gregory Hench, if you don't come up to scratch there's others aboard who will, get me?'

'Oh.'

'I'm not that bad looking.'

'No, no –'

'So watch it.'

He didn't answer right away. When he spoke it was to say, 'How about a drink, Gloria?'

'Oh, for God's sake. Past master at evading the issue you are. Get me a long gin-and-grapefruit if you must, but lay off the booze yourself.'

As ever on a long convoy, there was a necessity for the escort and merchant ships to take on fuel. Bunkers taken at the Cape would power them as far as the Azores, but the Azores under the Portuguese flag were strictly neutral. Fuel would therefore be taken at Ascension Island, where two deep-laden naval tankers of the Royal Fleet Auxiliaries would be in readiness to discharge into the tanks of the convoy as they lay off the port.

Ascension Island was now two days ahead, and the re-fuelling would take place before *Vindictive* and the damaged *Okehampton* with her single destroyer escort detached for the Rokel River and Freetown.

Maconochie discussed the operation with Kemp and his own Chief Officer and Chief Engineer.

'Not as easy as going alongside for fuel,' he said. 'We'll need all the fenders we can muster when the RFA ship comes alongside. They're big ships to handle, very deep draught of course. Do you see any problems from your point of view, Chief?'

French shrugged. 'So long as it's oil fuel, the intake's all the same to me. The rigging of gantries to take the pipelines, that's the deck, but my lads'll be there to see to the connecting up. No, I don't expect any problems.'

Maconochie nodded, and turned to Kemp. 'The A/S screen'll lie off to act as guardships, I understand?'

Kemp said, 'That's the ticket. They'll fuel singly after the rest of us have bunkered.' He added, 'It'll be a long job, of course, and the sooner it's done and we're away again the better I'll like it. We're going to be pretty well exposed, never mind the destroyers. And pretty damn immobile, not to say helpless – sitting ducks in fact.'

Kemp had fought the issue back at the Cape, wishing to enter Freetown for bunkers, but the brass had brushed his protests aside. U-boats, they had said – and this was true – tended to lurk outside the Rokel River. But plenty of convoys, Kemp had pointed out, had put into Freetown before now. The response to that, also true, had been that Kemp's was a big convoy to fuel from barges, which was all Freetown had to offer by way of facilities. That would take time, and because of the urgency of the troops' arrival in UK speed was of the essence. No notice was taken of Kemp's strong representations against what would amount to fuelling at sea, a technique that was bound to be developed in the future but which was currently in its infancy. Kemp knew that the Masters of the RFA were experienced in manoeuvring their heavy ships in confined waters, such as when going alongside the battleships and cruisers and aircraft-carriers of the Mediterranean Fleet, in the Grand Harbour of Malta. It was not easy to handle a 12,000-tonner in such constriction. But in carrying out the operation outside a port, with the ships to be fuelled lying, perhaps, in an ocean swell and heaving about on open waters . . . Kemp's imagination told him very many things, adverse things, that could happen. Using that imagination, as he had done on and off ever since leaving Simonstown, he saw a time when the Admiralty might devise a system of extended gantries that would carry the fuel-oil pipelines across, say, a cable's-length of sea, joining the tanker and the receiving ship at a fairly safe distance apart so that the risk of sides being scraped and damaged would be minimal. It might even be possible, given that safe distance, to carry out bunkering whilst under way. And Kemp wished fervently that he was not faced with the prospect, as he was, of heaving-to outside Ascension Island.

Sighing, he said, 'I suppose they know what they're doing. I refer to those who control our destinies. One of the senior bods at Simonstown gave me the impression of having just disembarked from the Ark. I'd not be surprised if the last time he took bunkers it was coal. And I'm not to be quoted on that, gentlemen.'

With unease in the Commodore's heart, the troop convoy steamed on.

TEN

There had been discussion about the body of the German POW: following the medical examination, the corpse had been placed in the ship's cold store. The discussion, between OC Troops, the two doctors, Captain Maconochie and Kemp, had been to decide what to do with the body finally. Carry it on for disembarkation at the Tail o' the Bank, or have a sea committal?

Maconochie was all for a sea committal. Seamen, he said and Kemp was in full agreement, didn't like corpses aboard ships. Not even in peacetime. They were largely a superstitious bunch and corpses brought bad luck. OC Troops disagreed.

'Evidence,' he said. 'Can't destroy evidence, right? I'm answerable to Canberra, maybe to your War Office. Because of the Geneva Convention, treatment of POWs. How do I come out of it, reporting a dead Nazi already disposed of?'

'I don't believe it's any skin off your nose, Colonel,' Kemp said. 'The facts are known, no one's attempted a cover-up, and the doctors have established the cause of death. The Geneva Convention's all very well, but we're here, at sea, with a body that could cause a lot of bad feeling among the seamen. Further, I think that from the POW viewpoint it would be better disposed of. I'm sure the incident is rankling along the German accommodation and it could fester. We certainly don't want that. What we want is a clean ending. Agree, Captain?'

Maconochie nodded. 'Very much so. I see absolutely no point in keeping that body aboard and I think the disposal should be done soonest possible.' He added, 'The weather's fair for burial now. As we make our northing later on, it very likely won't be.'

'That's your view,' Colonel Harrison said.

'It's the sensible one,' Kemp said sharply. 'With all due respect, Colonel, you don't know seamen. Maconochie and I do. We know their feelings, what makes them tick. And I'm for a sea committal.'

'You mean you've decided, have you?'

Kemp nodded. 'Yes.'

'It wouldn't occur to you to ask the senior officer of the escort, eh?'

Kemp said formally. 'Colonel Harrison, I am the Convoy Commodore. I make my own decisions within the convoy itself and I do not propose to bother the senior officer of the escort with matters that don't concern him. In short, I'm not passing any bucks.'

'So you're going right ahead?'

'With the permission of the ship's Master, yes.'

'Righto, then, so long as you take the can. Meantime there's the question that I reckon all of you people want to know the answer to. And that is, what's to be done about my RSM, Treddle. Now, a little bird's been telling me something, something that got overheard. That bloke Pumphrey-Hatton. He's been opening his kisser over matters that are nothing to bloody well do with him. Now, I don't take anything from that dried-up old has-been nor do I take anything from seamen who know bugger all about the bloody army. So I want you to know that what is done about my RSM is my affair and no one else's, right? I make that decision for myself and I reckon I've made it. Pumphrey-Hatton needn't have bothered his arse, because I'd made it already.' He took a deep breath. '*Nothing's* going to be done. We have a dead Nazi, and good on RSM Treddle's what I say.' He got to his feet, staring around truculently. 'That having been said, I'll say g'day to you all, gentlemen.'

He left the cabin. Kemp caught Maconochie's eye and gave a grimace. 'Honours even, I suppose. Got his own back . . . because we didn't go along with him from the word go.' He went on, 'They do have 'em in Australia! But so, I admit, have we.'

The departure of Colonel Harrison broke up the conference. Kemp, going back to the bridge with Maconochie, reflected that it was perhaps not so very surprising that Pumphrey-Hatton didn't appreciate the 'temporary gentlemen'. Kemp had learned that in civilian life, Harrison had been a car salesman. Probably a very successful one, if his pushing manner had originated in peacetime. And as for the RSM, Kemp was only too relieved not to have to interfere.

'A funeral, my dear. You remember – that German prisoner. It's necessary, you know.'

'It's upsetting,' Mildred Holmes said. 'Oh, I know he was a Nazi and may have helped to sink some of our ships, and that he was most dreadfully foolish to do what he did –'

'Well, then.'

She stuck to her point. 'No, Stephen, it's not a case of well, then. One can't help thinking of his family. Parents, possibly a wife and children . . . they'll all probably have heard he had been taken prisoner and will be thinking that at least he's safe from being killed. And now this. I call it very sad, even if you don't. I suppose soldiers see things differently.'

'You know they do, Mildred. Good God, you were a soldier's wife for long enough. A soldier's daughter too, as I said to that Northway woman, or was it Hench?'

'It wasn't either. You didn't say that.'

Holmes clicked his tongue. 'I think I said you came of a military family. Same thing.'

'It isn't the same thing,' she said in a rather high voice.

Her husband rustled irritably. 'Oh, don't be so . . .' He didn't go on; there had been a sound like a sob. 'Steady on, old girl, there's really no need to get so upset. Damn it, we're *fighting* the blasted Nazis, aren't we?'

'It's not just this – this funeral. It's everything about this voyage. The awful feeling that we might be sunk at any moment . . . and what's in store for us if we arrive –'

'*When* we arrive, Mildred. I've said so often, we're in good hands and we're going to be all right.' He added in what was intended to be a reassuring tone, 'You'll feel quite differently as soon as we pick up Ailsa Craig at the entrance to the Firth. Bring back happy memories. Remember the Turnberry Hotel? Golf, with good old Bill, first-rate course – Open standard, of course, same league as St Andrews, or Carnoustie, or Royal St George's, or Lytham St Annes –'

'Or Troon,' she put in, tongue in cheek.

104

'Oh, yes, Troon, of course. Remember the golfing week at Troon, back in '22 wasn't it – foursome with good old Bill and Arse-end Portlock and a feller called Bashy Longford? I often wonder what happened to Bashy Longford. Sherwood Foresters . . . said he'd once got a hole in one on the Old Course at St Andrews but I never quite believed him, he wasn't quite up to it.' Mildred would be all right now, he'd jollied her out of her mood, talking about old times. Nothing like old times and reminiscences. Mildred used to say that she might just as well have stayed at home when he went on his golfing weeks since she never set eyes on him all day, but of course that was a lot of tommy-rot. And she used to say she couldn't stand any more of good old Bill's laugh. It was certainly on the loud side, but still, it was jolly. He droned on now and never noticed that Mildred was crying.

The sea committal took place early next day, in the Morning Watch, the 0400 to 0800. Sharp on six bells Captain Maconochie went down from the bridge, with Kemp, to the after end of F Deck where Bosun Barnes had rigged a plank where a section of the guardrail had been temporarily removed. The body of the Nazi, sewn into canvas with fire-bars at the feet to ensure that the corpse would sink, was laid beneath a German naval ensign provided by Yeoman Lambert. Present were OC Troops, *Kapitan-Leutnant* Stoph, and an armed guard of the King's East African Rifles under the command of Sergeant Tapapa. Maconochie briefly read the words of the committal service, referring to 'our brother here departed', for there was no nationality in death, the plank was tilted and, with the engines briefly stopped so that the revolving blades of the screws should not suck the body down to be shredded into fragments, the canvas-shrouded corpse took the South Atlantic with a splash as *Kapitan-Leutnant* Stoph gave the Nazi salute.

After a decent interval, a matter of little more than a minute, Maconochie nodded to the bosun, who went to the sound-powered telephone and rang the bridge.

He spoke to the Officer of the Watch. 'From the Captain, sir. Engines to full ahead.'

The ship's halt had been very brief; she still had way on her and shortly after the telegraphs had rung on the bridge and had been repeated in the engine-room, the *Aurelian Star* was moving up to resume her station in the convoy. On the starting platform Chief Engineer French had just two thoughts: one more of the sods gone, and thank the Lord they were under engine power again. No one liked hanging about in enemy-infested waters.

Far to the north, a Morris Eight was parked in a road some distance xkaway from Chief Steward Chatfield's Southampton house, as was always the case when Cocky Bulstrode was making a night of it. A different street each time. No flies on Cocky Bulstrode, who as suspected by Chatfield was indeed a salesman, but not of furniture. Cocky Bulstrode was in the business of selling life insurance, being an agent of one of those insurance companies that sold door-to-door and made a weekly collection of premiums, mostly in small change. To accommodate this small change he carried a leather bag not unlike a schoolboy's satchel. At the time the German was being slid over the side of the *Aurelian Star*, and some twenty-four hours before the convoy was to heave-to outside Ascension Island, thus putting Cocky's hostess' husband at some risk of his life, this satchel hung by its strap from a hook behind the door of Chatfield's bedroom. In the double bed Cocky Bulstrode and Roxanne Chatfield lay, currently asleep but more or less still entwined. Both snored but were unable to hear each other. When one awoke, there would be a complaint.

It was Roxanne who woke first, and she awoke with a start that brought Cocky awake at almost the same instant so there were in fact no complaints.

Roxanne said, 'Oh, my God.'

'What's up, eh?'

'Nothing, not now. It's all gone. Nightmare,' she added in explanation.

Cocky always tried not to look at her first thing in the morning: her hair stuck up like the fuzz on a coconut and her breath smelled of too many fags, and she had no make-up on to hide the pallor. But he enquired about the nightmare nevertheless.

'My hubby,' she said.

'What about him?' He gave a light laugh. 'Not a nightmare that he'd turned up suddenly, was it?'

She shook her fuzz. 'No, not that. That he wouldn't ever turn up – not *ever*. He got sunk.'

'In the nightmare, love?'

'Yes. In that ship. The Germans had got him. Didn't have a chance. Down in the meat store, the refrigeration chamber he was, when them so-and-sos fired a torpedo at him. The door banged to, in the explosion like, and the door got a bit buckled. He was shut in, couldn't get out. He froze to death.' Roxanne shuddered. 'Ooh, it was that awful, it was reelly.'

'Sorry to hear it, love, very sorry. Only a dream, though. Best forget all about it now, eh?'

'I can't, it's still on my mind. It was really vivid, I see him go in, hear the door bang shut, hear the torpedo. I see him struggling like in vain, see his face, all cold and all twisted up with fear.'

'What you might call a frozen expression?' Cocky suggested, grinning.

She turned on him, fag breath and all, beat at him with small clenched fists. 'Don't bloody make a joke of it, it was reel. To me it was.' She added, turning away from him, 'Like an omen. Just like an omen.'

'No,' he said reasonably. 'Couldn't have been. Dreams are like that, daft mostly. Like I said – just forget all about it, love.' He cuddled her, for there was more he wanted before once again taking up his satchel from its hook and pounding what he called his book. But she stiffened in his groping grasp and said no, she didn't want it, not after that awful dream. She just couldn't. Not just yet, anyway.

'Tonight, love?'

'We'll see.'

'I'll come round anyway, usual time, all right?'

'All right,' she said in a voice that to Cocky Bulstrode seemed somewhat small, frightened even. 'I'm ever so worried,' she said. 'It's made me think, like. Anything can happen at sea, any time. Here one moment, gone the next. I never really thought about it like that, never. Not till now. I'd be all on my own, see. Lost. On me tod with a war on. Wouldn't I?'

Cocky was by nature cautious. 'Well . . .'

'That's what would happen. There'd be just you. I . . . I'd like to feel you were, well, around.'

'Yes,' he said. 'I understand, love. You can rely on me if the worst happened.' The worst, in Cocky's view, would be if hubby survived and came home when he wasn't expected, which could be very awkward indeed even though Cocky had a ready tongue. It would depend, of course, on what he and Roxanne happened to be doing at the time, just having a friendly drink, or – well. If it happened to be the latter then it wouldn't be funny. Cocky Bulstrode had seen photographs of Chief Steward Chatfield: he was big, a real heavyweight. Never, so far as Cocky knew, been a boxer but he certainly did have the build. It wasn't only Cocky's physical form that would be at risk, either: his insurance company had a reputation to keep up and wouldn't go much on agents who dallied with the clientele. Conversely, if hubby never did turn up, if he did get sunk like in the nightmare just ended, then Cocky might get stuck for life, which was definitely not his idea. Cocky was accustomed to roam with his book: Fareham, Cosham and down into Pompey where there were any number of lonely wives with husbands at sea, just like Southampton itself. No, he really wouldn't want a wife.

It might be prudent to stand off just a little. He might not turn up after all, come the evening. He could always plead pressure of work.

Having washed and dressed and had a good breakfast of Roxanne's ration of one egg and a rasher of bacon, plus toast and marmalade and *ersatz* coffee, he took up his moneybag, kissed Roxanne, circumspectly, in the hall and departed on his rounds, picking up the Morris Eight in the anonymous street a safe distance away.

In a different part of the United Kingdom worry of another sort entirely was taking place. In Kemp's home in Meopham not far from the port of Tilbury, peacetime home of the Mediterranean-Australia Lines' ships, Mary Kemp, lonely in the house now that John's old grandmother had died, waited for the telephone to ring and tried to control the shake in her hands. Early that morning there had been very bad news. A telegram had come from the Admiralty: one of their two naval sons, Harry, had been reported missing after his ship, a light cruiser on convoy escort duty in the North Atlantic, had been engaged and sunk by German aircraft as the convoy had come into the danger zone of the Western Approaches. 'MISSING BELIEVED DROWNED' the telegram had said. Waiting in despair until nine thirty when the Mediterranean-Australia Lines London offices would be open, she had spoken directly to the Chairman. Sir Edward had been very concerned: he would do his best to obtain more information from the Admiralty, where he had a number of contacts. He would telephone the moment he had any news.

So Mary waited. Waiting, she thought about the terrible state granny would have been in had she been still alive. Harry had always been her favourite, and he had been fond of her as well, her bedroom – she'd been bed-bound for years – always what he called his first port of call after arriving home from school or, more recently, on leave. Thinking of granny now, she found herself wishing her back alive so that they could be some comfort to each other. Loneliness was a scourge, the more so in wartime. As John Kemp, half the world away, had suspected, Mary missed even the peremptory thump of granny's walking-stick on the bedroom floor, the thump that announced some want or other to be instantly met. Granny had been a nuisance and a tremendous burden to a wartime housewife coping with rations and shortages of all manner of things and queues and bombs and a lack of help in the house, but she had been basically strongly supportive, kind and generous. She had also been someone to turn to when a couple of years earlier in the war another telegram had come, similar in content to this morning's, also announcing Harry missing presumed drowned. That had ended happily: Harry's destroyer in the Mediterranean had also been sunk whilst escorting a convoy, but Harry had turned up safe that time on the island of Pantellaria off the North African coast to become a POW and later had managed to escape.

The telephone didn't ring. Mary occupied her mind by writing out a list of chores for that morning: butcher to pay, rations to be bought there and at the grocer's, try for some fish, a pair of shoes to be soled and heeled, clean the kitchen range which used to be cleaned by Mary's version of Mrs Mopp but which wasn't any longer because Mrs Mopp had gone into munitions and was now rather hoity-toity . . . get her hair done because it was a mess, and see the local builder about some loose slates after a bomb had landed in a nearby field.

At a little after noon the telephone rang. There was, Sir Edward said, no further news.

'I don't need to tell you how very sorry I am . . . but you must not lose hope. I'm told by the Admiralty that there's every hope

Harry will have been picked up by another ship. It's just that up to the time I spoke to them, there hadn't been any lists available – naturally they have to wait for the full reports to come in.'

Sir Edward refrained from saying that, Harry's convoy having come under attack, there would be little likelihood of a sea rescue. But Mary said, in a dead-sounding voice, 'They never do stop to pick up survivors. I know that.'

'There are always exceptions, Mrs Kemp. It has to depend on the particular circumstances. I repeat, you must not lose hope. I really mean that. There *is* hope. You must believe me.'

She asked, 'Will my husband have been told? I'd really sooner he wasn't. Not while he's at sea, with so much to worry about.'

'I agree,' Sir Edward said. 'In fact he's not been told yet . . . the Admiralty has a human face, Mrs Kemp. They've considered the impact on a Convoy Commodore.' He cleared his throat. 'I did tell them . . . said I'd ask you –'

'Tell them not to tell him, Sir Edward, please. I – I'll do that myself when he gets home. That is, if I have to.'

Putting down the receiver, Mary Kemp went straight to the kitchen to start on the range. It was always better to keep busy. And of course there was always hope. Granny would have said the same.

After the sea committal the Nazi POWs were in a belligerent mood. They were accorded their exercise period as usual, under a heavier guard today, Sergeant Tapapa having reported that the prisoners were truculent whilst being escorted up from their accommodation.

'Sah!' he had reported to his Adjutant. 'They have called me unpleasant names and have only slowly and with menace obeyed my orders.'

'What sort of menace, Sar'nt Tapapa?'

'A waving of fists, sah.'

'But you were not struck?'

'Not struck, sah. Threat only, and noises. Loud voices, and some laughter at me, and things I did not understand.'

The Adjutant nodded. 'Very well, Sar'nt, I'll ask the RSM to add to the guard detail and I'll report what you've said to the Colonel.'

'Sah!'

110

'Carry on in the meantime. And watch it – watch carefully that the Germans don't try to get their hands on the men's rifles for instance.'

'Sah!' Sergeant Tapapa saluted and executed an about-turn that was as smart as any guardsman could produce. But he marched away an anxious man: the Germans had looked and sounded very hostile indeed, as though they were blaming him personally for the death of their compatriot. And, although he had not understood the words – and the riflemen under his command had understood even less, for none of them spoke even English – Sergeant Tapapa had known very well that the Germans had been jeering at the black skins.

In the office used for the trooping staff, the Adjutant of the rifles spoke to his RSM, asking for the guard to be strengthened.

'Very good, sir. Permanently, or just for this morning, Captain Harding?'

'Let's see how things develop, Mr Nunn.'

'As you say, sir.'

Harding asked, 'What's your view, Mr Nunn?'

'As to the Nazis, sir?' RSM Nunn was a very British RSM, seconded from the King's Royal Rifle Corps, the 60th Rifles. His back ramrod straight, he tweaked at the end of a waxed moustache and gave his opinion of the Nazis. 'Scum, Captain Harding, real scum. That cheering when the ammunition-ship blew up. It takes scum to do that, Captain Harding, sir.'

'Yes. But I think we shouldn't regard them all as scum, Sarn't-Major. Dangerous . . . prisoners, you know –'

'I'm aware of that, Captain Harding, very aware of that. The Nazis will be treated properly, scum or not scum, and we shall incur no complaints from those what regard the Geneva Convention as the equivalent of the 'Oly Bible or the blocks of stone brought down from the mountain by Moses. But I'll be keeping my ear to the ground, Captain Harding, sir, and my eyes front, back, and sideways.'

Harding concealed a grin. 'Meaning you expect trouble, Mr Nunn?'

'Trouble, sir, yes, that is what I expect. And now if you'll pardon me, sir, I'll see about giving extra backing to Sar'nt Tapapa 'oo's a good little bloke if black.'

The RSM marched away, left-right-left just as though on parade at the Winchester depot of the 60th Rifles. Harding hoped he wouldn't be putting a big sergeant-majorly foot in it. RSM Nunn had lost a brother serving under General Auchinleck in the western desert – a Desert Rat, blasted by the guns of Rommel's Afrika Corps.

ELEVEN

The convoy had slowed some while earlier in order to accommodate the damaged cruiser, the *Okehampton* having been forced to reduce speed so as not to bring too much pressure of water on the torn fo'c'sle plating. She had reported some casualties; and the damage had included the rendering unfit for use of the two seamen's messdecks situated in the fore part of the ship. Kemp watched her progress from the bridge of the *Aurelian Star*.

'We've lost more time than we allowed for,' he remarked to Finnegan. 'We'll be around fourteen hours adrift on our ETA at Ascension.'

'Meaning we arrive after nightfall, sir?'

'Yes, exactly. I don't fancy hanging around with engines stopped in the dark hours. Nor do I fancy taking oil fuel at night. We'd need yardarm groups – too much damn light to home the U-boats onto us. That's not on.'

'Not on at all, I guess . . .'

Kemp grinned. 'Have another guess, sub?'

Finnegan lifted his cap and scratched reflectively at his forehead. 'Guess as to what, sir?'

'What we ought to do about it.'

'Simple,' Finnegan said. 'Make a signal to the senior officer, suggest the convoy and escort steam in circles till daylight, then start fuelling. How's that, sir?'

'Two minds with but a single thought, sub, to coin a phrase, apart from the circles. No reason why we shouldn't steam up and down in our present formation. I don't know why the senior officer hasn't thought of it for himself.'

113

'It takes a citizen of the good old USA, sir –'

'Come off it, Finnegan, it's my idea too. I'm going to stick my neck out.' Kemp turned. 'Yeoman?'

Yeoman Lambert came across. 'Yessir?'

'Make, from Commodore to cs23, in view of delay in forthcoming ETA suggest convoy and escort maintain formation under way after arrival and throughout dark hours.'

'Aye, aye, sir.' Lambert had been writing the message down on his signal pad. Moving away, he began making the senior officer's call sign on his Aldis lamp. There was a speedy acknowledgement from the cruiser. Kemp awaited for the reply. It came within a couple of minutes. Lambert approached the Commodore and read from his signal pad.

'Commodore from cs23 sir. Your 1436. Do not propose to accept delay involved. Ships will take fuel on arrival and leave soonest possible. Time of origin 1440, sir.'

'Thank you, yeoman.' Kemp blew out a long breath. 'Well, it's his decision . . . his responsibility too. He's taking a damn big risk in –' He broke off as the senior officer's signal lamp began winking again towards the *Aurelian Star*. Lambert made the acknowledgement, took down the signal, and once again read it off to Kemp.

'Commodore from cs23, sir. My 1440. Yardarm groups will not repeat not be used. Fuelling will take place with the least possible light.'

Kemp exploded. He said, 'Of all the world's constipated minds . . . the RN sometimes take the prize.' He added, 'Yeoman, just forget you heard that remark, all right?'

Lambert grinned. 'Cloth ears, sir, never heard a thing.'

Kemp nodded. 'And you, Finnegan.'

'Sure, sir, Commodore. In the United States Navy –'

'Save it, Finnegan, I'm not in the mood to appreciate the wonders of America.'

Some ten minutes later the flagship's masthead light went into action, making a general signal to all ships, repeating what had already been made to the Commodore. Kemp had the feeling that at least he had galvanized the senior officer of the escort into a decision, even though in Kemp's view that decision was quite the wrong one. Unless cs23 was in possession of information as to the disposition of enemy forces that had not been made known to anyone else.

*

114

'There's been a lot of signalling going on again,' Gloria Northway said, sitting at the bar. 'What's it all mean, Greg?'

Hench shrugged. 'How would I know?'

'You're a man. Or supposed to be. Men know about these things, I always thought. Like they're supposed to know about cars and railway timetables and choosing from menus.'

'What's the connection with naval signalling?' Hench asked acidly.

'Oh, I don't know. Forget it.' After a pause she went on, 'It's just that I'm scared, I suppose. In case you don't know, dearest Gregory, I'm a bloody bag of nerves. You wouldn't notice, I suppose.'

'I hadn't thought –'

'No, you wouldn't, would you? Men don't, do they?'

'I don't know.' Hench, somewhat out of his depth, took refuge in ordering more drinks from MacInnes. The usual in each case. The two passengers served, MacInnes turned away and began polishing glasses, keeping within earshot while he did so. He knew what Miss Northway was leading up to if Hench didn't. Perhaps Hench did, he couldn't be that insensitive, but preferred not to let on for reasons as aforethought by MacInnes himself. Miss Northway's next utterance left no room for doubt, in MacInnes' ears anyway.

'You know what the doctors recommend for women with nerves, don't you, Greg?'

'Well . . .'

'Right first time. Bloody brilliant! Look, we've been into this before. You know we have. It's about time you did something about it.'

Hench dithered, took a gulp at his whisky. He didn't feel in the least ready for a romp in the hay. Once again he temporized. He muttered into his glass, 'I don't know what you really want, Gloria, I always –'

'You know bloody well,' she said venomously, then raised her voice. '*You know bloody well I want to be, in your stupid phrase, taken advantage of.*'

Hench noted that the Holmeses had entered the lounge whilst Gloria's voice had been at its highest. He also saw them both turn and leave again. As they did so, Captain Mulvaney of the Australian Army came across, grinning. He put a hand on Miss

Northway's bare shoulder. As she turned to him in sudden surprise he said, 'Where I come from, that's to say along by the Murrumbidgee, a man doesn't need to be asked twice. Get me, bloke?' he added to Hench. 'Best make up your mind, hadn't you?'

Hench got to his feet, putting a hand on the bar to steady himself. 'The lady's no concern of yours,' he said thickly. 'I suggest you take your paw off her pronto.'

'You do, eh? And what if I don't? What happens then, bloke?'

Hench gathered himself, looked belligerent. 'I'll deal with you.'

'You and who else, eh?'

'I – well . . .' Hench looked around the lounge as though seeking assistance. He said, 'I'll hit you. Then there'll be a scene. For the adjutant of the trooping staff to be seen fighting . . . it'll be a matter for the ship's Captain as well as your own OC Troops.'

Mulvaney's voice was contemptuous. 'Just like a bloody pom, run to mummy.' He removed his hand from Gloria Northway's shoulder; she had made no move to remove it herself. 'Be seeing you, lady,' he said. Giving Hench a two-finger gesture, he turned away, grinning at the ex-planter's discomfiture. Hench finished his drink and demanded another. He had a bad shake in his fingers, MacInnes noticed, as he pushed the refill across the bar.

'Handled like a man,' Miss Northway said, her eyes glittering. 'I don't think.' She turned away and left the lounge. Her very walk told Gregory Hench that there was no invitation to him to follow her. In a way it was a relief; in another way it was not. In any case there was always the bottle. He downed the refill fast and asked for another. As he was drinking it he became aware of someone standing by his side. Brigadier Pumphrey-Hatton.

'Hench, isn't it?'

Hench nodded. 'Correct.'

'I heard some of that, Hench. Australians – a very primitive lot, very rough diamonds. Damn good in a fight. I expect you realized that. That man was a damn sight bigger than you, h'm?'

Hench stared wordlessly. What the devil was it to do with Pumphrey-Hatton of all people?

'Don't brood, Hench. That woman's not worth it, you must realize that. Don't overdo the drink, Hench.'

'I –'

116

'It's risky. On account of the flies.' Pumphrey-Hatton seized Hench's arm. 'Tell me frankly: have you noticed any flies since Simonstown? Fly-blows in the glasses?'

'No, I –'

'No more have I, thank God! But you never know. Just a friendly warning, Hench. Heed it for your own good.'

'Well, thanks –' Hench broke off; Pumphrey-Hatton was on the move again with his jerky walk. Hench shrugged, met the eye of the bar steward. MacInnes winked but said nothing. Hench reflected that it took all sorts; and he'd heard odd stories about the brigadier.

In the chart room in rear of the bridge, Kemp listened at 1600 to the BBC's Overseas news broadcast. There had been air raids over London during the night, the usual thing, and although there had been some damage in Clapham and adjacent districts a number, unspecified, of German aircraft had been shot down. There had been heavy fighting in the western desert, the 8th Army and the German Afrika Corps exchanging artillery fire and the armoured columns engaging. A convoy entering the Western Approaches had been attacked by enemy aircraft but this attack had been fought off, though not without some loss, a number of ships having sustained damage.

After the news there was a food programme. The role of the humble potato was being changed once again. Kemp remembered his wife saying that when there was a shortage of potatoes there were Government-sponsored propaganda broadcasts urging those who wished to preserve their figures not to eat potatoes; when there was a glut, then the eating of potatoes was advanced as an excellent and nourishing food with no weight-inducing qualities.

So much for propaganda.

And so much for the news broadcasts, which Kemp had largely ceased believing. Always so many enemy aircraft shot down, always the damage to British cities and ships and men played down. It was no doubt necessary in order to keep up morale. Or was it? The British public had already shown that it could take it. They'd taken Dunkirk, they'd taken the Battle of Britain. Right at the start of the war they'd taken the sinking of the liner *Athenia*, laden with women and children bound for the safety of the

United States, they'd taken the sinking of the battleship *Royal Oak* right inside the supposed safety of the boom at Scapa Flow; they'd taken the blowing-up of the mighty battle-cruiser *Hood*, largest warship in the world. And much else beside.

Nevertheless, the attack on that convoy in the Western Approaches nagged at Kemp. 'A number of ships had sustained damage.' What ships – merchantmen or naval escort? And how much damage? How many casualties?

Back on the bridge with Maconochie, Kemp forced the news broadcast out of his mind. The tones of Alvar Liddell, or Gordon MacLeod, or Bruce Belfrage, or Frank Philips or whoever it had been, faded. Kemp wasn't the only man in the world with sons at sea, sons at risk of their lives twenty-four hours a day, seven days a week. There would be very many fathers and mothers reading unpleasant things into that broadcast and all the other broadcasts that had gone on throughout the terrible years of war.

During the afternoon of the following day Kemp spoke on the Tannoy to all the passengers and crew, a brief and informative announcement to still rumour and speculation as issued by what was known at sea as the galley wireless.

'This is the Commodore speaking, with the approval of your Captain.' He paused, clearing his throat. 'At a little after dark tonight the convoy will heave-to off Ascension Island. Whilst stopped all ships will take oil fuel replenishments from two fleet tankers, naval tankers – RFA *Brambleleaf* and RFA *Oligarch*. This operation will naturally be conducted as speedily as possible but at this moment I'm not able to say precisely how long it will take since this has to depend on a number of factors, among them the weather, which at present happens to be fair.' Kemp didn't go into the other factors, which included any enemy presence and the difficulties of oiling at sea in darkness, which could lead to collisions. Nor did he add that on the previous day a wireless transmission from the Admiralty's Operations Room had indicated that the battleship *Duke of York* was adrift on her original time of departure from the Clyde owing to a union dispute over the handling aboard of an item of engine-room machinery by the ship's company, a job that should by rights belong to the Amalagamated Engineering Union or whatever. The battleship's rendezvous would thus be delayed – which fact Kemp now believed had swayed the senior officer's decision not to hold up the convoy overnight but to get the ships as far north as possible, as soon as possible, so as to bring them under the 14-inch batteries of the *Duke of York* before there was an encounter with the *Stuttgart*. He went on, 'I shall not disguise the fact that there is some danger in lying hove-to, but the exigencies of the convoy make this inevitable. Because of this possible danger, I intend to send the whole ship to boat stations for the period of refuelling. I know this will be uncomfortable to say the least, but the first concern of us all is the safety of all aboard. That is all. Except to assure you that you are in very capable hands under Captain Maconochie.'

He clicked off the Tannoy, saying a silent prayer that the lifeboats wouldn't have to be filled and lowered.

Instructions had already been issued by Maconochie and were now being put into effect throughout the ship. Chief Officer Dartnell, with the bosun, went round all lifeboats, inspecting their equipment – boats' bags, Verey lights, spare rudders, compasses, emergency rations – and seeing the falls in good running order, checking the Robinson's Disengaging Gear in each boat. Before arrival off Ascension all lifeboats would be ready for lowering to the embarkation deck with the gripes slipped and their crews standing by, and the Carley floats would be ready in their slides for instant release. In the engine spaces Chief Engineer French made ready for the taking of fuel into his tanks; Purser Scott and Chief Steward Chatfield made their arrangements, the Purser and his staff placing the ship's cargo manifest, passenger lists, Portage Bill and cash into leather bags ready to be taken to the lifeboats. Chatfield mustered his overtime sheets for the catering department and made them ready for fast removal if the worst should happen. With them he put his silver-framed photograph of Roxanne taken during a stay at Butlin's Holiday Camp in Skegness, Roxanne in a gay and happy mood, the happier because a redcoat had somehow got into the background, a redcoat, young and romantic, at whom she had made eyes frequently during their stay. Stowing away this reminder of times past, Chatfield wondered if that perishing Morris Eight would be round at his house that night. And what if the convoy got knocked off during refuelling? Was there someone already waiting to step into his shoes, take over his home, Roxanne and all?

Like Kemp, Chatfield tried to cast worry from his mind as he carried on with his duties, detailing his second steward to have hands ready to assist the masters-at-arms in ensuring that all cabins and other below-decks spaces were vacated when the bridge passed the order for boat stations, seeing to it that those of his department needed for the running-out of fire hoses were all on the top line. There were a hundred and one things to be seen to and thoughts of Roxanne's carryings-on receded.

TWELVE

As Ascension loomed through the night, the convoy reduced speed to ease its formation into the position where the ships would lie off to await the tankers. As a single flash came from the escort commander's masthead light, Kemp said, 'That's it, Captain. We're in position.'

Maconochie nodded. 'Stop engines,' he ordered.

'Stop engines, sir.' The Officer of the Watch pulled over the handles of the engine-room telegraphs. Bells rang in the wheelhouse, were repeated below in the engine-room. 'Engines repeated stopped, sir.'

'Slow astern both engines, wheel amidships.' Maconochie watched his bearings as the *Aurelian Star*'s headway came off. As the troopship began to ease astern, the final order was passed. 'Stop engines. Engines to remain on stand-by until further orders.'

When this had been passed below, Maconochie had a word with his chief engineer on the voicepipe. 'Here we wait, Chief. I can't say how long – there's no sign of the tankers yet, for one thing. I may need full power at any time and at short notice.'

'We'll be ready, sir. Ready for anything.'

'I know, Chief. And thank you.'

When the Captain had closed the voicepipe cover on the bridge, French left the starting platform and walked around on the greasy, slippery deck plates, checking here and there, watching the long, probing necks of the oil cans as the greasers kept the bearings sweet, felt the close heat that seemed to radiate from the very metal of the great shining steel shafts that, when in

121

motion, turned the screws . . . those shafts were idle now. How long for?

Every moment was a time of danger if the enemy should be anywhere around. But if he was, then surely he would be picked up on the radar or the Asdics. The Commodore had made the point earlier that the a/s screen would still be guarding the convoy. Until their turns came to lie alongside the tankers to take on fuel, the destroyers would be continually under way, circling the convoy and keeping a continuous watch on the Asdics. And if an echo was picked up, the ships would quickly be got under way. Except, of course, those that happened to have the tankers alongside when the lurking enemy was picked up.

'A matter of luck, that's all,' French said to his second engineer who had joined him in his tour of inspection.

'What's that, Chief?'

'Nothing really. Just thinking aloud.' French explained. 'A matter of luck that it's not us who get caught short.' He gave a brief laugh, one with no humour in it. 'We've always been a lucky ship. So far, anyway. We'll just pray it holds – that's all.'

The second engineer nodded but didn't comment. They both knew – or could guess intelligently – what it would be like to be torpedoed whilst alongside a laden tanker, taking oil fuel through pipelines that could hardly fail to fracture or tear away from the couplings. Explosion, fire, a searing blast from the tanker and they would emerge from the engine-room and boiler-rooms, if they emerged at all, into a world of flame, and a sea aflame as well, a sea beneath a carpet of burning oil into which it would be suicide to lower the lifeboats or rafts, assuming any were left intact.

Nobody wanted to die, that went without saying. But the second engineer happened to know that Chiefy French had a very particular reason for wanting to stay alive. The two of them were good friends, with shared confidences, and the chief had opened up about his family problems, needing someone to talk to, someone he could trust. He'd spoken about the sons, Alan and Billy, and the pending police court – shoplifting. Billy was the ring-leader and a right tearaway by the sound of it, and French's wife seemingly couldn't cope. If French should be killed, the family could disintegrate. Probably the Chief was visualizing that at this moment.

A very nasty worry on a night like this. The second engineer echoed the earlier thoughts of the Commodore: the Navy back at the Cape must have been like Harpic – clean round the bend –to have made the decision to bunker outside a port at night.

Once again the B deck lounge had been cleared for the reception overnight of the Germans. Once again those Germans were under guard of the native riflemen. But this time Sergant Tapapa would if required be backed up by a half-company of the Australian troop draft. OC Troops had agreed with Captain Maconochie and the Commodore that security was of more importance than having all the soldiers sticking rigidly to their allotted boat stations.

'Flaming Nazis c'd make real trouble,' Harrison had said in the orderly room. 'Watch the buggers like hawks, all right? But don't *you* be too bloody obtrusive, Sar'nt-Major,' he added to RSM Treddle. 'We don't want to *cause* trouble. Or give the Nazis the excuse to *say* we caused it. Understand?'

Treddle nodded. 'I'll act like a lovely, cuddly little bloody baa-lamb, Colonel. That do?'

Harrison grinned and clapped the RSM on the shoulder. 'Wolf in bloody sheep's clothing more like. Just keep the wolf hidden, that's all.' He added in an incredulous tone, 'Lovely, cuddly little baa-lamb my arse! Just don't look the part somehow. Tell you what, Sar'nt-Major. The rifles' RSM – he'll be, as he'd put it himself, on parade throughout the night. Let him do the high profile bit, eh?'

RSM Treddle said, 'Reckon he'll do that without bloody encouragement, Colonel. Bloke's a walking stuffed-shirt, as full of bullshit as you can get without being a bull's bum. Oh, beg pardon, I'm sure,' he added as RSM Nunn appeared in the orderly room doorway, his tight-lipped face indicating that he'd over-heard the closing remarks. RSM Treddle grinned cheerfully. 'No offence, mate, eh?'

RSM Nunn disregarded the overture. His pace-stick held rigid and precisely horizontal with the deck beneath his left arm, he crashed his boots and gave Harrison a magnificent salute. 'Sir! Reporting for duty as may be required, sir. I have the German prisoners in mind, sir. I –'

123

'Funny,' Harrison broke in with a straight face. 'We were just talking about you and the Nazis, Sar'nt-Major. . . .'

'Sir!'

'What was that?'

'Sir! I said sir, sir.'

'Oh, right. Well, good on you, Mr Nunn.'

'Thank you, sir.' RSM Nunn looked baffled. 'Sir! If I may be acquainted with your proposals for the night, sir, in respect that is to the Germans, sir.'

'Right you are, Mr Nunn, but I reckon I'll have to leave that to my sar'nt-major here. Me, I need to go to the bridge. A word with the Commodore.' Harrison was already moving for the door as he spoke. He paused on the threshold and waved a hand at Treddle. 'See you,' he said, and vanished. RSM Treddle returned the wave to an empty doorway and grinned at RSM Nunn.

'Bloody jack-in-the-box, I reckon 'e is. Dinkum bloke, though, no bloody bull, just like one of the ordinary diggers is Harrison.'

'Ha,' RSM Nunn said.

'Come again, mate?'

'I said ha, Mr Treddle.' RSM Nunn did not approve of warrant officers who spoke familiarly of their colonels, no more than he approved of colonels who were just like one of the ordinary diggers, whom RSM Nunn understood to mean the rank-and-file. It was not like that in the British Army. He rose and fell for a while on the balls of his feet, back straight, service cap very square on his head, peak well forward so that he had in fact to keep his back straight in order to see. 'If you would be so good, Mr Treddle, as to inform me –'

'Cut the bloody formality, mate, why not? I'm Jim. You, mate?'

RSM Nunn remained very still. There was a pause. 'I do not approve,' RSM Nunn said heavily, 'of the use of Christian names on, shall we say, early acquaintance or like on parade. Neither am I "mate". My name is Mr Nunn, Mr Treddle, and that, I am of the opinion, we would do best to stick with. I've no doubt I make my meaning clear, Mr Treddle?'

'As bloody crystal, Mr Nunn. Now, where were we, eh?'

'The matter of the night detail, Mr Treddle.'

'Dead right, Mr Nunn, so we were.' RSM Treddle grinned. 'If you'd care to come down off of your high bloody horse, mate, we'll get on with it. All right with you, is it, eh?'

*

'It may be cold, Mildred. The nights often are, you know that. If I were you I'd take a jumper.' Colonel Holmes added, 'It's going to be a long night at boat stations.'

'I do think it's so unnecessary,' Mildred said.

'Oh, no. We have to take on fuel.'

'I didn't mean that. Though why at night. . . What I meant was this business of being at boat stations all the time. We would be just as handy sitting comfortably in the lounge, wouldn't we?'

Holmes sighed. Women seemed at times to lose all sense, all contact with the world of war. 'Perhaps, Mildred, perhaps. But the Germans are being mustered in the lounge so none of the passengers can use it.'

'That's another thing,' she said. 'I call it very dangerous to have Germans –' She broke off as the Tannoy clicked on in the alleyway outside their cabin, and the Captain came on the air.

'This is the Captain speaking. All personnel are to proceed to their boat stations and remain there until further orders. I ask all civilian passengers to give priority in the alleyways and on the accommodation ladders to the troops. There is no urgency and no need for any rush. You will be kept informed throughout the night as to the progress of the fuelling operation. That is all.'

The Tannoy went silent. Holmes extended an arm to his wife. 'Come along, my dear. We're rather slower than most I'm sorry to say.'

'Why not do as the Captain said, and give the soldiers time to get to their stations, Stephen? The night's going to be long enough as it is, you said so yourself.'

'Oh, very well, very well.' Colonel Holmes sat down again while his wife searched through drawers for a woolly jumper. The old man gave an involuntary sigh: they were both too old for this kind of thing and one way and another Mildred was taking it pretty badly, he thought. Not like her; she was used to army life in both an active service sense and a retired one. Back in Mombasa they'd led an army-oriented life in so many ways, still stuck to the old routines, down to the club for coffee in the mornings, possibly a luncheon party, siesta in the afternoons, drinks as soon as the sun went down, dress for dinner and then after dinner perhaps bridge. Part of all that was the stiff-upper-lip tradition of Britons abroad. What Mildred needed really was a strong whiff of the real old times before the war, when everything had been jollity and security and, well, *British*. What would do wonders for her would be an evening with good old Bill and Arse-end Portlock, fun and games and a lot of army talk and reminiscences, but that was wishing for the moon of course.

Holmes gave it ten minutes during which time the progress of the troops could be heard: crashings and bangings of equipment along the alleyways and heavy boots clumping up ladders for the embarkation deck. Then they emerged from their cabin, two elderly people, both rather frail and hesitant in a crowd, liable to stumble and fall if pushed. Holmes found himself thinking once again of Arse-end Portlock, wondering if he was now as decrepit as he was and then remembering, with something of a shock, that Arse-end Portlock had been killed by a bomb at Paddington.

As the Holmeses reached the embarkation deck something large was seen approaching the *Aurelian Star*'s port side, coming in from aft. Mildred clutched at her husband's arm. 'What's that?' she asked.

Holmes looked. 'It's one of the tankers, my dear, that's all, nothing to worry about. They're evidently fuelling us first. The Commodore's ship, you see.'

'Here she comes, lads,' Petty Officer Ramm said. He and Petty Officer Biggar, Biggar for'ard and Ramm aft, were under orders, along with their gunnery rates, to assist the troopship's deck party with the handling of the fenders, wires and ropes as the big tanker manoeuvred alongside. '*Brambleleaf*,' Ramm said. 'Med Fleet before the war – seen 'er often enough.' He was all set to reminisce now, impress the hostilities-only men with his memory and his service. 'Commander-in-Chief, 'e was Admiral Sir William Fisher, flying 'is flag in the old *Queen Elizabeth*. The *battleship*, not the Cunard liner. Flag Lieutenant was a bloke called Duckworth . . . poor old Fisher died a year later, caught a chill taking the salute at the King's birthday parade on Southsea Common, when 'e was C-in-C Pompey. Buried off the Nab, along with a load of other admirals what 'ad gorn before. Coffin aboard the *Curacao*, light cruiser. An' what's the matter with you, may I ask, Able-Seaman Sissons?'

Stripey Sissons smirked. 'Department of useless knowledge, PO. Them days is over.'

'More's the pity, and take that grin orf your face, Able-Seaman

Sissons, or you'll be up before the Commodore on a charge of bleedin' impertinence, you'll see.'

'Sorry I'm sure, PO.'

Ramm grunted. 'You may know it all, Stripey, in fact you do, but there's them as can do with a spot of naval 'istory.' Ramm's tone altered. 'Right, lads, stand by now, *Brambleleaf*'s coming on and there'll be lines flying around.' He bent over the guardrail, checking the fenders. Stripey Sissons, standing by to take the first of the heaving-lines, thought about pre-war. True, it was over and done with, but there had been some good times. Stripey had seen a good deal of the world – West Indies, China-side, Singapore, Home Fleet in the days, back in the twenties, when it had been designated the Atlantic Fleet. But, looking back, his commission with the Mediterranean Fleet, also back in the late twenties, had been the most memorable. He hadn't been married then, which meant among other things no mother-in-law; and life when ashore from the battle-cruiser *Renown* had held plenty of promise. Nights in Alexandria, nights in Gibraltar and other places, most memorable of all the nights ashore in Malta. Down Strada Stretta, better known to generations of roistering British seamen as the Gut; plenty of booze in the many bars, plenty of women in the rooms above the bars, a wee bit sleazy but never mind, you could always see the quack when you got back aboard after dipping your wick. The RN surgeons had had any amount of experience in that branch of medicine, you should just see the queues outside the sick bays of the fleet, every morning . . .

Stripey's dreams of heaven were cut short when a heaving-line from the *Brambleleaf* whizzed through the air, the monkey's-fist at its end only just missing his head. Stripey, who was agile enough never mind his age, caught it expertly and began heaving it in, hand over hand, until the weight of the attached rope hawser came on and with the assistance of Ordinary Seaman Featherstonehaugh he struggled with it across the deck to place the eye over the troopship's bitts. When the eye was in position Stripey shouted 'All fast' and seamen aboard the tanker hauled in on the sternrope. When Petty Officer Biggar, up for'ard, had secured the headrope and the springs were hauled taut, the hands aboard the troopship were fallen out to stand by their guns, the two petty officers keeping an eye lifting on the securing lines.

127

On the bridge Maconochie and Kemp watched the lie of the RFA vessel closely. Maconochie, having the direct responsibility for his ship, would remain on the bridge throughout the operation. So would Kemp, though with the convoy hove-to he would be handy enough catching up on some much-needed sleep in his cabin immediately below the bridge, ready within half a minute if and when required. If there were U-boats in the vicinity, plenty of early warning would come from the guardships currently steaming up and down in protection of the convoy. But with the rest of the ship at boat stations he would not go below himself.

As the two of them watched, RFA *Oligarch* was seen approaching the ex-liner next astern of the *Aurelian Star*. As in the case of the *Brambleleaf* she already had her own fenders rigged along her starboard side to supplement those of the receiving ship. Also as in their own case there were no hitches. Aboard the Commodore's ship the oil pipelines were already being connected and shortly the discharge into the troopship's tanks would begin. Kemp took a look all round the assembly of ships, using his binoculars in a slow sweep. Luckily the weather had held; there was a flat calm and scarcely any swell, just enough to make it essential for all the wires and ropes to be watched closely in case there was any heave that could put enough strain on the lines to part them. Kemp knew that it would be an anxious time for the masters of the tankers. Very fast action would be needed on their part to prevent a collision if a heavy surge should happen to come whilst fuelling was in progress.

Brigadier Pumphrey-Hatton was at the same boat station as Colonel and Mrs Holmes. He was dressed in his khaki-drill uniform with a heavy khaki pullover beneath his cork life-jacket. He seemed distrait, nervous, walking up and down his section of the embarkation deck below the lifeboat hanging from the davits with steadying lines rigged fore and aft until such time as it had to be lowered for taking its passengers aboard.

He halted alongside the Holmeses.

He said, 'Ascension Island.'

'Er – yes, Brigadier.'

'Lucky it's close. If anything happens.'

'Yes, quite. Very handy. It might not have been.' Holmes gave a chuckle; he had made a joke of a sort.

Pumphrey-Hatton said irritably, 'What d'you mean, it might not have been? If we hadn't been here, neither would *it*. Stands to reason I'd have thought.'

'Yes, that's true.' Holmes felt bewildered, as though he'd possibly missed something of military significance, thereby showing his age. 'I take your point, Brigadier.'

'I'm glad to hear it, Colonel, very glad. It is necessary to make an assessment of any situation, an appreciation don't you know. Good practice. Always tell my chaps that. No doubt you yourself did in your day.'

'Er . . . yes. Yes, I did.'

'Which was your war, Colonel? South African – the Boers?' Holmes felt shock. 'As a matter of fact, no. The Great War –'

'Ah. Well, same thing. You're all out-of-date now. In this one, you know. Agree?'

'I'm afraid I don't.' Holmes thought of good old Bill and Arse-end Portlock, who had both contributed to the war. 'I believe we do still have a useful role – or some of us do, some who are a little younger than I. I –'

'You're *disagreeing* with me?'

'Yes, I –'

'Don't, then.'

Holmes gaped. 'I beg your pardon, Brigadier?'

'You heard what I said. Don't damn well disagree with me. I happen to be right. There are too many damn disagreements and too many people not listening to complaints. I have had trouble with my bath water, did you know that?' Pumphrey-Hatton had pushed his face close to Holmes' and was staring belligerently. The old man took an involuntary step backwards, saying that no, he hadn't been aware of that.

'I spoke to that purser feller. Didn't do a *damn thing* about it! I told him my complaint was to be forwarded to the Captain for immediate action. Result, still no damn water coming through, either salt or fresh. You'd never think there was a war on. I shall represent it to that Australian – Harrison.'

'I see . . .'

'I doubt if you do. However – good luck to you. I hope you reach the Clyde, but I doubt if you will or your good lady either. If a convoy commodore can't regulate a damn bath, how in heaven's name was he ever given charge of a convoy?'

Pumphrey-Hatton turned sharply and walked away. Holmes shook his head in sheer bewilderment. It was unforgiveable for anyone to doubt their safe arrival home in front of largely scared civilians mustered at a time of danger at their boat stations. Holmes reassured his wife. 'Don't pay any attention, my dear. The man's as mad as a hatter. All that disjointed talk.' He shook his head. It was all very sad.

RSM Nunn was surveying the Germans assembled in the lounge beneath the blue police lights. He was doing so through the glass screen, from the deck outside. 'They appear docile enough, Mr Treddle,' he said, tweaking at his moustache.

'Could be deceptive, Mr Nunn.' RSM Treddle had lost the battle and had abandoned 'mate'. 'Can't always go by appearances, eh?'

'There's truth in that, Mr Treddle, that I don't deny.' RSM Nunn expanded. 'Take your lot, like. Very good fighters. Reliable in action.'

'Dead right they are. If they weren't, I'd be right up their arses. And don't get me wrong on that. You know what I mean. But so what?'

'So what, Mr Treddle?'

'So what, yes. I mean, I get the idea you were about to make a comparison. About appearances being deceptive, right?'

RSM Nunn, who had in fact been about to say that the Australians looked a right bunch, sloppily turned out and a sight too free-and-easy, refrained. It might cause offence since they were a touchy lot, especially if criticized by what they called pommies, or poms, which always put RSM Nunn in mind of a pomeranian dog. So he disregarded RSM Treddle's last query and instead drew attention to a POW lounging in a chair and smoking a cigarette. 'Tobacco, there,' he said, pointing with his pace-stick. 'Contraband! Passed by one of the ship's crew, I'll be bound. That must be dealt with, Mr Treddle.'

'Not by me,' RSM Treddle said at once. 'Now's not the time, mate.' That had slipped out past his guard. 'It can be investigated later, when they're back below. Not now. We don't want any trouble while they're up here, do we, eh?'

'Proper discipline must be maintained, Mr Treddle. I am aware of course that this is principally an Australian draft and that you personally are responsible to OC Troops. But if you will not take

130

action then it is up to me. I shall speak to Sar'nt Tapapa.' RSM Nunn, replacing his pace-stick beneath his left arm, marched towards the entry to the lounge, his boots banging the deck, left-right-left, right arm swinging. Treddle shrugged; if old starcharse wanted to stir things up, it was his loss. Treddle himself had had his say, cleared his own yardarm as the poms put it.

RSM Nunn had reached the entry when the Tannoy came on from the bridge. Captain Maconochie announced a contact by the A/S screen. Boat stations were now for real. To give point to his words and to alert any passenger or crew member who might have gone below in defiance of orders, the alarm rattlers sounded throughout the ship.

THIRTEEN

Maconochie called the engine-room. 'Disconnect, Chief. How much have you taken?'

'Around three-quarters full –'

'We'll resume later if all goes well. Meanwhile I'm casting off the tanker.' Maconchie banged the voicepipe cover down, then went at the rush to the port bridge-wing. Using a megaphone he called across to the RFA master. 'I'm casting you off, Captain. Hope to see you again when the panic's over.' He used the megaphone again to call down to his own decks. 'Unberthing parties stand by fore and aft. As soon as the pipeline's disconnected, cast off all ropes and wires from *Brambleleaf*. Tend all fenders as she goes.'

He met Kemp's eye. 'Just what I feared,' Kemp said, his face set hard. The naval command in Simonstown had made a boob that might cost the convoy very dear. He watched as the tanker slid away astern, her twin screws sending up a kerfuffle between the ships that helped to keep them apart. Along the troopship's decks the fenders were hauled back aboard. In charge of the naval party aft, Petty Officer Ramm was more outspoken than the Commodore had been.

'Bird-brained admirals, that's what, don't know there's a war on, half of 'em.' He paused, noting the tremor of the deck and the surge of water astern. 'Under way already – and thank God for it. Bridge didn't take long to get moving, I'll say that for 'em. I tell you –' He broke off suddenly. There had been a sharp crack from for'ard, followed a moment later by two more. 'Now, what the hell was that, eh?'

Featherstonehaugh said, 'Rifle fire, PO –'

'God give me strength, *Featherstone*haugh, I bloody know that, thank you very much! What I meant was who and why, and I reckon it's them bloody Germans. You and you,' he said to Leading Seaman Purkiss and the OD, 'get up to the bridge, at the double, stand by the Oerlikons. And remember, no firing without orders.'

Ramm was aware, as Featherstonehaugh started for'ard, of a kind of glitter in the OD's eyes and he remembered the lad's dad had been knocked off by the Nazis.

RSM Nunn had gone into the B deck lounge, pace-stick beneath his arm, cap on square as ever, very regimental, to sort out the crime of smoking and contraband. He had halted just inside the door from the open deck and had used his parade-ground voice.

'Now what's all this, then? That man there.' The pace-stick had been pointed. 'Smoking by POWs is not permitted, the more so as POWs do not have access to tobacco! Right! Now, extinguish that dog-end, that man, and then we'll see.'

He waited. The Nazi blew a long trail of smoke, grinning. Then he reached into a pocket and brought out a packet of cigarettes. He handed this to the man next to him, who took one and lit up. RSM Nunn's eyes bulged with anger. 'Matches,' he said in a loud voice. 'Likewise not permitted. Well?'

'Not well, British pig,' the first smoker said calmly. 'The fat murderer Churchill smokes cigars. We smoke cigarettes. The monster Churchill is also a pig.'

RSM Nunn advanced a few paces. 'Do you know what you are saying?' he enunciated. The speaker seemed to have good English but he might simply be mouthing what he'd learned back in his own country. He had to be given a chance.

'I know what I say,' the German answered. 'I speak of the mad Churchill, who is a wicked warmonger and will shortly be made to answer for his crimes against the Third Reich and the German people.' Then he stiffened to attention, clicked his heels, raised his right hand in the Nazi salute and said, '*Heil, Hitler.*'

This was echoed by the whole POW contingent.

'Right,' RSM Nunn said. 'That does it. I'm going to 'ave your guts for garters.' Armed only with his pace-stick, the Regimental Sergeant-Major advanced, pushing his way through the

Germans, who were now jeering and cat-calling, fast becoming an undisciplined mob.

'Sar'nt Tapapa,' RSM Nunn called.

'Yes, sah!'

'Where the devil are you, man?' Sergeant Tapapa was so far invisible.

'Here, sah.' Sergeant Tapapa appeared in the doorway to the open deck, looking frightened out of his wits.

'Get your men in here, Sar'nt Tapapa, you booby, with bayonets fixed and a round up the spout. Then follow my orders very closely, all right?'

'Yes, sah –'

'Right! First thing. Send a man to the orderly room and the bridge to report the state of affairs. That done, come up alongside o' me with your revolver ready. No one's to open fire, however, till I give the word. Or one of the officers does if they 'appen to get here in time. Now then, got that, have you?'

'Yes, sah!'

'Right, get to it, then. *Pronto!*'

RSM Nunn stood his ground stolidly while the mêlée went on around him. Within half a minute he was joined by the native riflemen, their black faces gleaming in the blue police lights that were the only illumination.

Harrison had gone at once to the bridge, where he was joined by Colonel Carter of the Rifles. They conferred with Maconochie and the Commodore.

'The situation's electric, I reckon,' Harrison said. 'I took a gander. My adjutant's gone along to take charge in the lounge. I reckon that RSM of yours,' he added to Carter, 'has kind of gone loony or something, bellyaching about a bloke smoking –'

'Mr Nunn's a first-class warrant officer,' Carter said crisply, 'but we'll not go into that now.' He turned to Kemp. 'In my opinion, sir, the POWs should be marched back below right away. My riflemen are in control so far but that may change quite quickly. I believe the Germans'll take a chance that no one's going to open fire, and try a break-out.'

'We certainly don't want shooting,' Kemp said, 'but I'll not have anyone shut down below when we're likely to come under attack at any moment. I –'

'There's civvy passengers at risk, Commodore.' This was Harrison. 'Me, I go along with Carter.'

'No,' Kemp said firmly. 'Those Germans are not going to be put below. To do that . . . it's not in the tradition of the sea –'

'For Jeez' sake,' Harrison cut in, 'balls to tradition, in a situation like this. What we –'

Kemp rounded on him. 'I have given an order, Colonel Harrison, and you will obey it. I'm giving another order and it's this: the Germans are to be made to understand that they wouldn't have a hope if the riflemen or your Australians were ordered to open fire. They must be told quite clearly that if they don't calm down, the order to open fire *will* be given – though I hope to God it doesn't come to that. And now, gentlemen, go away and carry out my orders and leave me to do my job – which concerns the safety of the convoy as a whole against possible attack.'

The soldiers turned away and went down the ladder, their faces saying clearly that they considered the Commodore to be entirely wrong. It was soon after they had left the bridge that the sound of rifle fire came from below. Kemp, awaiting further reports from the A/S screen and worrying about the state and readiness of the merchant ships as they got under way, shut his ears to it. The soldiers would have to cope. It was their job to guard the prisoners. And undoubtedly, on the face of it, the regimental sergeant-major had stuck his neck out rather too far. Kemp cursed the involvement of prisoners-of-war; he was a seaman, with a vital job to do, not a pongo or a warder.

He found himself wondering how Pumphrey-Hatton would have reacted, had he still been OC Troops.

Kemp had a feeling the brigadier might have made a better fist of it than Harrison. Pumphrey-Hatton was, after all, of the old school of military thought, and part of his code would be at least a degree of chivalry towards a defeated enemy, though in all conscience the *Aurelian Star*'s prisoners-of-war didn't appear to regard themselves as defeated. But in any event Pumphrey-Hatton's attitude would be very different from Harrison's; Harrison was brash.

As it happened, Pumphrey-Hatton was already involving himself. He had been startled by the sound of what he took to be revolver fire followed by rifle fire, quite a number of rounds, coming from the deck above. He had at once left his boat station and had climbed fast to B deck. There was a shindig coming from the lounge and he had seen that some of the big square ports had been shattered, no doubt by the rifle fire. He found Captain Mulvaney outside the main door.

'What's going on?' he asked.

Mulvaney told him. 'Bloke smoking. One of the black NCOs fired his revolver on the RSM's order and that did it, I reckon. There was a riot and the blacks fired over the Nazis' heads. I reckon –'

'Where is OC Troops?'

Mulvaney gave a jerk of his head. 'In there. Sorting it out or trying to.'

'Ask him to come out on deck.'

Captain Mulvaney pushed his bush hat back from his head. 'Now look,' he began in a tone that suggested he was speaking to a child. 'You don't want –'

'Kindly refrain from telling me to look, Captain Mulvaney, and from telling me what I don't want. Go and fetch Colonel Harrison. That is an order.'

'You've got no authority that I know of –'

Pumphrey-Hatton's voice rose. 'I am a brigadier of the British Army and I have given you an order. You will disobey it at peril of a Court Martial. Do I make myself clear, Captain Mulvaney?'

Mulvaney glared, muttered something indistinct, then swung away sharply and went into the lounge. A few moments passed and then he returned with OC Troops.

Harrison was tight-faced. 'You listen to me, Brigadier. I –

'On the contrary. You will listen to me.' Pumphrey-Hatton's tone was crisp and authoritative, his curious manner and his preoccupations with trivia seeming to have vanished. 'I may not be OC Troops any longer, but I have experience that, if I may say so, you lack. The whole ship is now faced with a very difficult situation, as you must realize. I have had experience of dealing with German prisoners in the western desert – Eighth Army, also under Australian command in Tobruk.' He paused. 'A day or so ago you asked my advice as to the duties and so on of OC Troops. I now apologize for my abruptness. I am asking you to allow me to handle this situation . . . on your behalf.'

Harrison's mouth opened and then closed again. He was still angry, wishing to tell the old geezer to stuff his advice and not act as though he were God. But something was stopping him. A riot that could now be held only by gunfire, a riot that could end in the killing of prisoners-of-war under the protection of the Geneva Convention would for sure rebound on him as OC Troops. He might just as well keep his trap shut and let Pumphrey-Hatton take at least some of the blame afterwards. He glanced at his adjutant, whose face told him he was keeping out of it so far as he could, then he turned back to Pumphrey-Hatton.

'Righto,' he said grudgingly. 'Advise away if you want to.'

Pumphrey-Hatton asked, 'Is the German officer, *Leutnant* Stoph, in there?'

Harrison said he was.

'Have him brought out. And the regimental sar'nt-major who I understand is involved. The rifles' sar'nt-major.'

'Too bloody right he's involved –'

'Just have him brought out, Colonel Harrison. And then we shall all shift up to A deck, rather than conduct proceedings in the view, and possibly in the hearing, of the prisoners.'

Harrison, fuming, gestured to Mulvaney. The Australian captain turned away and went back inside the lounge, returning after an interval with *Kapitan-Leutnant* Stoph and RSM Nunn, plus native escort. They all climbed to A deck, whence Pumphrey-Hatton had already gone. RSM Nunn slammed to attention in front of the brigadier with much banging of boots and a quivering salute. In rear of Stoph stood one of the riflemen with his bayonet fixed and his eyeballs rolling.

'Now then,' Pumphrey-Hatton said briskly, addressing the German officer. 'I understand there is a complaint.'

'There is much of a complaint,' Stoph said.

'You will address me as sir, or as Brigadier.'

'I will not address you as sir,' Stoph said superciliously.

'I see. Then I have to say that I am disappointed in you, *Kapitan-Leutnant* Stoph. Also surprised. I take you for an officer and a gentleman. For a professional seaman rather, perhaps, than let us say one of the *Gestapo* or the SS.'

There was no response from Stoph, who stood looking disdainfully at Pumphrey-Hatton, his tall body as straight as that of the RSM.

Pumphrey-Hatton went on, 'I believe there is a German Grand Admiral named Stoph, who retired from your service before the war. A Prussian, with a Prussian's code of honour.'

'My uncle, yes.'

'Then may I say that were I a prisoner, I would address your uncle as sir, or as Admiral,' Pumphrey-Hatton said mildly.

There was another silence. Then Stoph said, 'I understand. I shall therefore address you as Brigadier.'

Pumphrey-Hatton smiled. 'Good! A small but important point of etiquette is settled, and we can talk about your complaint. We can talk, too, about what is currently taking place in the lounge. Your complaint is to do with smoking, as I understand?'

'My complaint is to do with harassment over one of my men observed to smoke, *Herr* Brigadier.'

'Yes, I see. Not perhaps harassment but the establishment of discipline and the safety of the ship, upon which we all depend, your men included, *Kapitan-Leutnant* Stoph. I don't see it as any occasion for the sort of trouble that seems to have erupted. Do you?'

Stoph's eyes shifted. 'Perhaps no.'

'H'm. Sar'nt-Major?'

'Sir!'

'A word from you would help, Sarn't-Major.'

RSM Nunn stared at a fixed point over the brigadier's head. 'There was words, sir. Provocative words, sir, as to Mr Churchill who was referred to as being a pig, also as being a monster, sir. Also as being mad, sir. Such arose, sir, on account of my stopping the man smoking.' Nunn paused. 'The cigars, like, sir, see.'

'The cigars, Sarn't-Major?'

'Mr Churchill's, sir.'

'Really. Sarn't-Major . . . if you were a prisoner in Germany . . . I wonder what you might say about Herr Hitler?'

RSM Nunn lifted a hand and tweaked at the ends of his moustache. 'Yes, sir. I get your meaning, sir. Perhaps I was over-hasty, sir.'

Pumphrey-Hatton nodded. 'A little give-and-take, Sar'nt-Major, that's the thing. A storm in a tea-cup, I rather fancy.' He turned to Stoph. 'If the rifles are withdrawn, *Kapital-Leutnant* Stoph, have I your word that your men will quieten down and remain obedient to orders for your own safety while the convoy is in danger?'

Stoph hesitated, but only for a moment. Then he said, 'You have my word, *Herr* Brigadier. I thank you.'

Pumphrey-Hatton nodded again and turned to Colonel Harrison. 'Now it's over to you again, Colonel. I trust I've been of some assistance.'

He went away with his odd, jerky walk. He felt he'd settled something, defused a tricky and dangerous situation. Now he had other matters back on his mind and once the convoy was safe from possible attack he would make representations in the proper quarter. Really, these days it was one damn thing after another and just before going to his boat station he had discovered that the tank beneath the wash-basin in his cabin had not been properly emptied by his steward, a residue of water being left after his last wash. These things all added up to a very serious lack of discipline throughout the ship, as dangerous in its way as the Germans.

Pumphrey-Hatton had started down the ladders to the embarkation deck and his boat station when he heard more firing, this time heavier as though from one of the close-range weapons, the Oerlikons mounted in the bridge-wings or on monkey's-island above the wheelhouse.

As *Kapitan-Leutnant* Stoph had been ordered back down the ladder to B deck he had slipped on a greasy patch. He had lost his balance, pitching sideways and knocking RSM Nunn off his feet. A trigger-happy gunnery rate at the starboard bridge Oerlikon had, without waiting for orders, opened fire in a short burst, evidently taking the incident as an attack on the RSM. The bridge personnel had been taken off guard and had reacted too late. As the burst ended, Kemp himself seized the man and wrenched him bodily from the straps. The rating was Ordinary Seaman Featherstonehaugh.

One of the Oerlikon shells had taken an escorting native rifleman in the left shoulder; another had hit *Kapitan-Leutnant* Stoph, who was lying on the deck. The rest of the burst had gone harmlessly aft.

FOURTEEN

Petty Officer Ramm, hearing the Oerlikon in action, had gone at the double to the bridge. He saluted the Commodore.

'Sounds like trouble, sir,' he said breathlessly. He looked at Featherstonehaugh, standing quietly in the bridge wing. Again there was something funny in the OD's eyes. Or could have been the moonlight streaming across the bridge into his face.

'Trouble's right,' Kemp said. 'This man fired without orders. Sub-Lieutenant Finnegan will make the charge and carry out a preliminary investigation once the convoy's in the clear and he'll be brought before me subsequently. Until then, he's to be held in arrest.'

'Aye, aye, sir. Where's he to be placed, sir?'

Kemp hesitated. He had no wish to place any man in cells at sea, still less so in current circumstances. He said, 'Contact the Purser, Ramm. There's always a cabin or two kept empty for emergencies of one sort or another.'

'Aye, aye, sir.' Ramm saluted again. 'Right, Featherstone-haugh – about turn, quick march, down the ladder.' He added to Kemp, 'I'll send up a replacement right away, sir.' He clattered down the ladder close behind the OD. When he reached the bottom he said in a low voice, 'What d'you want to go and do a thing like that for, eh, lad? Bloody daft.' Then, quickly, he said, 'Don't answer that. Forget I asked. You're what they call *sub joodyce* now.'

The rifleman was in a bad way as reported to OC Troops by the medical officer. The shoulder was shattered and there had been a

140

serious loss of blood plus some ancillary injury to the head on the left side. Emergency surgery would need to be carried out and it was too early yet for any positive prognosis. The German, Stoph, was not badly hurt: nothing beyond a graze to the right upper arm beneath some torn clothing. He had been concussed by striking his head on a mushroom ventilator when he'd fallen and he would be kept under guard overnight in the sick bay for observation.

Soon after the doctor's report had reached the bridge a series of explosions was heard away on the convoy's starboard beam.

'Depth charges,' Kemp said. 'And a perfect night for attack. Has that rating been fixed up, Finnegan?'

'Yes, sir, I guess so. When the attack is over he'll be accommodated in a cabin on F deck, armed sentry on guard outside. Meantime he's back on the after three-inch. Petty Officer Ramm's acting as watchdog. I gave that the okay, sir, all right?'

Kemp nodded. 'Sensible, Finnegan.'

There was a grin. 'Trust the US Navy, sir, Commodore –'

'Stop boasting, Finnegan, and watch out for torpedo trails.'

'I'll do that thing, sir, Commodore.'

'Which I take it is American for aye, aye, sir.'

'You bet it is,' Finnegan said.

'In that case,' Kemp said heavily, 'it's time you learned English, young man.'

Finnegan grinned again. They understood one another well enough. The explosions continued, growing more distant. Half an hour later there was a blue flashing lamp from the senior officer of the escort. Yeoman Lambert reported, 'Enemy losses believed to be three U-boats, no losses to convoy or escort. Have broken off action.'

Kemp said, 'Thank God for a good result. Tell the guns'-crews, Finnegan. They can stand down but remain handy. Yeoman, make to the senior officer from Commodore, propose to resume fuelling.'

Over the next fifteen minutes the convoy resumed its formation for completion of taking bunkers, turning back through 180 degrees for Ascension Island.

Finnegan thought ahead to his forthcoming session with Ordinary Seaman Featherstonehaugh, which would take place next forenoon. He had no liking for that task; he, as well as Kemp, knew the rating's recent history. If the Nazis had killed his, Finnegan's, dad he would very likely do the same thing if he got the chance. But the moment that line of thought entered his mind, he conscientiously dismissed it. That would be prejudging the case: there was so far absolutely no evidence that Featherstonehaugh had been aiming for *Kapitan-Leutnant* Stoph.

Nattering whilst the ship was once again taking oil fuel from the *Brambleleaf*, Petty Officer Ramm did what he shouldn't have done which was to discuss what had happened with Petty Officer Biggar. He had no qualms about prejudgement. 'Avenging his dad,' he said firmly. 'Stands out a mile. Bloody rotten shot, that's all.'

'Took 'is chance, like.'

'Wouldn't you?'

Biggar scratched his head. 'Dunno. Maybe.' He thought for a moment. 'Yes, I just might, I s'pose. But only when I knew I was going to get away with it. I'm not that bloody daft.'

Ramm nodded. Himself, he didn't believe the OD had a hope in hell of getting away with it. His dad – circumstantial evidence they would call that. Ramm wondered what the penalty would be; and pondered on what Biggar had said. In the last war, so it had been rumoured, officers on the Western Front, officers who'd been rotten bastards to their men, had on occasion taken a shot in the back during an advance on the Jerry trenches. It was different at sea: Featherstonehaugh had been much too indiscreet. Daft, really.

Kemp paced the bridge while the interrupted oiling continued and the tanker, having completed fuelling the *Aurelian Star*, moved off the troopship's side and proceeded to the next of the waiting ships. Kemp had much on his mind, not least the stupid action of Ordinary Seaman Featherstonehaugh. To go into action without orders was bad enough; to project gunfire towards a prisoner-of-war, unarmed and giving no trouble, was conduct of the worst kind. Featherstonehaugh could say goodbye to any prospect of a commission. Kemp would be immensely sorry about that; but there were no two ways about it. It was, however, not that alone that now weighed heavily with the Commodore. Kemp was in a fair way to blaming himself for both Featherstonehaugh's predicament and the injury to the native rifleman.

None of this would have happened if he had heeded the opinions of Colonel Carter and OC Troops that the POWS should be taken back to their quarters below.

He had perhaps been obstinate.

He paced on, his face set into hard lines. No use having regrets now; what was done was done and that was that. But his self-recrimination could be reflected in the view he would be taking of Featherstonehaugh's action when the rating came up before him. He must not allow that either. Whatever he, Kemp, might have done, Featherstonehaugh's action stood on its own demerits.

Kemp, as he came to Finnegan hunched in the starboard wing of the bridge, stopped his restless pacing. He said, 'Your investigation, Finnegan. The shooting.' He paused. 'First thing after dawn action stations, Finnegan. I want all this settled soonest possible.'

The shooting had naturally reacted on the civilian passengers. Mothers had become extra protective of children, in most cases holding them tight. The children themselves were scared. They knew there were Germans aboard, and they had mostly heard scary tales about Germans from fathers who had fought in the trenches of the Western Front in the last war. Germans were Huns, warlike, ferocious as the giants and ogres and hobgoblins in Grimm's Fairy Tales. The nanny of one of the children had said they had horns like devils, and forked tongues that went out and in like serpents. They spitted children on their bayonets, and roasted them over fires like the fires of hell that would burn them up one day if they didn't say their prayers.

One small boy, known to the Holmeses back in Kenya, voiced some of this in a loud whisper to a girl of about his own age and was overheard not by his mother but by Colonel Holmes, who intervened.

'What nonsense, Billy. Whoever told you that?'

The boy looked up at him round-eyed. 'Nanny did.'

'Then Nanny had no business to. Nanny's quite wrong, Billy.'

'Nanny's never wrong,' the boy stated firmly. 'Mummy said so.'

'Really.' A matter of discipline, of course. You always stood by your NCOs in front of the soldiers. Holmes cleared his throat. He said, 'Certainly Nanny is always right when, for instance, she

143

says it's time to go bed, or . . . er . . . things like that. She really doesn't know very much about the Germans, Billy, take it from me.'

The boy stared him in the eye. 'Nanny knows all about witch doctors.' Nanny, of course, would have been black. The boy went on, 'She says they push red-hot needles into your eyes.'

'The witch doctors are –'

'No, silly, the Germans.'

At this point the small girl started crying and gave a shriek for her mother. Mother appeared from the lee of the boat's falls, together with Billy's mother, who said she hoped Billy wasn't being a pest but she knew he would be all right with the Holmeses. 'Come along, Billy –'

'The boy's no trouble, Mrs Moriarty,' Holmes said. 'But he has some strange ideas about the Germans –'

'That's Nanny,' the mother said. 'She's rather alarmist.' The children were gathered up and removed. Alarmist, Holmes remarked to his wife, was scarcely the word for such horror stories. Modern mothers, he said, didn't pay half enough attention to their offspring, leaving them too much to their nannies. Then he remembered his own childhood days. What with boarding school and Nanny, he'd scarcely seen his own mother, just an hour a day after tea before he and his younger sister were gathered up and returned willy-nilly to the nursery. But that had been before the Great War when Germans had not yet become monsters, were indeed quite socially acceptable since their Kaiser was a grandson of the Queen-Empress . . .

Farther along the embarkation deck Gregory Hench was comforting Gloria Northway. She had become almost hysterical when she'd heard the rifle fire, more so when the short burst from the Oerlikon was heard. Hench had put a protective arm around her and she had snuggled. She was snuggling still; Hench felt he had stolen a handy march on the Australian, Mulvaney.

Brigadier Pumphrey-Hatton received a message from the Commodore: Kemp's compliments and he would appreciate it if Pumphrey-Hatton would find it convenient to come to the bridge. Pumphrey-Hatton would. He went up immediately. Kemp said, 'I just wanted to thank you, Brigadier. I understand you defused a very nasty situation.'

'Potentially nasty, yes. Tact – that's all. The Australians are not tactful. No more was that RSM – but RSMs are seldom renowned for tact, excellent fellows though they are. I'm glad to have been of service. Well, that's in the past, or I hope it is. I'd like to take the opportunity of drawing your attention to my wash-basin . . .'

Pumphrey-Hatton had indeed been of service; Kemp listened patiently to the woes of the wash-basin and the bath water and a recap of the electric fan and the flies. It took quite a while and when Pumphrey-Hatton had left the bridge Kemp shook his head in bewilderment as to how the brigadier's finicking could possibly add up with the firm way in which he appeared to have taken charge of the German problem. Of one thing, however, Kemp was determined: when his voyage report went to the Admiralty after arrival in the Clyde it would contain a glowing report of Pumphrey-Hatton's action for forwarding to the War Office. It might do the man some good in whatever he was due to face in London. In spite of all Kemp hoped very much that it would.

When Pumphrey-Hatton, leaving the bridge, moved aft to take a look astern at the rest of the convoy, many of the ships still awaiting one or other of the tankers, he came face to face with Leading Seaman Purkiss.

He stopped, drawing himself up. Each stared into the other's eyes. It was Purkiss who looked away. Pumphrey-Hatton said, 'You're the damn blackguard who struck me in Simonstown. Don't attempt to deny it. I recognized you instantly. What have you to say about it before I call the master-at-arms and have you placed in arrest?'

Purkiss swallowed, and remembered an important tenet of life on the lower deck, this tenet being that however bleak the prospect you never admitted to anything. You let the buggers prove it for themselves. Since, when an officer was involved, you were going to be found guilty anyway, you couldn't lose out by taking a chance that just might come off, however unlikely. So he pulled himself together and answered smartly.

'Never set eyes on you, sir. 'Cept in the distance like, sir. Not at close quarters, what I'd 'ave 'ad to be to clock you one, sir.'

'I said you were a blackguard. Name?'

'Purkiss, sir, leading seaman –'

'Now you're a liar as well, Leading Seaman Purkiss. Two crimes I make that. However, with the convoy in possible danger

145

and the likelihood of action stations, I shall leave the matter until the situation changes.'

Pumphrey-Hatton marched away. Purkiss let out a long breath and wiped the back of a hand across his forehead. Then he went for'ard in search of Petty Officer Biggar.

Biggar was worried but said, 'He'll have a job on his hands to prove it. Just you and me. So we stick together, no perishing admissions. His word against two of us. Look on the bright side, Purkiss. Make out it's a case of mistaken identity.'

'But you said earlier, 'e'd recognized you too, PO.'

'Yes, that does complicate it sure enough. I'll think of something . . . I still say, stick to what we says is the facts, all right?'

'All right,' Purkiss said gloomily. He was in deeper than Biggar; all Biggar had done was to do sod all when as a PO he should have taken action, made a report. A different matter from a Court Martial offence. Biggar might lose his rate, he, Purkiss, would not only lose his rate but his freedom as well for an indefinite period. Could even be six months or more in a civvy jail, like say Barlinnie in Glasgow on arrival in the Clyde. Striking an officer was about the worst thing you could do, short of desertion. Purkiss wasn't too sure what powers of punishment the Commodore had; he could no doubt punish summarily or by warrant but if the punishment was more than ninety days there might have to be reference to a higher authority such as the Flag Officer in Charge, Greenock, and God only knew what an admiral might inflict.

Next morning, a day of fair weather and calm seas and no further contact reported from the destroyer escort, Ordinary Seaman Featherstonehaugh was brought out from the cabin where he was being held and was taken under escort to the port side of the Captain's deck below the bridge. With Petty Officer Ramm in attendance, acting as naval master-at-arms, the routine was gone through as it would be aboard a warship.

Ramm gave the orders as the OD was marched in by Leading Seaman Purkiss, to whom the proceedings were by way of a rehearsal for his own arraignment.

' 'Alt, off cap.' Ramm turned to Finnegan. 'Ordinary Seaman Peter Ewart Featherstonehaugh, official number P/JX 187153, sir.

Did at 0123 hours of this day, open fire with the starboard side bridge Oerlikon without orders to do so.'

Ramm stood back. Now it was over to Finnegan. Ramm wondered if subby was going to lean over backwards to favour a rating who was in for a commission and whose old man had been an officer. It should prove interesting. Finnegan, however, had had further words with the Commodore. Kemp had stated the obvious: the charge was an extremely serious one and could turn out even more serious if the native soldier should die. The man was still on the danger list according to the doctors. Thus Finnegan was to do no more than bring out the basic facts. He was not to allow Featherstonehaugh to incriminate himself along the lines of possible motive.

He asked Featherstonehaugh if he had anything to say as to the charge.

'Only that I did open fire, sir.'

Finnegan, standing with his hands behind his back, nodded. So much was indisputable. He addressed Ramm. 'Petty Officer Ramm. Were instructions given that there was to be no firing without orders?'

Ramm temporized. He had no wish to harm Featherstonehaugh. He said, 'It's standing orders, sir, always is, that fire is never opened without orders.'

'Yes. But more precisely, Petty Officer Ramm. On this occasion. If you follow me.'

'Yes, sir,' Ramm said reluctantly. 'Before sending the ack-ack crews to the close-range weapons, sir, I issued the order for no firing unless specifically ordered.'

Again Finnegan nodded. 'Featherstonehaugh, were you or were you not, aware of this order?'

'I was, sir.'

'And was it,' Finnegan asked, knowing the answer, 'countermanded by anyone on the bridge?'

Featherstonehaugh shook his head. 'No, sir.' He paused briefly. 'I opened fire, really without thinking, when I saw the trouble on A deck.'

'Right,' Finnegan said. It would be as well if the OD offered no further evidence at this stage. Finnegan said, 'Commodore's report,' and nodded at Ramm. 'Carry on, please, Petty Officer Ramm.'

'Aye, aye, sir.' Ramm saluted. 'Commodore's report, on cap, salute the officer, about turn, double march, down the ladder, fall in on A deck.' Finnegan watched him go, feeling immense sympathy for what must be Featherstonehaugh's state of mind. Slowly, he climbed to the bridge. He found Kemp in his usual place, standing in the starboard wing, body braced against the guardrail, using his binoculars to scan the seas and the ships moving along sedately, the shepherd watching his flocks by night and day. Finnegan saluted the turned back.

'Commodore, sir?'

'Yes, Finnegan.' Kemp turned round, lowering the binoculars to the limit of the codline preventer. 'Well?'

'Placed in your report. Full admission.'

Kemp gave a short laugh. 'Obviously! Nothing further?'

'He opened fire without thinking, sir. What I'd call an automatic response, I guess. Do the same myself.'

'We're not considering hypothetical situations, Finnegan, or what you would do.' Kemp paused. 'What's your opinion?'

Finnegan shrugged. 'Guy's honest and straightforward, I guess. And if he did aim for the kraut . . . well, killing krauts is what the war's all about. Isn't it?'

'Not prisoners-of-war, Finnegan. Clear your mind on that, for God's sake! And don't get sentimental –'

Finnegan's eyes widened. 'Me, sir? Sentimental?'

'Yes, you, sir. Sentimental. Sympathy doesn't come into this . . . though God knows I do understand.' Kemp's mind was with his two sons, serving the King at sea as he was himself. If one of them should be killed, and he had a Nazi in his sights, POW or not . . . he couldn't be sure what his reaction would be. Probably responsible enough; he was too old, too accustomed to command, too experienced in controlling his feelings to let those deep and instinctive feelings get the better of him. But a younger man, a much younger and more callow man, might respond quite differently and in that category he had to place his own sons. Either of them, given a similar set of circumstances, might have been in Featherstonehaugh's shoes. Once again, as Finnegan stood there waiting for him to go on, Kemp forced the mental images from his mind. He was jumping the gun. Featherstonehaugh, he reminded himself for the tenth time, very likely had had no such intention.

148

He looked at his wrist-watch. He was about to tell Finnegan that he was going below to his cabin for five minutes when a rating came up the bridge ladder and approached with a signal form in his hand. 'Cypher from Flag Officer Gibraltar, sir.' He passed it over. Kemp glanced at it and handed it to Finnegan.

'Prefix Most Immediate, Finnegan. See to it at once.'

Finnegan went below to get his decyphering tables out of Kemp's safe. He was back on the bridge within twenty minutes with the plain language version. Kemp read, cs23 *repeated Convoy Commodore, German raider Stuttgart reported in position 30 degrees east 22 degrees 25 minutes north, course south, estimated speed 25 knots, now disappeared into fog. Time of origin 0933 GMT.*

Kemp called to Maconochie and went with him to the chart room, where Maconochie noted the positions of his own ship and the raider. Laying off the distance between, he said, 'Around 2200 miles ahead. Closing speed . . . forty knots. A little over two days.'

'And then that's it,' Kemp said. 'That's it – and no word of the *Duke of York*.'

Commodore and Captain went out to the open bridge. Nothing was said between them, but Kemp's mind was racing. The heavy guns of the *Stuttgart* . . . the convoy had nothing to match them. All would now depend upon the arrival of the Home Fleet battleship from Scapa Flow. If she failed to turn up, the convoy would be decimated. The only heavy ship the convoy had was the *Vindictive*, due shortly to detach to her Freetown base. No doubt she would be ordered to remain, but her guns too would be no match for the *Stuttgart*.

Kemp and Maconochie waited now for messages from the senior officer of the cruiser escort. In the meantime there was a tacit agreement that it was as yet too soon to warn the passengers as a whole. The report would of course be communicated to oc Troops, but it was to remain strictly in the confines of the orderly room until Kemp broke silence throughout the ship.

FIFTEEN

The orders had come quickly from cs23: the convoy would alter course north-westerly in the hope of bringing the ships to the westward of the *Stuttgart*'s estimated course. With luck, they would stand clear of the raider, then alter again to make the rendezvous with the *Duke of York*. As they made their northing there might be an aerial reconnaisance by the enemy long-range Focke-Wulfs and if they were picked up then the *Stuttgart* would inevitably be homed onto them. If there was an encounter the convoy would be scattered on orders from the Commodore, and the escort would stand and fight to the last, putting themselves between the enemy and the valuable troopships and cargo vessels. In the meantime *Vindictive* would detach in accordance with previous orders: she had reported to the senior officer of the escort that she had insufficient oil fuel in her bunkers to remain at sea beyond Freetown, not having fuelled off Ascension since she had intended taking on fuel at her Freetown base.

Kemp cursed, but said, 'Fortunes of war, Maconochie. We've all been relying on the *Duke of York* turning up before we met the *Stuttgart*.' He paused, then turned to Finnegan. 'Exercise guns'-crews, Finnegan, till they drop.'

'I'll do that, sir. But they can do the drill in their sleep by now.'

Kemp grunted. 'I'm glad to hear it. If we scatter, they'll be all we've got.'

Captain Mulvaney, having promulgated Colonel Harrison's orders for engagement to the Australian company commanders, went below to fulfil an engagement of his own. He tapped at Gloria Northway's cabin door.

She was irritable. 'What's been keeping you?' she asked.

'Routine. Work. Not like some.' Mulvaney had sealed lips by order, though he failed to see the point. All aboard were going to have to know sooner or later, unless the Commodore intended saying nothing at all if they managed to evade the *Stuttgart*. Maybe there was sense in that.

He threw his bush hat onto a chair and stripped off his khaki-drill jacket. Miss Northway watched him sardonically. She said, 'Don't bother with the trousers.'

He stared, trousers waistband already slackened. 'Eh? What d'you mean, don't bother with the trousers?'

'What I say. Something's happened.'

'What's bloody happened?'

'Don't sound so damn truculent, and don't make out you're that dumb. Men who come from whatsit, the Murrumbidgee, didn't come down with the last shower. Or that's what you once said.'

Mulvaney ticked over. 'Bloody hell, girl, so that's it, eh?'

'That's it,' she said. 'Sorry, but there it is. Time of the month and all that.'

'Bloody sudden,' Mulvaney said angrily.

'That's the way it goes. Caught on the hop.' She added, 'There'll be other times before we get to the Clyde, don't worry yourself.'

Captain Mulvaney resecured his trousers, put his tunic on again, took up his bush hat and stormed out of the cabin. Bloody women, he thought, they're all the same, lead you on and then go and get the curse. Or maybe she hadn't; maybe she'd just changed her mind . . . but he didn't think she had. Captain Mulvaney from the Murrumbidgee was a real man and women didn't turn real men down. Not in his experience. But she should have got her dates worked out better and not got him all worked up in anticipation. That rankled. Sod the woman.

He didn't see Gregory Hench at the end of the alleyway when he stormed out of Miss Northway's cabin, but Hench saw him very clearly and it gave him a jolt. Hench had intended going himself to Gloria's cabin. He'd had a sudden feeling things might turn out all right and he'd meant to take advantage before that particular urge subsided.

151

Now he turned away. It *had* subsided. He knew he would be no match for Mulvaney. After that sighting, he simply couldn't. He went instead to the B deck lounge and ordered a large whisky.

Brigadier Pumphrey-Hatton's mind nagged away at the wretched matter of the two ratings involved in the fracas at the Cape, men of whose names he had made a note on recognizing them. He had yet to decide what to do about them. Currently they were probably laughing at him behind his back. Meanwhile, having observed the extra gun-drills currently in progress, he had another ground for complaint, since he realized the significance of the drills as the Commodore's assistant stood by the exercising, sweating crews with a stop-watch in his hand. The closing-up, the opening time after time of the breech-block, the thrust of the ram as an imaginary projectile and charge were loaded, the shouts of the petty officers as the breech-blocks were slammed shut and the gunlayers swung onto imaginary targets . . . the repeated exercising of the misfire procedure, for ancient naval guns were prone to misfires at critical moments . . . it all had the unmistakable sound of much urgency. To Pumphrey-Hatton urgency meant only one thing: the German raider was believed to be in the vicinity.

And he had not been informed.

As a matter of courtesy he should have been. The Commodore and OC Troops were slighting him. He began to tremble as that realization came to him. He might have no official standing aboard the *Aurelian Star* but he remained a brigadier of the British Army on active service and as such he was not going to be disregarded.

He stalked away towards the orderly room, shaking, his anger boiling up inside him. On the way he passed the entry to the B deck lounge. He hesitated, then turned back. He went inside, went to the bar, where he stood in preference to sitting like a lounge lizard on a stool. He felt vaguely unwell. Not gin today. 'Brandy,' he said to the bar steward. 'Courvoisier.'

'No Courvoisier, sir. Only Van der Humm.'

'Damn. All right.'

'Coming up, sir.' MacInnes turned away. Pumphrey-Hatton became aware of a person on a stool nearby.

This person wished him good morning.

'Good morning. Hench, isn't it?'

'That's right, Brigadier.'

'I remember. Told you not to overdo the drink. And that awful woman. No good to you at all, Tench.'

'Hench –'

'Don't damn well argue. I'm sick and tired of being damn well disregarded.'

Hench gave a laugh. 'Snap.' He sounded bitter.

'What?'

'Snap. So am I. Fed up with being –'

'Ah. You, too? That woman?'

'Yes,' Hench said viciously.

The Van der Humm arrived. Pumphrey-Hatton took it, examined it closely, then knocked it back and demanded another. He said, 'I did tell you. If you can't take advice, then you've only yourself to blame. I think I also said, don't do anything silly. Remember?'

'No,' Hench said.

Pumphrey-Hatton shook with anger. 'Damn stupid,' he said in a high, almost hysterical voice. 'I . . .' His voice tailed away and suddenly he seemed to crumple. He slid to the deck, knocking over a stool. The Van der Humm spilled over his uniform, the glass broke.

Hench stared. 'My God,' he said. He remained as though rooted to his stool. MacInnes came round the bar, asked Hench for assistance. Hench didn't react; it was old Colonel Holmes who came across and helped MacInnes to carry the limp form to a settee. MacInnes felt for a pulse. 'Alive,' he said. 'I'll put out a call for the doctor.'

Yeoman of Signals Lambert had happened to look in at the w/t office when the leading telegraphist was picking up an overseas broadcast from Germany. The tones of the broadcaster were nasal. 'Lord Haw-Haw,' Lambert said. 'Stand by for a laugh, eh?'

William Joyce, British subject, traitor who spread propaganda for Adolf Hitler, trying to undermine the morale of the home front, had long been dubbed Lord Haw-Haw. Earlier in the war he had constantly asked the question over the air, 'Where is the *Ark Royal?*' in reference to Britain's newest and largest aircraft carrier, the inference being that she had been sunk and the British

153

public had not been told by a cowardly Admiralty. In fact, though she had later been sunk by submarine attack a little east of the Gibraltar Strait, she was at the time of Lord Haw-Haw's queries very much in being. That had been one of Lord Haw-Haw's boobs; but mostly he had been extraordinarily accurate in his war news. It was supposed that he had any number of informers inside Britain who made clandestine radio contact with Berlin, men and women who described with deadly precision the air attacks that had been made the night before. Lambert himself had heard Lord Haw-Haw speak of local damage, Pompey damage: Haw-Haw had told Britain of the massive attack by the *Luftwaffe* on the Royal Naval Barracks in early 1941, when the petty officers' block had been demolished by a land mine, with more land mines smashing onto the parade ground and the air raid shelters beneath. Lambert had heard him speak of a terrace in Arundel Street that had taken a direct hit and had mostly gone up in flame and rubble. Lord Haw-Haw had spoken of the demolition of Palmerston Road in Southsea, of the total destruction of what had been Handley's Corner. Lord Haw-Haw had known his stuff. He had said in that peculiarly offensive nasal tone, 'The naval officers of the Portsmouth base and their families will never again dilly-dally over coffee and biscuits in Handley's cafe next to the china and glass department nor use the old-fashioned lift like a mobile parrot's cage . . .'

To naval personnel serving overseas such a broadcast would have struck home very forcibly. And it had been the same all over the country. The result could have been devastating, could have impressed people with the perspicacity of Germany's all-seeing eye, could have made them fearful of their own neighbours. But that had never happened: Lord Haw-Haw had become a comic turn even though he was known to speak the truth on most occasions. He had become compulsive listening, enlivening many an evening of short rations and a huddling in thick clothing over almost non-existent fires in winter. He was as popular as Tommy Handley in It's That Man Again, as popular as Much-Binding-In-The-Marsh.

'What's he on about now?' Lambert asked.

The leading telegraphist put a finger to his mouth. Lambert listened.

'. . . told me by, let us say, a little bird. Are you listening, down there in the South Atlantic?'

Lambert stiffened, stubbed out a fag-end in a handy ashtray. Lord Haw-Haw went on, 'Are you listening, Commodore Kemp? Are you still acting the good shepherd of your convoy aboard the *Aurelian Star*, bound for the Firth of Clyde, and home? If you are listening I have, I'm sorry to say, some bad news for you.' There was a pause. 'Your son, Sub-Lieutenant Harry Kemp, has been drowned at sea when his ship was sunk by action of one of our U-boats. . . .'

Lambert's face had gone white; he listened for a moment longer, but Lord Haw-Haw had gone on to other matters, describing the fate of more than a hundred people, men, women and children, in a cinema in south-east London that had taken a direct hit the night before.

'I'll be buggered,' Lambert said in a voice little above a whisper. 'That's bloody horrible.'

The leading telegraphist said, 'Typical, is that. Will the Old Man have heard?'

'Not on the bridge, no. I wonder . . . will somebody tell him?'

The answer was a shrug. 'Wouldn't care for the job myself, Yeo.'

'Nor me neither. I'll have a word with Mr Finnegan, see what he thinks – leave it up to him. He and the Commodore, they seem to understand one another.' Lambert paused. 'I reckon he'll *have* to be told, and you know why as well as I do. That Haw-Haw . . . he knows where we are, what our orders are for the Clyde. You know what that means, eh? What with the bloody *Stuttgart* and all . . .'

'Heart attack,' Dr Grant said succinctly. He stood up. 'Get him down to his cabin,' he said to MacInnes. 'I'll treat him there. He'll pull through, I believe, it's not too serious.' He added. 'Can you rustle up a couple of hands with a Neil Robinson stretcher?'

'Yes, sir. Leave it to me, sir.'

'Sister Forman'll go with the stretcher party.' MacInnes got on the phone to the second steward, and two men came up within the next couple of minutes, carrying a stretcher. Pumphrey-Hatton was carried below, the ship's nursing sister walking beside him along the cabin alleyways. Outside in the lobby was

Petty Officer Biggar, and Biggar happened to see the face in the stretcher as the party came past him, out of the lounge door to head for the ladder down to the accommodation decks. Biggar moved away thoughtfully and went in search of Leading Seaman Purkiss, who was having a smoke by the guardrail aft, it being stand-easy.

He retailed what he had seen.

Purkiss gave a low whistle. 'May let us off the 'ook, PO.'

'Yes. If he 'appens to kick the bucket, that is.'

'How did 'e look, eh?'

'White. Or sort of parchment. Face gone all thin like.'

Purkiss nodded. 'Not too good?'

'No, I'd say not. So here's hoping, eh? Looks like the good Lord'll provide.'

Purkiss clicked his tongue. 'That's bloody blasphemious, PO.'

'Much you care, eh? And don't be bloody impertinent, all right?'

Finnegan came up the ladder to the bridge. Kemp asked, 'How's the invalid now, Finnegan?'

'Haven't enquired, sir. But I guess he's okay. The doc didn't seem worried, so Sister Forman said.'

Kemp grinned. 'So you did make some sort of enquiry? If only as an excuse to chat up the nursing sister.'

Finnegan didn't comment; there was a formality about his manner. He began to fidget and said, 'Commodore, sir.'

Kemp raised an eyebrow. 'Well?'

'I guess . . . well, if I could have a word.'

'With me?'

'That's so.'

'Here I am,' Kemp said impatiently, 'so go ahead.'

Finnegan hesitated, not meeting Kemp's eye now. He said, 'In your cabin, sir?'

Kemp frowned. 'In my cabin? What have you been up to, young Finnegan?'

'Nothing, sir. It's not me. But I guess it's – it's important.'

'Oh, very well, if you must.' Kemp called across to the Officer of the Watch that he would be in his cabin if required, then went down the ladder with Finnegan.

*

Pumphrey-Hatton, given a sedative, slept for some hours. When he awoke, Sister Forman was sitting by the side of his bunk. Jane Forman was a cheerful girl with a placid expression that the uncharitable called cow-like. Her figure tended to stoutness. Being cheerful, and seeing the signs of life as the patient's eyes opened and he stared around somewhat vacantly, she spoke brightly.

'How do we feel now?' she asked.

Pumphrey-Hatton focussed. 'I don't know how *you* feel, my good woman. I feel bloody.'

'That's only to be expected. We'll feel better soon, won't we?'

'How the devil do I know?'

'Because I say so.' Sister Forman had been put out by being addressed as 'my good woman'. She went on, 'Now we'll make you all comfy, shall we.' She lifted Pumphrey-Hatton's head gently and fluffed at the pillow, straightened the sheet over the recumbent body. 'There. That's better, isn't it?'

Pumphrey-Hatton said disagreeably, 'Will you kindly tell me what's wrong with me?'

'That's up to Doctor,' she said in a reproving tone. 'He'll be along just as soon as I tell him we've come round –'

'Oh, for God's sake, woman! Kindly remember I'm singular, not plural. *I've* come round. *We* haven't. And I've had a heart attack. Haven't I?'

Sister Forman busied herself at the wash-basin. 'Well,' she said. 'P'raps Doctor will say that, I don't know. But we're – you're doing very well so there's no need to worry about –'

'Oh, go away, woman, and fetch the doctor.'

'Oh, very well.' Looking hurt Sister Forman left the cabin. Pumphrey-Hatton glared after her. He disliked being fussed over and he disliked nurses; they were a bossy, interfering bunch. And he had no intention of finishing the voyage in his bunk. Confined to his cabin he would be angered beyond measure by his electric fan and his wash-basin, and there might well be flies in the vicinity of the equator, and he had yet to deal with his attackers, Biggar and Purkiss. He felt groggy when he tried to sit up, and he broke out in a profuse sweat. But that nurse woman had said he'd feel better soon. One had to assume she knew her job. When he felt better he would get up and that would be that, nurse or no nurse, doctor or no doctor. After a while, staring at the deckhead, he saw a fly. Worse than a fly: it was, he believed, a bluebottle. He couldn't have that. By the side of his bunk was a magazine, a very old copy of the *London Illustrated News*. He reached out and rolled it up.

Sister Forman was reporting to Dr Grant that her patient had woken up and seemed likely to prove a difficult and very rude man, when Pumphrey-Hatton, standing on his bunk and feeling groggier than ever but flailing away at the bluebottle, if such it was, suddenly clutched at his chest and fell, landing in a heap on the cabin deck.

The news went quickly round the troopship, together with Dr Grant's theory of what had happened, reconstructing from the rolled-up magazine, the continuing presence of the bluebottle on the deckhead, and the well-known antipathy of the brigadier towards flies and such.

'Killed by a blue-arsed fly,' Leading Seaman Purkiss said in something like awe that Petty Officer Biggar's thoughts had borne fruit so quickly. 'Would you bloody well believe it, PO?'

'It's fact, anyway. You don't speak ill of the dead, I know that and respect it like. But I can't deny it's a relief. Almost like it was meant to 'appen. Providence, see?'

In the chart room aboard the *Stuttgart* a conference was being held. Present with the Captain were his navigating officer, the gunnery and torpedo officers and the radar and communications officers.

The *Stuttgart* was now within twenty-four hours' steaming of the northbound convoy. Captain von Bellinghausen's face was formidable as he outlined his plan of attack, emphasizing with blows of his fist on the chart table the great glory that would accrue to the Third Reich and to his ship's company if an important troop convoy was successfully attacked. A number of Iron Crosses of the Military Division were likely to be awarded.

'I propose to open fire the moment the convoy is sighted, gentlemen,' Captain von Bellinghausen said. 'The first point of aim is to be the ship of the Convoy Commodore – the *Aurelian Star*. At the same time as I open fire with my heavy batteries the escort will increase speed towards the convoy.' The raider was accompanied by four destroyers, one on either bow, one ahead and one astern acting as rearguard. 'They will go in amongst the ships of the convoy and will fire their torpedoes. We must naturally expect opposition from the convoy's escort, but as you know, gentlemen, the British escort has no battleship, whilst its light cruisers have no armament that can match our eight-inch batteries.' He paused, seeing that his gunnery officer was anxious to speak. 'Yes, Schürer?'

'The British battleship *Duke of York*, Herr Kapitan. Is she not –'

'There has been a signal a matter of minutes ago from the Naval Command in Wilhelmshavn, Schürer. The sailing of the *Duke of York* was delayed. So very British a delay – a dispute with their trade unions. We in Germany are fortunate that our Führer has never in Germany permitted such stupid disputes. *Heil, Hitler!*'

The dutiful chorus of *heils* came. Von Bellinghausen continued. 'The British battleship is believed to be currently no closer than five hundred miles westward of Cape Finisterre. We shall not be bothered by her, and we shall destroy the convoy. When that has been achieved, then we shall head at once, but not directly, for Germany. There will be many warships searching for us, but we shall set our course westwards towards the vicinity of Venezuela and then head east and north for the Denmark Strait. There will be dangers but we shall overcome them – with the assurance that the Reich has God on its side. God and our Führer, gentlemen, cannot be defeated.'

There was a lengthy dissertation on the various technical details of navigation and ship-handling after the attack, talk about frequent alterations of course and other ways of evading the British who would be bent upon a swift revenge. Von Bellinghausen refrained from drawing any comparisons between the sinking of the British battle-cruiser *Hood* and the subsequent swift pursuit and destruction of the mighty *Bismarck*; there was nothing to be gained from gloom. The *Stuttgart* was going into the attack and afterwards she would steam safe home to glory and that was all about it.

When the conference broke off the various heads of departments went about their duties to their parts of ship. In the big turrets the gunner's mates put their guns'-crews through their paces for the hundredth time; the torpedo crews were exercised time and time again aboard the *Stuttgart* and the destroyers of the escort. In the engine-rooms extra checks were made of the propelling machinery and all bearings were examined and given an injection from the oil-cans. The telegraphs were checked, dummy runs to ensure that orders from the bridge were transmitted to the starting platform without delay due to any mechanical fault. All the electrics were checked and double-checked throughout the ship. Every man worked at the peak of efficiency. The honour of the Third Reich was the guarantee of that; a notable blow was to be struck, hammer-like, at Britain and the monster Churchill to the glory of the Führer and his so-victorious Navy.

Next morning, after dawn action stations had been fallen out the final accolade reached the *Stuttgart*: a cypher had been received in the main receiving room deep below the ship's armoured belt. Captain von Bellinghausen, when this signal had been de-cyphered, read it himself to all his ship's company over the internal broadcasting equipment.

'May God be with you,' von Bellinghausen read in a voice that shook with the emotion of the moment, 'in your so splendid bravery and loyalty to the Third Reich that will last a thousand years.'

It was from the Führer himself. The ship rang with cheering.

SIXTEEN

Finnegan left the Commodore's cabin, went into the pantry next door and spoke to Kemp's steward. 'Commodore's had bad news, I guess, Horton. Wouldn't hurt to take him in a whisky.'

'Commodore doesn't drink at sea, Mr Finnegan –'

'I know. Just this once, all right?'

Finnegan went back to the bridge, had a word with the Officer of the Watch. Captain Maconochie was in the wheelhouse, using the voicepipe to the engine-room. Finnegan moved into Kemp's position in the starboard wing of the bridge. He was very concerned about the Commodore. Kemp had said little, had seemed to be in a state of shock. That was far from surprising. Finnegan had stressed that since the name was known, Harry Kemp must have been picked up and that anyway the word had come only from Lord Haw-Haw, who could be, probably was, wrong. But Kemp had known all about Lord Haw-Haw's curious ability to get at the facts. He'd heard that from his wife among others. On leave once, Mary had told him that Lord Haw-Haw had announced, after German aircraft, chased by Spitfires, had ditched some bombs over a nearby village, that a certain Mrs Brampton, address given, had had her house taken out by a direct hit. Mrs Brampton, Lord Haw-Haw had said, had two daughters named Lilly and Lucy who attended Queen Anne's School in Caversham, Reading. Mrs Brampton had been killed but her husband Tony, who worked in the Bank of England, had been away for the night and was safe. Lord Haw-Haw had added, as a sort of throw-away line, that Mrs Brampton's bridge-playing friends would miss her.

Mary had been one of the bridge addicts and had known just how correct all the details were.

Kemp, standing by the square port of his cabin and staring out across the troopship's fore decks, hadn't moved when Finnegan had asked in embarrassment if there was anything he could do. Finnegan had had to repeat the question.

'Thank you, Finnegan. No.'

Finnegan had then left him alone with his thoughts and his anguish.

Within the next quarter of an hour Kemp was back on the bridge. His face, very pale, was set into hard lines that deterred any expressions of sympathy. The only reference he made to the broadcast from Germany was made obliquely to Maconochie.

'There seems a likelihood that the *Stuttgart* is homing onto the convoy, Captain. We could be in action at any time after about the next twelve hours. Before that happens, we'll need to carry out a sea burial. Pumphrey-Hatton. I shall attend, of course.'

Maconochie nodded. 'I suggest the afternoon watch. Three bells.' He paused: currently this was a fraught situation. He said, 'I'll have the bosun informed.' Bosun Barnes would have to see to the preparations, the plank, the Union Flag, the canvas shroud, the bearer party. Bearers were, it seemed, on the Commodore's mind as well.

He said, 'We'll have to liaise with Harrison. Or Carter – or both. The bearer party must come from the military.' His tone was expressionless. 'Pumphrey-Hatton . . . a difficult man but very much a soldier. I'm wondering if he'd prefer a native guard or an Australian one. I believe he'd have preferred the rifles. Same sort of traditions as a regiment from home.' Kemp half turned his head. 'Finnegan?'

'Yes, sir, Commodore?'

'Take soundings. We don't want to hurt any feelings.'

Finnegan went below and made contact with both colonels. The sea committal was carried out as planned at three bells in the afternoon watch. The bearer party was provided by the riflemen, Colonel Harrison being only too glad to spare his Australians the duty. It was, however, the Australian padre who conducted the service with both Kemp and Maconochie in attendance. Among the immediate attendance were Colonel and Mrs Holmes.

Mildred had been reluctant; she disliked funerals and there was something extra about a funeral conducted in the midst of possible terrible danger to them all; but Holmes had insisted. It was their duty: the late brigadier had been one of themselves.

During the short service it was observed that the Commodore had tears in his eyes. By this time all aboard knew the reason why. Mildred Holmes remarked *sotto voce* to her husband that Lord Haw-Haw ought to be shot.

'After the war,' Holmes said, 'he will be.'

The absence of the heavy cruiser *Vindictive* had made itself felt once she had detached for the Freetown base. There was a naked feeling, a feeling of being exposed. The biggest warship now left was the escort carrier *Rameses* and she hadn't a great deal of speed and manoeuvrability, and her guns were not of heavy calibre – her Barracuda torpedo-bombers and her Seafire fighters, the naval equivalent of the land-based Spitfires, were her armament. They might well be called upon. Before the light faded that afternoon, they were. A signal was flashed to the Commodore from the senior officer of the escort, informing him that *Rameses* had been ordered to fly off one of her Barracudas to spot ahead, searching out the oncoming German raider. If contact was made, the Barracuda would refrain from attacking and would return to the carrier to make its report. *Rameses* would then fly off her full squadron and the convoy would deviate westwards in an attempt to stand clear of the *Stuttgart*. It would be up to the Commodore thereafter if and when he ordered the merchant ships to scatter.

'Always a tricky decision,' Kemp said. 'There's danger either way. You can stay and maybe form a compact target, or you can risk being caught without the escort. So we'll play it by ear when the time comes.'

There was another point to be considered now: the signalling between the Commodore and the escort would have been noted from the troopship's decks and obviously the flying-off of aircraft from the carrier was going to be very plain to see. Kemp said, 'The time's come to give them the facts, Captain.'

Maconochie agreed. Kemp, as signs of activity were seen on the carrier's flight deck, went to the Tannoy in the wheelhouse. His words were brief and to the point. 'This is the Commodore speaking. *Rameses* is about to fly off aircraft on a spotting mission.

Troops must not crowd the starboard side to watch, since to do so would bring us too heavy a list.' He paused, cleared his throat. His voice was unaccustomedly husky. 'It is believed the German raider is coming down upon the convoy from the north. You may all be sure I shall take avoiding action in good time once the *Stuttgart*'s position is known. I am expecting to rendezvous with HMS *Duke of York* shortly.'

That was all; 'shortly' was but a hope. Kemp believed the battleship to be still well to the north. It was perhaps too much to hope that she would intercept the *Stuttgart* before the latter picked up the convoy. But if by some chance she did, then her big guns should make short work of the German.

Within the next ten minutes a lone Barracuda was seen to be taking off from the carrier. The sound of its engines was heard aboard the *Aurelian Star* as she cleared the flight deck and gained height, heading north to seek out the enemy. Gregory Hench heard it from his stool in the B deck lounge, the stool to which he seemed anchored. Miss Northway heard it as she came up from her cabin to take a walk on deck and worry about the immediate future. She was looking for Captain Mulvaney but failed to find him amongst the troops thronging the upper decks. In the lounge she joined Hench: any company was better than none. Hench sat gloomily, nursing a double whisky just provided by MacInnes. He looked up as Gloria Northway joined him. He said, 'Speaking again, are we?'

'Don't be stupid. And don't sulk. You've been sulking ever since –' She broke off, realizing what she'd been about to reveal, not that it mattered all that much.

'Ever since what?'

'Nothing, nothing, Greg.'

'Ever since that loud-mouthed Australian screwed you.'

She laughed. 'He didn't, as a matter of simple fact.'

'Oh, yes?'

'Yes. I mean no, it's a fact he didn't. He turned up at the wrong time.'

'Wrong time?'

'Oh, don't you be thick too. Anyway, he seemed offended and took himself off. Now he's sulking too, I think.'

Hench had ticked over. He said, 'In a few days' time he won't be.'

'Maybe not,' she agreed. 'That is, if we're still around. You heard the Commodore's broadcast, I take it?'

He nodded, and ordered another large whisky and a gin for Gloria – why not? He might as well lose with a good grace, especially if they were all going to die within a day or so. He said, 'Nothing we can do about it. Except wait and see.'

'And pray.'

He jeered. 'You, pray?'

'I'm going to, Greg,' she said seriously. 'I may not be used to praying and I'm darn sure God won't be rating me very high, but . . .'

'But what?'

She took the gin from MacInnes and sipped. Then she said, 'I heard one of those Aussies talking, Greg. He said there are no atheists in a fox-hole. I think he was right.'

Hench didn't answer; he stared down into his whisky, into the comforting amber glow. Maybe that was his God. If you were going to die, what better way to go than pissed as a newt so you felt no pain? He signed a chit for another large Scotch.

Below decks, others worried about the prospects for a safe arrival in the Firth of Clyde. The Holmeses worried, though the old colonel tried not to show it. It was, of course, Mildred whom he worried about rather than himself. He was a soldier. Death in action was always on the cards for a soldier from the moment he left Sandhurst or his regimental training depot. A wife was different. But if one of them was left – either one – what would become of the other? Holmes couldn't begin to visualize life without Mildred. Love and companionship apart, he would be lost. He couldn't even boil an egg – had never had to. Servants in pre-war Britain, native houseboys in Africa . . . life on his own in England would be insupportable. And Mildred, if she was left and he had gone? Of course it was easier for a woman, women were domestic creatures anyway and they could cope better. But she would be in a financial mess, only a widow's pension to live on, a pittance when based on his service pay of so many years before when the pay of officers had been itself a pittance.

After the Commodore's broadcast Holmes put his arms around his wife and held her close. He told her that he loved her; she said she knew that though it had been a long time since he'd said so;

165

and she loved him. She said quietly, 'If you go, Stephen, I shall follow you. I mean that.'

'Oh no,' he said. 'No. Don't think about it, my dear. It isn't going to happen. Commodore Kemp –'

'He's not God,' she said. Holmes could think of no adequate response to that.

Once again Chief Steward Chatfield was gathering up his overtime sheets and other documents concerned with payments and stores requisitions. Never mind a sinking if it came, the Superintending Chief Steward ashore in Liverpool would demand all relevant bumph. Life – or death, come to that – was like that, you always had to show a chit.

The photograph of Roxanne went in with the bumph; she would be nicely cushioned by the stewards' overtime. Chatfield was still worried about that Morris Eight as he prepared to face German gunfire and maybe leave Roxanne a widow though possibly not a sorrowing one. Chatfield's mind switched to his home: all his furniture, his bits and pieces, things that had come down from his mum and dad, from his grandparents too. Things that in many cases had not appealed to Roxanne. The stuffed owl beneath a glass dome that had been his dad's pride; the reproduction of a painting, *The Monarch of the Glen*, in which an antlered stag on a mountain-side stared arrogantly at a bit of Scotland; an antimacassar, pink and blue stitching, that his gran had laboured over for hours; a chocolate tin that had been presented by Queen Victoria to his uncle along with all the other troops on active service in the Boer War; a po that his dad had bought in Arundel and was said to have been used by Queen Victoria on one of her visits to the Duke of Norfolk at Arundel Castle. It was now in Chatfield's parlour, in use as a receptacle for a pot plant. Things like that, all treasured, though not by Roxanne. Roxanne didn't like what she called antiques; she was all art deco, modern stuff. Now, if he went, the stuffed owl and all the rest would no doubt pass to the sod he still didn't know was called Cocky Bulstrode. Either that, or it would all be chucked out as junk.

It was a nasty thought, with the bloody *Stuttgart* no doubt all set to blow the *Aurelian Star* out of the water. It wasn't bloody right. Wasn't bloody right at all. Chief Steward Chatfield reflected on the air raids on Southampton. Maybe a bomb would sort out the Morris Eight. The Lord, Chatfield understood, moved in a mysterious way and in so doing was wont to sort out the good from the bad. Chatfield had always been an honest man. Well – more or less; he was, after all, a chief steward and perks were perks, anyone knew that.

Within minutes of the returning Barracuda's approach to the carrier's round-down and its hook being caught by the arrestor wires stretched across the flight deck, Kemp had been informed by the lamp flashing from cs23's bridge that contact had been made with the *Stuttgart*, which was approximately seventy-five miles ahead of the convoy's track and steaming south at an estimated 25 knots. While Kemp and Maconochie conferred with Chief Engineer French and the officers of the trooping staff, the torpedo-bomber squadron took off from the *Rameses* and headed north on their killing mission. Kemp was reserved as to their chances.

'The German's got fairly massive ack-ack,' he said. 'And Barracudas aren't all that manoeuvrable. We'll still be very vulnerable.' Already the convoy had altered away from the raider's track, steaming west-nor'-westerly and maintaining the zig-zag against possible U-boat attack. 'We may be lucky and miss her – it's a chance either way. We may come inside radar range, in which case she'll home onto us, but –'

'Are you going to scatter the convoy, Commodore?' This was OC Troops. Kemp shook his head.

'Not yet, Colonel. Time enough for that when we get a further report from the aircraft.'

'Not much time surely? Closing speed, what, 40 knots or so? She'll be on us within a couple of hours.'

'Yes, I know. If she finds us. But she'll be engaged by the escort, don't forget. The escort's the only screen we have and I have to consider that.' Kemp's face was grey with tiredness and anxiety: he could be making the wrong decision, he was always aware of that. But there were the risks inseparable from any scatter order, the over-riding risk that individual ships on their own could become easy prey to a U-boat . . . the whole idea behind the convoy concept was that there was safety in numbers. Not always, though; and it was Kemp's responsibility to decide.

As the conference broke up, Kemp thought suddenly about Featherstonehaugh, whom he had yet to see. It wasn't fair on anyone to keep him hanging on but certainly now was not the time. Once the threat from the *Stuttgart* was over and done with, the matter would be a first priority.

The reconnoitring aircraft had not approached within range of the *Stuttgart*'s AA armament; but she had been spotted by the German lookouts shortly after the radar had picked her up on the screen. Captain von Bellinghausen was not unduly worried: the presence of a carrier with the convoy's escort had been known but von Bellinghausen had full confidence in the ability of his anti-aircraft gunners to deflect any bombing or torpedo attack. Those gunners would put up a virtually impenetrable shield of lead and shrapnel, and the British would go down like ninepins.

Nevertheless, it was plain that the British convoy would now know for certain of the presence of the *Stuttgart*; therefore it would be necessary to re-think the situation, just a little, in order to outwit the enemy. Von Bellinghausen tried to, as it were, insert himself into the mind of the British commander. The British were a wily race; where the German, or at any rate the Prussian, mind was straightforward and forthright, the British mind twisted and turned so that it was very difficult indeed to determine what they might be expected to do next . . .

Captain von Bellinghausen spoke to his navigating officer. 'Clearly the British will alter course.'

'Ja, *Herr Kapitan*.'

'In which direction would you expect them to alter, Friske?'

Friske said confidently, 'To the east, *Herr Kapitan*, in order to remain closer to the shore of Africa. There is the British base at Freetown in Sierra Leone –'

'You believe they may run for Freetown, Friske?'

'It is possible, yes, *Herr Kapitan*.'

Von Bellinghausen stalked his navigating bridge; he was deep in thought. There was truth in what Friske had said, but von Bellinghausen was doubtful. If to run for the safety of the Rokel River and its filthy native Kroos in their deplorable dug-out canoes with persons defecating over the sides was what the British would think that he, von Bellinghausen, would think . . . then their duplicity would have to be matched by his own wits.

The British might in fact move westerly while the *Stuttgart* moved easterly and then he would miss his prize.

It was a quandary, but not for long. Von Bellinghausen made up his mind. 'Friske,' he said, 'we alter course south-westerly. I believe the convoy will attempt to escape on a north-westerly course, hoping to outflank us and then to make their rendezvous with the battleship from Scapa Flow.'

'*Ja, Herr Kapitan.*' The navigating officer bent to the voice-pipe and passed the orders to bring the *Stuttgart* onto what was to prove a closing course with the convoy.

SEVENTEEN

The convoy had increased speed to the west-nor'-west, each ship managing to squeeze out the extra three knots that was the most Chief Engineer French could extract from his own engines. More than that and they would rattle to pieces, he had told the Commodore, might even be at risk of shearing the holding-down bolts, he had added – which was an exaggeration but not so far from the truth all the same. The ship had been continuously at sea from the beginning of the war and never enough time in port for a full engine-room overhaul.

On the bridge Kemp and Maconochie, as the sun went down in a brilliant scene of orange and green, scarlet and purple over the shores of South America far to the west, maintained an unbroken vigil of the horizon behind the ship. Their binoculars searched for the first signs of the enemy: the masts and then the funnel, indicating a ship as yet hull-down . . . and then the emerging upperworks, the bridge and the gunnery control tower, then the heavy fore batteries of the raider. The *Stuttgart* had the legs of them; once sighted, the uneven battle would be joined at once, starting with the cruisers of the escort. The destroyers and the aircraft carrier had altered to take them onto a course to intercept the enemy, while the cruisers, remaining with the convoy, stationed themselves between the merchant ships and the bearing from which the raider might be expected to appear. If the raider was sighted the cruisers would make smoke, laying a screen to hide the convoy and confuse the aim of the German gunnery controllers.

It wouldn't really help much; but it was all that could be

done. And if the German did appear, then Kemp would scatter the convoy.

The *Stuttgart* was sighted by the lookout at the foremasthead just before the sun, with a farewell blaze of colour, dipped below the horizon, sending a shaft of blinding golden brilliance across the water and silhouetting the ships against the backdrop.

Kemp said, 'Make the executive, Yeoman.'

Yeoman Lambert doubled to the signal halliards and hoisted the ready bent-on flag signal for the convoy to scatter. A few moments later thick black smoke began rolling from the cruisers' engine-room uptakes as the stokers in the boiler-rooms opened the taps to send a surge of oil fuel into the furnaces.

Two minutes later, invisibly to the ships behind the smoke-screen, there was a series of flashes as the German batteries opened.

Aboard the *Aurelian Star* and the other troopships, all hands except those required at their action stations – the naval guns'-crews, the ship's officers and engineers and those needed to man the pumps and fire hoses and so on – had been assembled at their boat stations and the embarkation deck was filled with troops and the civilian families. Gregory Hench had been prised from his bar stool by the Chief Officer, the latter making his rounds of the ship before reporting to the Captain that all crew and passenger spaces had been cleared.

Except, so far, for Hench.

'Out on deck, Mr Hench.'

'I'm all right here, thank you very much.'

'Don't thank me,' Chief Officer Dartnell said. 'The bar's shut down, or have you not noticed?'

'I've noticed.' Hench waved an arm, indicating three glasses of whisky lined up. 'Precautions.' He gave a belch.

Dartnell said, 'Out. That's an order.'

'And I,' Hench said indistinctly, 'am a fare-paying passenger. All right?'

'All wrong,' Dartnell answered crisply. He laid hold of Hench's shoulders and lifted him bodily from the stool. 'Fare-paying passengers cease to exist as such in an emergency. And when I say out, I mean out. *Out!*'

Hench made a disoriented swipe in the direction of the

171

whisky glasses. 'And you can leave those behind,' the Chief Officer said.

As, under propulsion, Hench went through the door to the open deck there came a distant whine, one that grew quickly louder as it made its approach, not more than a matter of feet above the *Aurelian Star*'s mastheads. On the bridge, the officers and ratings ducked instinctively. As a moment later Kemp straightened he heard an explosion, saw a gigantic burst of flame from a ship steaming away south on his port beam. Finnegan was at his side. '*Buckfast Abbey*,' he said. 'Dry cargo, foodstuffs mostly.'

Kemp levelled his binoculars. 'Fore part gone,' he said tautly. 'She won't make it . . . looks as though the hit was aft of the collision bulkhead. I'll give her three minutes. And God damn Hitler.'

It was in fact a little over three minutes before the freighter began her plunge. The Master had signalled that the German shell had smashed away the collision bulkhead and his pumps were unable to cope. With her fore part shattered, the *Buckfast Abbey* went down bows first and then, as the waters spread aft throughout her length, she settled briefly. Kemp saw men trying desperately to launch a lifeboat, but before the boat could be got into the water the ship went lower very suddenly and the boat, still on the falls of the davit, went down with her. Kemp saw men struggling in the sea until there was a blast of steam from her engine spaces, followed by a dull internal explosion and then she had gone.

In the meantime, the *Stuttgart* continued firing, the shells coming closer.

Hench was more than three parts drunk. He lurched about, bumping into the other passengers at his boat station. He seemed scarcely aware of the gunfire. He was by the after fall of his allotted lifeboat when the *Aurelian Star* was hit aft, a shell taking the after deck-house above the engineers' cabin alleyway. The deckhouse crumpled and fire started. The after gun's-crew were blown flat. Petty Officer Ramm was caught by a flying jag of red-hot metal that sliced through his neck. The head rolled grotesquely, fetching up against the ready-use ammunition locker. Stripey Sissons lay apparently lifeless, with both legs blown away and blood gushing from the stumps. As the rest of the gun's-crew stirred, Leading Seaman Purkiss got groggily to his feet and looked around. He saw the PO's head, and retched. Then, taking a grip, he said in a shaking voice, 'Right. I'm in charge now. Back on the gun, those that can. You, Featherstonewhat's it. Take over gunlayer.'

'Me?' Featherstonehaugh was dazed.

'Yes, you. I don't feel so good.' Suddenly, Purkiss went down flat on the deck, groaning in agony. Featherstonehaugh got down beside him. There was a spreading patch of blood from the leading seaman's stomach. The face was deathly white. Featherstonehaugh shouted at the top of his voice towards the embarkation deck, shouted for medical assistance, then went back to the gun. As a bright moon came out and beamed through the clearing smoke he could see the *Stuttgart* bearing down on the scattering ships of the convoy. She was still out of range of the troopship's inadequate, out-dated armament. Not that it mattered; Featherstonehaugh saw for the first time that the barrel was twisted into a cat's cradle and the whole mounting was tilted sideways.

On the bridge the orders had gone down for the fire parties. As the medical orderlies provided by the Australians arrived aft with Neil Robinson stretchers, a party of seamen dragged the hoses to the burning remains of the deck-house and began playing on the flames. Featherstonehaugh, in the absence of any orders, doubled for'ard to back up the crew of the fore three-inch. And Gregory Hench, whose drunken clumsiness had pitched him over the guardrail when the German shell had hit, drifted helplessly astern to wallow in the South Atlantic until a fin, slicing through the water, found him and turned for the kill. His screaming end was seen from the decks. One of those who witnessed it was Gloria Northway, though at the time she didn't know it was Hench. She gave a low, keening sound at the sheer moonlit horror of it and collapsed in a faint at the feet of Captain Mulvaney.

Kemp said, 'The German's making short work of the Barracudas, Finnegan. Four down.'

'That's right, sir. I –' Finnegan broke off as another of the cargo vessels was seen to be hit aft, a tearing explosion that had almost certainly damaged her rudder and screw. As if in confirmation the freighter swung, and began turning in a circle until she slowed to a stop. A minute later Kemp saw a flash of flame and billowing smoke from the German: one of the cruisers had scored a hit just for'ard of her bridge.

As the smoke cleared Kemp was able to see the damage: the shell had taken one of the heavy gun-turrets and the gun-barrels had drooped as if weary of action. That turret wouldn't be firing again; and one of the searchlights on the German's bridge seemed to have been put out of action in the blast.

'One up to us, sir!'

Kemp nodded. There was a glimmer of hope; if the cruisers could put more guns out of action . . . but where, in Heaven's name, was the *Duke of York*? After the raider had been sighted, wireless silence on the part of the convoy and escort had no longer been relevant and the troopship's wireless room had picked up the signals from the escort commander, indicating that the convoy was under attack. If the *Duke of York* was anywhere in the vicinity, she would surely be steaming towards them at maximum power. In theory at any rate she should show with her massive gun power at any moment.

In theory . . .

By now reports were coming in from aft: the fire was coming under control. There was no significant damage below decks. As yet there were no further hits on the convoy; the *Stuttgart*, with that one turret out of action, was being closely engaged by the escort. But, as Kemp was about to use the Tannoy to give what reassurance he could to the troops and civilians, two of the cruisers, *Marazion* and *Lydford*, were hit. *Marazion's* bridge was taken fair and square, and the director on the foremast came down mast and all on the wreckage. *Lydford* was hit on the starboard side amidships. There was a burst of smoke and flame and she took an immediate list.

Kemp felt drained of all emotion. First his son, then the possible – probable – loss of an entire convoy. And all he could do, with his popgun armament, was to stand by helplessly and watch it all happen. Or he could do the other thing, the heroic thing, and emulate Captain Fogarty Fegan of the armed merchant cruiser *Jervis Bay* and close the enemy with his popguns barking – they couldn't be said to roar – in selfless but doomed defence of his convoy. Should he?

174

It was a hard decision but an inevitable one: no. Fogarty Fegan had had no troops embarked. No civilians, no women and children. Because of them, Kemp had to stand off and await the arrival of the *Duke of York*.

Old Colonel Holmes was doing his bit. He asked permission of Purser Scott, in charge of his boat station, to absent himself so that he could circulate and talk to the riflemen in whose regiment he had served for so long, and so long ago. He spoke Swahili and he had been a familar figure, latterly as a guest, around the KEAR depot for longer than he cared to remember. So he walked, a little stiffly because of his age, among the assembled riflemen. He spoke to Sergeant Tapapa and the other NCOs, assuring them that help would arrive, that the German devils would not win and that they were in the safe and capable hands of men who knew the sea, who had sailed it all their working lives in peace and in war. He spoke to Regimental Sergeant-Major Nunn, asking if the native troops were likely to believe what he had said.

'Sir! Yes, sir, I believe they will. You are a respected gentleman, Colonel Holmes, sir, what I might call a father figure to them lot. With respect, sir.'

Holmes laughed gently. 'Yes. I'd sooner be a brother, Mr Nunn, but of course we all grow old.'

'Sir! That's a fact, sir.'

'I only hope I'm not letting them down. Giving them a false appreciation of the situation.'

'I'd say, sir, it's the only line you could have took. They want to be, well, fortified like, sir.' Nunn was standing as if on parade, ramrod-straight, immaculately turned out, Sam Browne gleaming with spit-and-polish, inevitable pace-stick at the correct angle beneath his left arm. He was, Holmes thought, almost a caricature of himself, of any pre-war warrant officer. Nunn went on, after clearing his throat rather noisily, 'Sir, if I may be so bold as to ask, sir, what do you think of the situation? Between ourselves like.'

Homes pondered for a moment, then asked, 'You don't want any devil-talk, I take it?'

'Me, sir? Oh no, sir, which is why I enquired like –'

'Yes, quite. Well, Mr Nunn, I rather think you know the answer for yourself, without my underlining it. Don't you?'

'I think I do, sir, yes. May I take the opportunity, sir, of asking you to take my respects to Mrs Holmes, sir. And my respects to you of course, sir. It's been a long association, sir.'

'Yes, indeed it has, Sar'nt-Major.' Holmes held out his hand knowing that this was the RSM's way of saying goodbye in case there was no other opportunity. The RSM executed a difficult manoeuvre. Grasping his pace-stick even tighter, he slammed his right hand to a quivering salute, brought it down to shake that of Holmes, saluted again, then brought the hand down to the 'attention' position at his side, fingers clenched, thumb in line with the seam of his trousers.

Holmes said rather sadly, 'Don't give up hope, Mr Nunn. And God be with you.'

'Sir! And with us all, sir.'

Holmes turned away before the RSM could see that his eyes were becoming moist.

All the while the distance between the scattering ships of the convoy was becoming greater, but still the raider seemed to be stalking the Commodore's ship, one of the biggest prizes of the attack, probably unaware that the troopship carried German prisoners-of-war.

Finnegan remarked on this. 'If they don't know, that's surprising. Seem to know everything else about us.' Having spoken, he wished he'd kept his big mouth shut: the Commodore would have got the reference. But all Kemp said was that they probably did know but were disregarding the facts.

'War, Finnegan. I dare say we'd do the same. In war, you kill, because that's what you're there for. You can't afford to be squeamish.'

Finnegan didn't respond. He knew he would hate to be killed by his own side. But of course the Old Man was right. You couldn't afford to be choosy. Hundreds of thousands of civilians on both sides had been and would continue to be killed in the air raids, another thing to be accepted as inevitable. It had become a dirty war.

Kemp said, 'Go below, Finnegan. Let me have a report on the prisoners.'

Finnegan went down the ladders to B deck. All seemed well, and was reported so by Captain Mulvaney who was also checking on orders from OC Troops. 'Well but restive,' the Australian said. 'Buggers cheered when we took that hit.' His voice was savage but he said, 'Reckon it's natural really. Tell you one thing: I'd bust a gut laughing if a Nazi shell landed in the bloody lounge.'

'Not for long you wouldn't. If that happened, the shell'd be likely to plough right down through the ship's innards. We haven't got armoured decks.'

'Too right, bloke, too right. Maybe I'll send a negative on that thought, addressed God.' Mulvaney frowned, dug into a nostril with a finger. 'That old bloke. Know who I mean? Dug-out colonel –'

'Yes.'

'Weird old geezer, been gassing away to the troops, all about how safe we're going to be. Like hell we are! I'd say we don't have a snowflake's chance in hell, that's what I'd say. How about you, eh?'

Finnegan said, 'Fifty-fifty. We just have to stay afloat till the *Duke of York* turns up.'

Mulvaney jeered at that. 'Which she won't. Not in time, anyway.'

Finnegan went back to the bridge, giving the Commodore the report as ordered.

The attack was kept up throughout the night hours. The *Stuttgart's* escorting destroyers had moved in quite early on, weaving at speed past the depleted British escorting force, coming in with their torpedo-tubes ready. Two more of the merchant ships had been sunk by those torpedoes, but the destroyers hadn't had it all their own way. The DEMS gunnery crews aboard the merchantmen had scored a couple of hits on the bridges of destroyers that had closed the convoy unwisely, and some damage had been done, one of the enemy vessels turning in a wide circle as her bridge personnel were blown apart, and ending up slap across the rearing bows of the Commodore's ship. The German had been sliced in half by those heavy bows, 24,000 tons of steel moving at full speed had been too much for the thin sides and she had gone down in two separate halves that for a brief time had banged their way down the *Aurelian Star's* port and starboard sides. There had been further torpedo sorties by the

177

Barracudas from the carrier, engaging the German ack-ack and helping to keep the raider at a distance from the scattered merchant vessels by blowing a hole in the stem just below the waterline, thus forcing the ship to reduce speed. But the end for the Barracudas came when a German shell smashed away the carrier's bridge superstructure and another penetrated her starboard side and fractured her aviation spirit pipelines rigged ready for refuelling when the aircraft landed on. The *Rameses* went up with a deafening roar, an envelope of flame, and a shower of debris some of which spattered down on the decks of the *Aurelian Star*. The airborne torpedo-bombers were left without a base, left to fly around aimlessly until their fuel ran out and they were forced to ditch.

Pessimism, as a fiery dawn came up, had gripped the bridge of the *Aurelian Star*. Though slowed, though harried by the British destroyers, the *Stuttgart* now looked set to obliterate the whole convoy. The fleeing ships could be picked off one by one. At intervals through the night shells had come close to the Commodore's ship, close enough to send heavy spray flinging over the decks, drenching the guns'-crews and the troops at their boat stations. One hit had taken the foremast fair and square, and the smashed remains had come down across the bridge, by some miracle injuring no-one but the lookout in the crow's nest, smashing the woodwork of the wheelhouse and chart room. The ship's carpenter and his mates were working to clear away the debris when an urgent shout came from the yeoman of signals.

'Ship hull down, sir, bearing red one-oh. Looks like a battleship, though I can't be sure yet, sir.'

A miracle? Kemp ran for the vertical ladder from the bridge to monkey's-island before realizing monkey's-island was no longer there. He turned back to the yeoman of signals. He said, 'The moment she's within signalling distance, make the challenge without further orders.'

'Aye, aye, sir.' Lambert went on watching, feeling the shake in his hands, the nervous tension building up: that battleship, if such it proved to be, could be the *Duke of York*. It could equally well be a German.

Cocky Bulstrode, in the evening of that same day, was in

Portsmouth on business. He had a prospect, a chap he'd met quite casually in a pub in Southsea, the posh part of Portsmouth. The pub was the India Arms in Castle Road. He'd subsequently worked on this contact, getting his confidence by exchanging confidences of his own, possibly indiscreetly but then Southampton was quite a fair distance from Pompey. Cocky had discovered two things: one, that his contact was a man with tastes similar to his own, i.e., the man liked a little on the side and they'd had a quiet giggle over this, sort of comparing notes of conquests. Two, that his prospect – Alf Smith by name – was a civvy working as a technician in an Admiralty department, situated in Fort Southwick on Portsdown Hill just behind the town. This department was concerned with wireless telegraphy and the receipt of codes and cyphers together with non-secret messages. Neither Cocky nor Alf had ever discussed this, neither of them being spies nor having any interest whatsoever in information that was none of their business; but on the evening of Cocky's visit to Alf's home to sew up a life insurance policy, Alf came across with some information that was very relevant indeed.

'You did say, Mr Bulstrode,' he whispered when his wife had left the parlour to make a cup of tea, 'you did say you had a, well, bit of stuff in Southampton?'

'That's right, Mr Smith, yes.'

'Wife of the chief steward of a ship called –'

'The *Aurelian Star*, yes.'

Alf looked round: the parlour door was still shut fast. 'Convoy under attack, South Atlantic. Commodore's ship, this *Aurelian Star*. Big losses believed but no ship names given. Anyway, not that I overheard.' Alf paused, and gave Cocky Bulstrode a nudge in the ribs with an elbow. He also winked. 'Could leave the coast clear, eh, Mr Bulstrode?'

'Er . . . yes. Yes, indeed, and I'm much obliged.' Cocky was in something of a mental whirl; his worst fears could possibly be about to be realized. He concluded his business as quickly as was decently possible and then, with the signed contract in his money bag he returned to the Morris Eight and drove back to Southampton but not to Roxanne Chatfield, whom in any case he hadn't visited since she had become possessive, going to the pub to avoid her incessant telephone calls. Now he wouldn't be

179

seeing her again, not ever. Much too risky to a man who valued his freedom and his spare cash.

'Acknowledged, sir. Correct reply.'

Kemp breathed easy: the battleship was not German. He said, 'Get her signal letters, Yeoman.'

Lambert was using his signal lamp again when there was a startling yell from Finnegan. The battleship was now coming into view through his binoculars. 'Oh, gee . . . oh, gee whiz . . . oh, daddy-oh!'

Kemp swung round. 'I beg your pardon, Finnegan?'

Finnegan gave a yelp, a sort of war-whoop. 'It's the good old United States Navy! It's the *North Dakota*! Oh, gee . . .'

Kemp grunted. 'Custer rides again,' he said. He levelled his binoculars. The Captain of the *North Dakota* was evidently a man of quick understanding and quicker decision. There was a flash followed by billowing clouds of smoke as the American's for'ard turrets opened and moments later, as the great projectiles winged across the seas between, big spouts of water rose around the *Stuttgart*. The *North Dakota* was seen to swing so as to bring all her guns to bear, and then she opened in the form of a broadside. Salvo after salvo; and when the range and deflection came spot on the German blew up in a shattering roar, split from stem to stern as her magazines opened her up like a sardine tin.

One of Kemp's first duties was to have Ordinary Seaman Featherstonehaugh brought before him officially. The proper formalities were gone through. Kemp listened and then pronounced; the situation had been eased by the shot native now being on the way to recovery. 'I have good reports of you, Featherstonehaugh. You had a nasty experience at the after gun . . . and Petty Officer Biggar reports that you stood up to action well enough.' He paused. 'I propose – there being no evidence to the contrary – to accept your own story. I accept that you acted instinctively to put a stop to what looked like a breakout. On that score the case is dismissed.' He paused again. 'The fact remains, however, that you fired without orders to do so. That is a very serious charge and one that should normally be beyond my powers to deal with summarily. However, I propose to use my discretion and allow you the likelihood that you acted in the instinctive way I've referred to already. Now, I can't say what view the members of the Admiralty Interview Board will take in regard to a potential officer who acts without orders, but I suppose there's a chance they may remember Lord Nelson . . . as for me, I propose to stop your leave for fourteen days.'

Featherstonehaugh had looked much relieved as well he might. But, as Kemp began the task of rounding up the convoy's surviving ships and shepherding them back into their formation, he had plenty to ponder. Had he handled the matter wrongly? Had he risked backing a potential officer who might impetuously lead men into unnecessary danger, an officer who at some vital moment might make the wrong decision? Well – that was in the lap of the gods now. He, Kemp, had made his own decision and that was that. But the affair still nagged at his mind as, some twelve hours later, they picked up the *Duke of York* and exchanged signals, after which the *North Dakota* detached to resume her original course; Finnegan was still cock-a-hoop about the arrival in the nick of time of the US Navy . . . feeling half inclined to shut him up, Kemp decided to allow him his natural enthusiasm. They had indeed been given salvation.

When some fourteen days later the convoy picked up Ailsa Craig, the great seagull-whitened rock at the entry to the Firth of Clyde, Kemp's heart was heavy. Within hours now he would be at anchor off the Tail o' the Bank, off the town of Greenock where news might be awaiting him, where there would be a telephone available to reach Mary. This could be the worst landfall of his career. When Maconochie brought his ship to anchor later that morning, the Commodore's lips were moving in silent entreaty to his God. Throughout the ship, throughout the remains of the convoy, many other people had their worries, the worries that would come home to them when they disembarked. Old Colonel Holmes and his wife, taking their leave a little later of the Commodore, had a defeated look. They had seen Greenock town, dour and grey under a leaden sky with a hint of lashing rain. So very different from East Africa. They left the ship aboard the tender for Prince's Pier, where they bought third-class railway tickets for austerity and obscurity and a sort of obliteration of so much of their past. Miss Northway had tagged onto Captain Mulvaney, who was determined to ditch her as fast as possible though she didn't know this because he had promised faithfully to call her the moment he got leave to London. Chief Engineer French, when Maconochie rang down Finished With Engines, was worrying about the mail that would probably give him news of what the magistrates had done to his two boys. And Chief Steward Chatfield, who though he didn't know it had nothing to worry about now, was mentally attaching a bomb to the Morris Eight.

There were a number of letters for Commodore Kemp: an Income Tax demand, a tailor's bill, letters from both his sons posted some while ago . . . two from Mary, one from the Chairman of the Mediterranean-Australia Lines. No telegram from the Admiralty. Hopes rose. He opened his wife's letters first. One told him the first news, and that there had been no confirmation either way. The second was very brief: would John please telephone as soon as he possibly could after arrival? Reading that, Kemp went very white. There was no telephone connection when at anchor; that privilege was reserved for the flagship buoy. Kemp went ashore to RN headquarters and used a telephone to his home. The second letter from Mary had warned him. His hand shook so badly that he could scarcely hold the receiver steady when the confirmation of the bad news came. The German Admiralty had reported Harry picked up alive; but he had died shortly after, presumably from exposure or wounds received.

Kemp would be home the following night; that was the fastest he could make it, there being unavoidable convoy matters to attend to and an obligatory visit to the Admiralty on the way south.

First there was something else: the bar of the Bay Hotel in nearby Gourock: the Naval Officers' Club in Greenock would scarcely do. He had a need to get drunk. He wouldn't go the whole hog; but the pain had to be eased.